The Mu

Kevin L. Hostbjor

The Musher Man

ISBN:

DEDICATION

For my wife, Terri. Her patience is remarkable.

ACKNOWLEDGMENT

Encouragement. Paul and Julie Green for supporting my earliest desires to write this book, and Joe Fuchs for trusting me to do so. To Steve and Rita Charles, thank you for never forgetting to remind me how I wanted (needed) to do this.

Beta Readers. To my friend and mentor, John Filicetti, for reading my earliest draft and not burning down my house. For my Cousin Gail and her husband Pat Donavan, thank you for the comments and edits; your support is appreciated. With one hand on a Dragon's Gate beer and another paging through The Musher Man, I thank Eloise Bell for her insightful assistance. And to my sister-in-law Celia Keith and her son Nate, thanks for your Montana perspective.

And finally, thank you to Eric James, Senior Manager, Amazon Book Publishing Pro. You brought me into this wonderful publishing world, giving me the opportunity to share this story with others. The Amazon publishing pro team is amazing, particularly Sabrina Brown, Author Consultant and project manager for The Musher Man. Thank you, Sabrina. You're the best.

CONTENTS

ABOUT THE AUTHOR

Kevin L. Hostbjor grew up on the West Coast (best coast) and, after a long stint in the United States Navy, landed in the Pacific Northwest. A graduate of the University of Washington with a Bachelor of Science in Metallurgical Engineering and City University with a Master of Science in Project Management, Kevin settled into a gratifying career as a Project Manager Professional (PMP), concluding with the Army Corps of Engineers. He lives in Spokane Valley, WA, with his wife, Terri and two whippets, Loki and Brewer.

Page Blank Intentionally

"I should have listened to Momma. She warned me."

Panacaea Clarke, November 1967

ENDINGS

CHAPTER 1

DENNY

Grasmere, Canada, September 1971

I both dreaded and looked forward to returning home. Four years ago, I left my safe and tranquil place after the worst day of my life. Now, I feared what I would find.

"Will they even remember me?"

I turned away from my cousin, took three steps from his truck, and received the answer. An over-excited Pixie and Copper led the assault. When they launched into my arms, I stumbled backward and landed on my backside in a puddle of garden runoff. The remainder of the team came to my rescue, and each of the nine dogs took turns giving me paw cardiopulmonary resuscitation everywhere on my body at once.

Seven minutes of licks and doggy CPR later, my white Navy uniform had turned to dark, muddy splotches as individual paw prints blended, becoming indistinguishable. In addition, a layer of tangled fur covered my front. It complimented my now grubby backside. Only my face remained clean, wet, but clean, as each dog made several concerted efforts to inspect and clean it. I could swim for an hour and get less moisture in my ears. Of course, getting dog slobber in my ears was more fun than pool water and much more sanitary. Watching me flounder, Aunt Diane laughed so hard she peed her pants and excused herself to change.

When I managed to get to my feet, Pixie sat with my white sailor's cap in her mouth. Somehow, it managed to avoid the muddy chaos, save for a bit of slobber where she held it in her teeth. My new badge of honor. I took the cap from her, placed it on my head, snuggled it down, and rubbed her ears.

"You're a good girl, Pixie. I've missed you so much."

Her tail fanned.

Aunt Diane came back, donning fresh gardening coveralls, pant legs rolled up to her knees, and wearing sandals. One hand holding her heaving tummy, she slipped the last strap over her shoulder and wiped her face with the back of the other. Wet baking flour smeared down both cheeks, making her a sad, laughing clown. My failed muddy hands, caked in fur, stopped patting my chest and fell to my sides. "It's not that funny."

She chuckled back between uncontrolled gasps, "Oh-ho-ho, yes, it is," and motioned for my Cousin Paul. "Kennel the dogs and carry Denny's duffle bag into the house." She shook her head and smiled at me. "You need to get cleaned up."

Reluctant to leave my dogs after my long absence, I followed my aunt into her kitchen. As I stepped in, she pointed to the floor. "Drop your pants and top here, fur boy."

***

Showered and changed, I found two giddy faces waiting for me at the kitchen table. Aromas from my aunt's family-famous venison stew assailed my nose, and my stomach answered with an audible prayer. In between swallows, we laughed about Pixie, my dog team, and their excitement to see me. Loath to bring up memories and answer their questions about my experiences in Vietnam, I diminished my discomfort with a short "I'm just glad it's over and I'm back," and moved to change the subject.

I pulled a letter from my bag and set it on the table in front of my Aunt Diane.

"Can you mail this for me? I wrote it to pass time on the bus. It's to our family lawyer. I wanted him to know I'm back from Vietnam, alive and well." I shook my head, chuckling. "Well, mostly."

"It also lets him know I'll be staying here for a few months."

I hoped to recharge my batteries and recover from the stresses of the war before going home. Waiting for the snow had a secondary purpose; I never wanted to be separated from my dogs again.

"Speaking of Abe, I've heard nothing. What's he said about Pan's killer?"

Paul lowered his head and dropped his spoon. Stew splattered. My aunt got up, pulled a bottle of milk from the fridge, and wetted a kitchen rag. She stood for a moment, one hand resting on the white jug sweating on the counter, the other massaging moisture from the damp rag. Looking out the kitchen window, her chest expanded and contracted. She turned to wipe up the splashes of stew. Her other hand still gripped the jug, knuckles turning the color of milk.

"We haven't heard anything about Panacaea's killer. It's as if no one cares."

"Wait! How can that be?"

She looked up at me. "He's called a few times to ask questions or make suggestions about the farmhouse, but even when asked, he says he knows little about your mother's murder and nothing about the killer."

"I don't understand. When Paul and Uncle John took me down to catch the bootcamp bus, we stopped at his office. I didn't see him but left a detailed letter of what I witnessed. Abe should know everything about the killer by now."

THE ARRANGEMENT

CHAPTER 2

DENNY

Stryker, Montana, October 1967

Bits of pickle, lettuce, ham juice, and smeared mayonnaise lay dribbled on the counter. As the last piece of pickle slipped to the floor, I grumbled a sigh.

"Making a sandwich for lunch shouldn't be so difficult. Or messy. How do you do it?"

I took a breath and started to clean up my spilled mess.

While washing the utensils, I glanced up at the wallpaper trim around the top of the kitchen walls. The trim always intrigued me with its alternating figures of farm equipment, tractors, combines, and such, repeating around the room. The images included one horse peering over a fence. Since we moved in, I often wondered why a horse would be included in a design with nothing but farm equipment.

Then it hit me.

The yellow background of the trim gave a sunny disposition to the blueish and black trimmed figures and tried to blend into the faded yellow of the kitchen walls. The full design made me think about the people who built the house and worked on the original farm. Life for them must have been much different than ours. More difficult.

My mother looked up, swallowing a sip of tea. "Practice."

Turning, I saw her sitting at the table. Yellow light flickered on all sides of Panacaea Clarke's smiling face, framing her. With her heritage, she often pondered the creamy color of her skin. Her long, straight, braided, shiny black hair and sparkling dark eyes provided the only clues to our Haitian ancestry.

Dressed for a typical day in the farmhouse and never one to display her natural assets, she wore her favorite unadorned white blouse, fastened one button short of her neck. She tied up the sleeves with a blue lace bow high above each elbow.

"It took you forever to learn how to tie those bows with one hand."

"One of the many challenges of living alone."

I nodded and smiled, "You look nice."

Although her nicer outfits are a little unnecessary for a woman in an old farmhouse out in the Montana woods, Panacaea always kept herself presentable.

"You never know when a client might arrive," she turned her head and sighed. "They could come at any hour, on any day. Unless I'm working in the garden, I need to be ready."

Below her light blue capris, she wore an old, worn, and comfortable pair of black and white oxfords. She had white socks folded down to her ankles. They even had blue trim. She squinted and clicked her heels together, chuckling.

"There's no place like home," I told her she could be on the cover of the Saturday Evening Post.

"If only!" she laughed, and grateful eyes smiled back. "We're on the wrong side of that rainbow."

Over everything, she draped a faded and stained apron hanging loose around her neck, untied in the back. She often loosened the thing when drinking tea or reading at the table to prevent the straps from pulling on her neck. Knowing she would need it when finished, she kept it looped around her neckline, hanging to the side, and pooling on the linoleum floor.

Okay, considering the tatty old apron, no picture for the Post today.

The working farm had been active for a long time before falling into decay, and the three-bedroom house could not support all the people necessary for its former operation. Next to the barn and workshop, an extended addition answered the matter.

"The old bunkhouse is working out well for my team," I spent days disassembling the bunks and used the slats and supports to build small stalls. "With the old bedding and blankets, each dog has their own spot for unencumbered rest."

The old bunk room also explained why the house had an oversized kitchen, pantry, and stove. The farmhands ate meals at the kitchen table, and someone prepared large meals. A small room to the side of the pantry showed faded outlines where an old milk/cream separator and other equipment once operated. A small chamber pot sat in the corner for those winter evenings to avoid a dark and uncomfortable walk outside. A set of narrow stairs, through a corner door, led down to a basement.

"I'll be in the workshop if you need me. I have some repairs to make on my sled before the big snow," I turned to leave the kitchen and grabbed my coat in the vestibule. "My dogs need some work before the snow too."

"Take your time," she took a breath and exhaled. "It's not like customers have been lining up at the door." She raised her eyebrows. "I've a funny feeling today will be different."

CHAPTER 3

PANACAEA

If asked, I had no answer for why I broke Momma's rule. Something about the tall, handsome boy weakened my unwavering regimen.

He smiled, "They call me Billy."

Although his handsome smile warmed me, his dark eyes steeled over my body as he rolled his shoulders and swallowed air. He wore a large, gaudy belt buckle shaped like a football.

I closed my eyes and took a slow breath.

His cowboy boots had some sort of animal skin ripples; the light flickered on the burnt orange leather. He turned around in a slow spin, brandishing his green and yellow letterman jacket. His bootheel left a dark mar on the porch floor where he whirled. I noticed his jeans showed faded wear on both hip pockets: one rectangle, one circular. In addition, he had multiple small frays on his knees.

Arrogant and pathetic at the same time.

He explained how the emblems and patches on his jacket showed he excelled at high school varsity football. He pointed at each in turn.

"Track and baseball too."

In tones somewhere between pleasantry and indifference, I offered two words.

"Nice jacket."

His right cheek gave a momentary flinch as he smiled, showing perfect teeth and a gaping maw. I closed my eyes for a moment and took another breath.

Billy had a simple request. "Can you give me something to make me more confident and competent in the big game?"

He rolled his head until his neck gave an audible snap. "Look, I have the physical skills to be a top-notch football player."

From the way his apparent muscles filled his jacket, I guessed he could be right.

"This is hard for me to say out loud, but the last three years of poor coaching and mediocre team performance affected me more than I want to admit."

He sighed.

"I need an edge. I need a boost. I need a good game, a really good game."

More pathetic than arrogant.

"For as long as I can remember, I've wanted to play professional football." He puffed up his chest. "It means everything to me." He went on to say how he needed to make the pro football draft to make his dream a reality. "To make the draft, I need to get to the National Football League combine."

I have no clue how or why the football league used a combine and assumed some farming equipment manufacturer sponsors the league.

Billy claimed his better-than-average play on a poor-performing team had gone unnoticed. "We lost nine of ten games last year, and the potential of even a skilled player on a horrible team making the NFL draft is almost impossible." He dropped his arms; both of his index fingers began rubbing his thumbnails.

"After last season's dismal performance, the university hired two new coaches," Billy told me that the coaches managed to turn the team around, and so far this year, the University of Montana Grizzlies won all but one game. "Although the team has improved a great deal, my season has not reached a level enough to draw the attention of pro football teams. It's my senior year, and I only have four games left."

He wanted a boost. He wanted an edge. He wants to go out in a blaze of glory.

The blond boy teetered in my kitchen, rubbing his hands together, skittering from one foot to the other. His forehead crinkled, and he spread the fingers of his right hand on his chest, eyes misting.

"Please. Help me. We're getting ready for the Brawl, and I gotta have a good game. If ever a pro scout comes to watch us, it's when we play Montana State."

He told me it's their annual rival game called the 'Brawl of the Wild.' I have no television and no appreciation for football, and I believe anything referred to as a 'brawl' has no business in my kitchen.

As I crossed my arms and pursed my lips, a severe wrinkling on his forehead threatened to join his eyebrows together. "Couldn't you please give me something for the next four games?"

I looked at the young man, relaxed my face, and shook my head. "No!"

Blinking, Billy took a breath and rubbed the back of his neck. "Please!"

"No!"

"I'll pay extra." He put his arms out, fingers splayed, eyes clouding.

Closing my eyes, I shook my head. "Look. I know of only one thing to help you. It's quite strong and dangerous if misused."

He laced his fingers and whimpered. "Please, ma'am, please. No one else can do this for me. I'll be careful."

It must have been the handsome young man's awkward attempt at a sideways shuffle or his near prayer.

I exhaled and raised a pointed finger. "One dose. Only one per week. Any more is out of the question." I spread my arms, mimicking his earlier movement, and squinted. "Come back each week for the next dose."

Folding my arms across my chest, I tilted my head forward and raised an eyebrow, my eyes reading his.

"Ma-mam-ma'am. Thank you, but I can't get back here each week. The trip takes me the better part of a day to drive both ways from the university to Whitefish, and you're another half hour further." His eyes began rolling, his head turning back and forth. "The next game is in Missoula, but we travel for the last three, and I have tons of classes during the week. I just can't get back here every week."

Drooping his shoulders, he lowered his head and voice, "Besides, the more trips I make out here, the more likely someone will see me, and I … if someone does … I don't want to have to explain why I've come to see you." He exhaled and closed his eyes. "I'm sorry." He swiped the back of his hand across his cheek.

I must be a sucker when it comes to a man crying. "Okay. How much do you weigh?" as he raised his head, his right cheek flinched again.

"About 215 pounds. But it's all muscle." He patted himself on his chest and made a guttural sound.

"Come back in four hours."

Billy smiled again. Somehow, his maw grew more teeth. "How much money should I bring?"

"What's this worth to you?"

He thought for a moment and, with another flinch, "I have $40 in my wallet."

I sighed again, nodded, and waved him off, "Four hours."

Forgive me, Momma.

CHAPTER 4

BILLY

The drive to the witch's homestead took about 45 minutes when we drove up here early one-morning last summer. My girlfriend, Becky, had some bizarre directions, and we drove by the place without realizing it. Her handwritten directions indicated to turn at a red barn, and we never passed any buildings. We took a slower drive on our return down the country road and discovered the mysterious missing barn.

"Shit, Becky. You'd think they could've told us the damn thing was a mailbox."

Minutes after we turned off the gravel road, the homestead appeared in a large clearing, and an actual red barn came into view.

Well, the faded structure might have been red once.

Across from the barn, a moderate farmhouse sat to the left, next to an almost fenced garden. At one time, the dirt-streaked house could have been described as white. Above the shallow peaked porch, a solitary window with shade drawn down halfway stared down at us.

Becky chuckled, "It looks like the face of a weeping cyclops with a frowning moustache."

Wisps of steam escaped glimmering patches of moss on the roof.

What a dump!

Back then, we brought one of Becky's friends to see the medicine woman. Her curative reputation spread among the young women of the community, and Becky's friend needed help on a particular and immediate personal issue. Like me and Becky last summer, boyfriends often accompanied their girlfriends on their occasional visits for help. For that trip, however, she asked Becky to bring her to keep her boyfriend from knowing. Becky put her hand on my shoulder as they got out of the car.

"Stay here. She doesn't allow boyfriends inside."

Although we boys had to wait outside, conversations with the girls on the drives back to town offered insight into the curative tinctures and poultices the medicine woman produced. For this visit today, I wanted no one to know I came to see the Haitian-Montana witch doctor.

Because many of the girls had trouble with the witch's odd accent, few could pronounce her name, whatever it was. Someone referred to her as Pansy, and the name stuck with all the kids.

Several of the boyfriends returned to the homestead and tried to get potions from Pansy, too, for acne or to stay alert when taking midterms or final exams. She always refused.

The medicine woman also had a reputation for beauty. Her good looks, her Pansy nickname, and her refusal to provide any help for the boys facilitated an unwarranted reputation by many of the local high school boys. They told fabricated stories of indiscreet, late evening visits. When drinking beer and partying out at the lake, the stories became more lurid with each telling as each boy tried to best the other. I knew they all lied. Most of those chumps will still be virgins when they get married.

Knowing the route now, this trip to the witch's den took about 25 minutes. I rolled up the farmhouse drive from the access road off the highway, trailing clouds of dust, and stopped. A spray of loose gravel peppered a clunky old green Ford pick-up, parked facing an outbuilding and weathered barn. Like everything else, it had more rust than color. Its lowered tailgate revealed an old gas can in its truck bed.

It faced the other direction last time. So, they must still use the old rig.

Although the distressed red barn had seen better days, it had square and plum corners and straight rooflines. Someone must be maintaining the buildings. Although a dump, I will admit, with a little paint, the old place could look good.

Okay, a lot of paint. Looking around, I decided there was no way I was parking my beauty near the junky truck or these crappy structures.

Stopped in the middle of the gravel clearing between the buildings and the house, I got out and walked toward the back of the house, where Becky and her friend entered. Angled off between the truck and the farmhouse and in front of the garden, a creaky windmill strained upward next to a makeshift temporary water tank. It groaned in aggravation; one blade was missing. After giving it another glance, I believed it would miss my car if it fell over.

The original water tank lay crumpled on its side, its support poles rotted and broken. A small replacement tank, sitting on old, stacked railroad ties, provided water to the farmhouse. Although the tank overflow filled a water trough, I saw no evidence of farm animals.

The porch had a brand-new replacement screen in an old screen door, though it missed its storm door. I pulled it open and stepped onto the shaded porch. The cramped space had dirty boots, a broom to one side, two coats, and an apron on pegs or hooks in the back corner.

Look, the witch has a rocking chair.

It sat opposite a stool with a short table with coffee stains and dents in between. The table had a tattered and wrinkled paperback book lying there, splayed open, print side down.

As I knocked, the door opened. Even with the stories going around, the pretty witch standing in the doorway surprised me. I thought her skin would be darker. Braided hair rested on her left shoulder. One sparkling eye stood out through a peaked eyebrow. She crossed her arms.

Oh boy. Here we go.

Because of the types of helpful ointments and other remedies, my girlfriend said the medicine woman provided in the past, I figured she could help me too. If she did, I would be an exception. My smile always worked on Becky and the other girls, so I gave her my best one.

I wore my old high school letterman jacket, like always whenever I come back to Whitefish, to remind my old alma mater chums of the glory days. I enjoy impressing the younger gals, too. The damn thing failed to impress anyone at the university, so I got used to leaving it in my car at college. As planned, it worked on the witch. Add one more adoring fan to my stable.

But damn!

She still blocked the doorway to keep me from entering. No problem. I would appeal to her good nature. From what Becky and the girls said, I knew she had one. Taking a breath, I smiled again and began my story.

"I'm not the one at fault here. The team sucked last year, and my professional career is at stake." She just stood there, watching me, eyes squinting, hands laced in front, thumbs twiddling.

Shit! She's not buying my sob story.

I crumpled my forehead to the point my scalp began to cramp. The pain hurt like hell and helped me tear up. With luck, I could cry or at least pretend.

Crap.

She continued standing there, resisting my charms. I watched a show on TV a while back, an episode of Twilight Zone, I think. The actor put his arms out, pleading for his life. The move worked for him. I saw a flicker in her eyes when I mimicked the move. Her forehead relaxed.

Touchdown!

Well, at least I made a field goal. With the way she had been stonewalling me, I would be happy with a first down. Then she caved and told me she had something strong and dangerous.

Cool! Just like me.

Clasping my hands, I begged and told her she had to help me. Watching Twilight Zone is all the education I need.

He scored, and the crowd went wild.

It took a moment to convince her to give me enough of the 'dangerous stuff' for all four games. She bought the story of my busy class schedule and didn't need to know I skipped most of them anyway. She stroked her braid and asked about my weight.

And he scored again. The crowd cheered as he tossed the football into the stands.

When asked what I thought this would be worth, the answer came to me in an instant: about a million bucks. Prepared to go five hundred, I let her know I had 40 bucks in my wallet.

She told me to leave and come back.

And they said it couldn't be done.

CHAPTER 5

PANACAEA

The boy came back on time. He stepped into the kitchen, the squeaking threshold announcing his arrival. Billy had an open grin on his face; his eyes participated in the smile. He stood there, feet spread, fists on hips.

"Have I made a mistake, Momma?" I exhaled.

"There are four packets here. Take only one for each game."

I reached out to grasp his face, pinching his chin between my thumb and forefinger. To make a point, I pulled his chin down and looked him in the eyes, my eyebrows raised.

"Only one."

Billy repeated my words with a slur, my hand still holding his jaw, "Only one."

"More than one could yield an undesirable result," releasing his chin, I squinted. "It could be dangerous. Unpredictable. Understand?"

He nodded. "Got it. One per game."

I handed him the four packets.

"Mix this with a full cup of water or tea," I told him and added a caution. "Nothing bubbly." Grabbing his chin again, I waited for him to focus his eyes on mine. "Make sure the contents dissolve before you drink it.

You want this to absorb into your system through your stomach. Do this, and you will notice the benefits of the tonic begin after an hour or two," he looked away, and I patted his cheek to regain his eyes. "The effect can last up to another ten or so, depending on your level of activity. Heavy exercise or work shortens the impact."

His eyes shifted to one of my candles, and he arched his eyebrows.

"Pay attention!"

I thumped his forehead with the heel of my hand.

"This is important. If you are resting, the effect will last longer. This temporary enhancement peaks in the middle. So, try to consume each packet around four hours before the game."

When he nodded again, I patted his cheek with my open palm.

Billy took the packets and dropped $40 on my table. He turned and left without a word. He left without saying thank you. He left me shaking my head.

"What have I done?"

CHAPTER 6

BILLY

On 28 October, I had the best game of my life, running over 100 yards and scoring our only touchdown. We beat the Northern Arizona Lumberjacks, ten to seven. In the locker room after the game, the head coach awarded me with the game ball. I thought about my secret purchase while getting dressed, smiled, and patted the pocket of my coat. I could feel a lump where the tart herbal supplements remained hidden.

My little packets of powdered courage.

***

Leaving the locker room late on my way to the bus for the Brawl a week later, I remembered needing to take my supplement. In the coach's office, I grabbed his coffee pot and poured the last remnants of the morning coffee into a small cup. As I tipped the supplement packet over the cup, the coach passed the door.

"Why aren't you on the bus? Get rid of that and get going," the coach said.

Swirling the liquid, I drank it in several quick swallows and left. The potion stung my throat, no doubt due to drinking the hot beverage too fast. I chewed lumps of undissolved grainy sludge. The bitter taste lingered on the back of my tongue. The heat hit me quicker this time, giving me an overpowering urge to move my body, something difficult to do while stuck on a bus. My mind was wheeled with game possibilities.

I can feel it working already, and my confidence is booming. Nice.

During the drive to the Missoula game, the assistant coach walked down to where I sat. The abundant warmth from the boost of elixir coursed through my body, and I ached, wanting to reach the field and crush the opponent; crush anything. I wiped the sweat from my forehead as the coach leaned down and whispered.

"Scouts from both the Green Bay Packers and Baltimore Colts called and signaled their intention to attend the rivalry game. Just be yourself. You'll be fine."

Everything comes down to this one game. To hell with what the damn witch told me. Scouts from two teams will observe the 'Brawl of the Wild,' and I want to impress both of them.

Despite her warning, I decided to take a second packet of powdered courage. How does she know if the stuff is dangerous or undesirable? What does she think could go wrong? I bet she only wants to keep me from winding up with superhuman strength and speed.

If one packet of courage is good, two must be better.

In about 30 minutes or so, we'll be in Bozeman and start warming up for the game. Not that I need to warm up, sweat's dripping from my nose. There will be no opportunity for me to mix another packet of tonic and sneak in the drink.

I reached into my coat pocket and snuck another one of the medicine woman's tinctures. Keeping my hands hidden inside my coat, I tore open the packet, reached up, and poured it dry into my mouth. I tried to chew and dissolve the substance as my mouth fought the sudden sour and gritty dryness of the powder.

Wait! I have a Coke in my bag.

I popped the top off and took warm gulps to wash the bitter taste out of my mouth. Swallowing, my tongue and throat burned, and I began choking.

Several faces turned as I gasped and gave a harsh cough, so I raised my coke, waved it, and received numerous nods and laughs as I bellowed out, "Wrong pipe," with a strangled burp.

When the team bus arrived, I placed my hand on my chest and could feel my heart thumping, pat-ah-tat-ah-tat. Drums in my head echoed the rhythm.

By game time, my faith in myself percolated like a vibrating boiler on the verge of exploding. The gauges on the boiler's control panel are pegged in the red. Lights flashed. The steam vent struggled to release the excess pressure. The vent failed. Who cares? I feel great; strange, hot, sweaty, but great. Hot damn! My gears are not in drive; they are in overdrive.

My double dose plan is working to perfection.

Although I felt no pain in my head from the pressure building in the pounding boiler, I could sense it enlarging from the increase in pressure. I began to lift above the field like a rising circus hot-air balloon. Weightless now and soaring above the field, I watched from a distance, my feet dangling.

Down below, I see ants scurrying around in slow motion. I raise and lower my feet as if smashing several ants with each stomp. The ants changed to tiny football players and back to ants.

Wait! Why can I see ants?

If I'm in a circus balloon, there should be a gondola basket below my feet. I tried looking up to see if I floated under a parachute rather than a balloon and could see nothing but groups of bright lights spaced around a dark sky. Damn. Wincing and blinking, I gazed back down, looking for some more ants to smush. No ants.

What am I doing here? Oh yea, stomping ants.

Why waste time on this grass, with these people, these ants? Football is beneath me, far beneath me. Searching for more ants while looking down from my lofty and elevated hot-air perch makes the waste of time clear. Palpable.

College is beneath me, too. Everything is beneath me. Soon, I will be beyond its reach. Rise up, my wonderful balloon. Keep rising. Lift me away.

Wait! The insects below are moving again and getting larger. No, not insects, not ants. The tiny football players began to grow bigger and bigger and move faster and faster. They keep growing and getting closer.

Wait! Somehow, I'm standing on the grass among them.

How did I get here?

Blinking twice, I bent over, joining other players, staring at the cold ground. Do they see ants, too? Are they searching for ants? What happened to the ants? Did I squish them all? I can see individual blades of grass now. I see my feet. Oh wait, there are other feet. How many? Two, four, five, and now they are moving away.

Hey, I am still counting.

My mind went wild with buoyant clarity on everything in my life. My head bobbled around from one thought to the next, from one idea to the next, never staying with one thought or one idea for more than a few seconds. I had no need to dwell any longer. I had lucid thoughts with clear and complete ideas. I had quick thoughts and brief ideas, amazing thoughts, and brilliant ideas.

There is nothing I could not do. Nothing.

I can do anything I want to do. Anything.

Later, the guys groused about my bumbling play after play. They told me I either failed to move, went the wrong way, or botched the ball handoff. The head coach benched me after the fifth offensive play. I have no memory of the game. Who cares anyway? I do remember sitting on the end of a bench by myself, laughing at the futility of the unnecessary movement of insects and stomping more ants.

For the remainder of the game, I sat alone, smiling and laughing at the ridiculousness of the players, the field, and the world, ripe for the taking.

Ripe for my taking.

I can take anything at any time. Anything. Any time.

Round and round after round, I went. I could smell the prize of success waiting for me. I could feel the brass ring in my grasp. Sitting there, enjoying my carousel ride, I could see my breath and reached up to wipe the sweat dripping from my steaming forehead.

The Montana State Bobcats won the Brawl, fourteen to eight. We lost. The scouts left the ballgame early in the first quarter. There would be no draft and no professional football career. Due to inactivity, my supernatural confidence remained when the bus arrived in Missoula.

No problem. Who cares? I love it.

Getting off the bus, I noticed the two coaches in a heated conversation, hands flying. The head coach came up to me.

"I've seen swimmers get out of a pool and have less moisture on their face. You haven't strained a muscle all evening. And I know exactly how to wipe that smug look off your face," he spoke aloud so everyone could hear. "You're off the team."

I laughed.

THE MISARRANGEMENT

CHAPTER 7

PANACAEA

November 1967

The vestibule floorboard squeaked.

Like before, Billy came in from the back side of the house. Unlike before, he entered without knocking. I became aware of his presence from the squeak and because cold breezes from opening the kitchen door tended to pass across the table side of the kitchen. I set down my book.

Seldom used, the front door faced the country road leading to our driveway and opened to a small living room. The wallpapered room had a green ivy-patterned design; a large rectangle of bright wallpaper scooted up one wall where a bookcase or armoire once stood. A faded old green divan, left behind by its previous owners, sat against one wall. A woven blanket lay across its cushions, hiding tiny burn holes in the fabric, and two ornate, cream-colored doilies did the same, covering both armrests. A small table in front of the divan held a scented burning candle.

I love candles.

The room reeked of cigarette smoke, and the candle helped obscure the stale odor. Although I have scoured the kitchen and other rooms, taking the time to do a deep cleaning of the parlor, unused except for those occasional times when I have more than one customer at a time, is low on my priority list.

In rare instances, when winter temperatures fall below freezing and a tincture takes a while to brew or prepare, I allow accompanying boyfriends to sit in there to stay warm rather than sitting in idling cars. Only rare instances, mind you. If the stale cigarette smell in the parlor bothers them, they are welcome to go back and wait in their car.

I might just keep the foul smell.

Entering unannounced, he moved to lean against the doorframe, one hand grasping his buckle. With his forehead furrowed, nose scrunched, and lips in a tight frown, Billy no longer looked charming. Traces of early snow trailed behind him through the vestibule, and I saw no sign of his beloved letterman jacket and thought it odd for him to be without his pride and joy fashion accessory. Lines of sweat dripped down his neck. His hair clung to his forehead.

My spacious kitchen, the largest room in the house, has a small table with two unmatched chairs. The aluminum chair has three rubber footers; the fourth leg has a glued-on slug of wood. The other chair, made of wood, shows rough gnaw marks on the lower support spindles, indicating someone's pet found them attractive to chew. We bought them and the sideboard at a secondhand store to help fill the room. Scuff marks and indentations on the checkered linoleum floor indicate the former occupants had a much bigger table capable of feeding a group of eight to ten people.

By his clammy brow, I knew the weather had no impact on him, and from the wide, empty distance in Billy's eyes, I dreaded what he wanted. Standing there with his chest heaving, I felt sure he came back for something besides another packet of herbal confidence. He wants what all arrogant and entitled young men want from a woman alone. By his sneer and the twitching of his cheek, it occurred to me he might try to take it. He lowered his hands and took a step forward.

I raised my shaking right hand, palm toward him. "Stop! Tell me you didn't take more than one dose!" His face gave no reaction to my words. "I told you, one dose only," he snorted and shuffled another step closer, and I repeated. "I warned you, one per game. You said you understood."

The corner of his mouth turned up, one eye squeezed low, and he took another step. I hopped up and moved to keep the table between us. My sudden jump forced my chair back, tumbling into the hallway. Its aluminum legs pinged against the hallway door frame, the wooden slug popping off. It pitter-pattered away until tittering to a final smack. In the heat of my kitchen, perspiration streamed down Billy's face, his t-shirt drenched. The smell of liquor wafted across the table as he exhaled.

Did I tell him no alcohol?

The side opposite the sink and window contained a series of cabinets suitable for pots, pans, and dishes for a small crowd. Most remained empty, except for those with bottles of assorted sizes and lids or other materials used for portioning out my supplements.

When he moved one way, I shifted the other as we maneuvered

around the table. Billy bumped into the cabinet, and two jars crashed to the floor, shattering. His smirk twitched, and his eyes widened. He stopped the dance shuffle, reached down, and flipped the table over. My coffee cup toppled to the floor, spilling light brown liquid, and the book landed on the counter. The candle arched through the air and smacked into my kitchen window. The window cracked while the candle landed in a cinched fold of the dingy curtain tied to one side. The pale yellow and blue curtain began to brown and smolder, effusing a musty vapor, swirling to the ceiling.

Backed into the stove, he came for me. He grabbed my neck with both hands and squeezed. Leaning in, he bent me backward. I pulled on his wrists but with his iron grip. I found it impossible to break his grasp. The awkward position hurt my back, and my eyes bugged and began tearing up. I tried to call out and could only manage a weak whimper and gasped for a breath.

I reached for something, anything, and found the handle of a pot bubbling on the stovetop. I managed to grab its handle and swung it with intensity. The side of the pot struck his head with an audible thud. He yelped, released my neck, and stumbled backward. His eyes rolled, and his arms windmilled sideways, catching my forearm and causing me to lose control of the pot. Its contents splashed down his left shoulder and arm, scalding him. He screamed and collapsed, following the pot to the floor.

Turning my attention to the curtain, now aflame, I grabbed a lower corner to yank it down into the sink. The discolored curtain needed replacement anyway. I doused it with a quick splash of water and looked back to see Billy sprawled on the floor, motionless.

"Oh my."

Leaving the kitchen for a quick moment, I hurried to the herbal lab to gather my medicine bag, brought it back, and put it between the legs of the upside-down table. As I kneeled to the floor, I grabbed a kitchen towel hanging on the oven handle and sopped up the remnants of the pot's liquids, a bit cooler now, and most of the spilled coffee. The cup lay in several pieces next to the kitchen counter. After rolling up the soiled towel, I lifted Billy's head and placed it under his neck for support.

Once again, the kitchen threshold creaked, and I looked up to see a familiar young man. He had long dark hair over his shoulders and brown skin. He wore faded and worn Levi jeans, a winter hunting vest, and working boots. Tufts of dog hair adhered to his coat and pants. Standing with shoulders forward, he gestured to the kitchen disarray and the young man on the floor.

"I hear scream. I come."

"It's okay. You can be yourself. He passed out." Denny stood up straight and entered. "Go grab a washroom towel and come back to help me," he returned with the towel and knelt beside me. "What do you see here?"

He examined the unconscious boy and the mess for a moment and spoke. "Based on the redness on his arm, I'm guessing he got scalded by whatever spilled from the pot over there. It spread more at his shoulder and less so, down his arm." His hand motioned over the arm. "His shoulder and upper arm might blister." He pointed to redness on the side of Billy's head.

"He will have a nice lump here. I assume his head hit the floor when he fell."

I smiled. "Excellent. The pot had one of my tinctures simmering and reducing. We are fortunate. I made a small batch." I took a deep breath and exhaled. "He'll have at least two-degree burns." I pointed to a shiny area on the floor. "Be careful. I wiped the towel through the spill, but the floor could still be slippery." I grinned again and shook my head. "He did not get the lump from the floor. I hit him with the pot." I closed my eyes and breathed again. "He attacked me and had his hands around my neck. I grabbed the one thing I could reach."

I looked at Denny, his mouth falling open.

"Now, how do we treat him?"

He looked up, squeezing one eye and tipping his head.

"Do we need to treat him? He attacked you."

Nodding, I took another long breath. "Look at his injury. You know we help anyone who needs actual medical assistance when they cannot help themselves, even if they do not deserve it," I turned Denny's head and looked into his eyes. "Remember, the heart of a person is demonstrated by how they treat someone in need or weaker than themselves, and the quality of your heart and mind are in your actions when given the opportunity to help someone, even a bully, not in the reasons why he should not be helped."

Denny bobbed his head, and we both turned our attention back to the incapacitated man sprawled on the floor.

"Besides, I believe he took a multiple dose of my special tonic and went out of his mind. Mixed with alcohol, I am quite sure he had no control over his actions."

I pulled one of my tincture jars from the bag, opened it, and scooped up two fingers of an opaque, green gelatin substance. Prying his mouth open, I wiped the bulk of the gel across his tongue and scraped the remainder on his teeth. Closing his mouth, I stroked his throat, encouraging him to swallow. "This should help clear his head."

I returned my scrutiny to Denny. "Now, what about his wounds?"

"First, we should get this shirt off his shoulder and flush some water on the burns to cool the wound," he glanced at the corner of the kitchen by the door. "The water barrel drinking ladle should work well."

"Good, good. Get my scissors from the bag to cut his sleeve. Take care in case the fabric sticks to any injured skin."

Denny sliced the shirt from sleeve to collar. In a few gentle minutes, he peeled it back, exposing the scalded shoulder. "His shirt took the brunt of the spill," he leaned in for a closer look. "Maybe the shoulder will be okay, and the blistering will stay on the upper arm."

Smiling in agreement, I told Denny to shake out the towel. "When I lift his arm, slide it under to soak up any excess water. If we get water on the remnants of this spilled oil, we will be sliding around on the floor all night."

After cleaning the ladle, Denny took several slow minutes irrigating the wound, making a second trip to refill the ladle. "That should do. I'm sure some of the tincture remains on his arm," I smiled and nodded. "I use this one for skin rashes and itches anyway. Remnants of the salve might encourage his recovery." Still smiling, I turned toward Denny again. "What next?"

Anticipating my question, he answered without hesitation. "We should put a light dressing over the wound to protect it. If the burn blisters, it could get infected," he turned and paused for a moment, looking at the back door. "Then, we need to get him to the emergency room in town. They can take over his care. We should consider an ice pack for his head."

We dressed his arm with a loose protective sleeve of medical gauze covering the wound, and Denny fashioned a length of it around the boy's neck as an improvised sling. "Go get one of your heavier shirts. We need to put something on him to keep him warm. Then we can take him to town." Denny left the kitchen and scurried out to his room off the workshop.

After several minutes, he came back with an old flannel shirt. "We bought this one at the secondhand store. You said I could grow into it," he chuckled. "It's still way too big and might never fit," Denny said, chiding me on my thrifty purchase. "His car is most of the way across to the barn, in the middle of the driveway, and too far for us to carry him. I'll move it closer."

"You don't have a license to drive," I checked Billy's pockets and chuckled as I pulled out his car keys and tossed them to Denny. "I won't tell if you don't."

Catching the keys, he smiled. "Even so, you'll have to drive his car to town," Denny started sniggering. "I'll follow in the truck and hope I don't get stopped."

"What's so funny?"

"He has a new car; you'll have a proper heater. Other than off, our truck has two heat settings, hot and too hot, depending on how far you roll down the windows."

I had to join in on his laughter. "You are right about that."

Denny went out to move the car closer to the steps of the kitchen porch. He left it running and went back to his outbuilding room to get his heavy coat for the journey. When he returned to the kitchen, I signaled by waving my hand and placing a finger across my lips.

He nodded, slumped, and shuffled in. He lowered his gaze and mumbled, "I help, Pan."

Billy sat on the wooden chair at the upturned table, favoring his left arm. His right leg spread straight away from the table while the other knee bobbed up and down, his bootheel tapping a staccato rhythm on the slick linoleum. He wore Denny's old flannel shirt, with his good arm through a sleeve and two buttons fastened. The other sleeve hung limp against his side, and his left thumb looped between the buttons to help steady his arm.

"Who's this?"

"Denny," I told him as I grabbed the other kitchen chair in the hallway. "He helps me with my garden and other things around the old place. I needed his help to carry you to your car and called for him when I moved it closer to the porch."

I set the chair by the table, and it wobbled, the missing slug causing a short leg.

Billy arched his eyebrows. "Pan?"

"Denny can't pronounce my whole name. He just calls me Pan."

Billy harrumphed. "So, this is dog-boy. I heard about the retard you had out here. I thought them just stupid stories made up by the girls."

He spit on the floor near Denny's feet.

CHAPTER 8

DENNY

In our first years in Montana, Pan provided most of her medicinal support to members of the Flathead Indian Reservation. They needed medical care more than anyone else in the area. Without an official medical office in town and without advertisements in local newspapers, it took a while for word of mouth to filter out to the local populace.

Except for her tribal visitors, I try to stay out of sight whenever any of Pan's female customers come by for help and always when their male friends accompany them. They often showed up at odd hours. Coming from both the Whitefish and Eureka areas, the young women would meet Pan in her business office.

I call it a kitchen.

The small farmhouse had three bedrooms, the one downstairs converted to Pan's personal library, herbal lab, and apothecary. She uses the kitchen stove whenever tinctures require heat and keeps most of her creations down in the basement, where the temperature remains constant. It functions as a root cellar.

Guests or patients needing to stay for a few days use the second upstairs bedroom. One of those guests caused her to use the triangle angle-iron ringer hanging from the front porch. Late one night, she needed help delivering a baby.

I came running when she rang.

As a relationship facade, I have a large and comfortable room off the farm workshop and use the convenient location to care for my sled dogs. It also provides a straightforward excuse and an easy place for me to go and avoid customer's boyfriends. Over the years, young women visitors would catch glimpses of me working in the garden or training my pooches.

Being of mixed race, black and white, single, and associated with an unusual occupation, Panacaea Clarke had enough trouble with community acceptance. I am half Kootenai, and she worried I would be targeted by cruel town kids. She wanted to keep me from attending the local schools and told me about some of the things she overheard the girls saying. Pan is right about most things.

No. She is right about everything.

Pan began homeschooling me after we arrived in Montana, and to complement the safeguard, she allowed (I should say encouraged) her customers to believe I am a simple-minded orphan she rescued as a small child. Pretending is easy, and I sometimes tease her when we are alone by putting on my act. In truth, my studies have gone well, and under her tutelage, I met all high school graduation requirements before my 17th birthday.

After years of pretending, calling her Pan became a habit. We both decided that doing so would prevent me from calling her mom in front of someone by accident. To me, calling her Pan became my warm and loving way of saying mom.

Our quaint little homestead sits a few miles over a hill from the state highway, situated between Whitefish and Eureka, Montana. Although closer to Whitefish, Pan established all our financial and legal contacts in Eureka. She liked the name. Unlike Momma, she trusts banks, and we drive to Eureka most weeks to make deposits or withdrawals and purchase groceries and other necessities. I received my graduation certificate during one of those trips.

On my 18th birthday, we took a rare trip to Kalispell for me to register for the draft. We also stopped to chat with a First-Class Petty Officer at the local Navy recruiting office.

CHAPTER 9

PANACAEA

The young man at the table sputtered. “Who needs his help?”

“I do! Until a moment ago, you were unconscious. I needed Denny’s help getting you into your car so I could drive you to the emergency room in Whitefish.”

“I don’t need your damn help. Or his,” he stood, grimaced, and repositioned his damaged arm.

“Your keys are in the car. It’s running.”

He stood, glaring at me. “You’ve ruined my life, Pansy!” He spit again and clomped out the door.

We watched him leave and heard his car accelerate down the driveway, spitting gravel and slushy snow. I sighed. “Momma was right.”

Denny turned to me. “What now?”

I smiled and tipped my head. “Well, amongst other things. We should arrange to get you a driver’s license.”

***

We moved to Montana from New Orleans, where my Haitian mother, Momma Clarke, immigrated with her parents from Port-au-Prince years ago. Momma Clarke’s parents both practiced Haitian Voodoo; her father was a third-generation Voodoo priest (or houngan, a male Haitian priest), and her mother a remarkable and talented female priest (or Mambo).

During our many evening talks, I entertained Denny with stories about our family history. "Momma Clarke told me she learned to speak English as part of President Franklin Roosevelt's Good Neighbor Policy." On hot evenings in Port-au-Prince, she worked to teach her parents what she learned of the language. "Although both children of privileged Haitian families, Houngan and Mambo Clarke had differing perceptions on the United States occupation of Haiti." As Momma told it, by some accounts, the occupation by US Marines did more damage than good, and depending on your perspective, the Roosevelt policy could be called the one good thing resulting from the long and unwelcome occupation.

I bumped up my eyebrows.

"She certainly believed it."

One of Mambo Clarke's biological grandfathers came from Germany. His family settled in Port-au-Prince in the early 1900s. Because the German nationals integrated within the Haitian community and married into many of the prominent Haitian families, their community grew to control the bulk of the modern Haitian economy.

Denny always paid attention.

"She had German blood. Is this why Momma had lighter skin?"

I nodded.

"One of the reasons. You also have German blood."

"As time passed, jealous American businessmen contended the local Haitian-German community became sympathetic and helped the German military by participating in their intelligence networks," my mouth curled and I shook my head. "They imbued the idea to US Government officials, who came to believe the Haitian Germans made regular and direct reports to Berlin. It wasn't true, but with growing national apprehension and boiling civil strife engulfing political factions within the Haitian government, the United States believed the stories and embarked on an occupation of Haiti, with a mission, promoted in part, to protect the Caribbean islands from hostile Germans."

Houngan Clarke's parents, both Haitian, fell outside of German influence and supported the US occupation from its outset.

"Although the US government conscripted many Haitians into construction projects, the initial backlash from the transgression softened as some improvements to infrastructure and facilities began showing positive results."

I looked at Denny. "Do you understand the term conscripted?"

"No."

"It's like a military draft, but in this case, it tended to be more forcibly applied. And as it happens, as in many prescribed situations, when forcing people into an environment without giving thought to the impact on community relations, progress began to falter."

Letting out a deep breath, I frowned at Denny. "Bullies come in all shapes and sizes."

I patted Denny's hand and told him about how the senior Marine leadership transferred to Europe in support of World War 1. The remaining non-commissioned officers used Haiti as more of a personal playground than a duty station and island under their care and protection.

"Because my great-grandmother had skin lighter than most Haitians, she drew the attention of off-duty Marines and, when walking alone, tried to avoid them and their rude behavior and banter."

"One evening, her avoidance attempts failed, and the future Mambo Clarke resulted from one of the many forced interactions with intoxicated Marines and unlucky local women who caught their bloodshot eyes," I winked at Denny. "This is another reason why Momma had lighter skin."

"So, please understand, my first historical awareness of American Marines painted an ugly picture."

The eventual Clarke and Caliste marriage became a Haitian version of Romeo and Juliet, as their two families never got along. For too long, they had been on opposite sides of the political divide, and their marriage did nothing to resolve those differences and bring the families closer together. The couple stayed in Haiti for several years until discordant family pressures forced them to flee.

Nodding to Denny, "In many things in life, there comes an event or a moment when one knows it's time to move on. It can sneak up on you or happen in an instant."

"After arriving in America, my grandparents opened a small shop in a former New Orleans apothecary. As you know, the shop filled one end of the ground floor of an old brick business building and included living quarters above the store, where we lived."

Denny smiled remembering. He loved hearing the stories.

The exterior had an old, carved mortar and pestle emblem above the entrance door, representing the earlier pharmacist business proprietor. Mambo Clarke appreciated the symbol and felt it bore a strong connection to her work, too. "Just like me, she would crush and grind constituent parts of her tinctures and often used a mortar and pestle in her work. She liked it so much; she adopted the symbol as her own and had the old symbol repainted and lacquered."

"This is the shop you knew so well."

The store catered to other Haitian immigrants and many locals seeking beneficial healing and spiritual help of a more colorful variety. Although she had a heavy accent, Momma Clarke helped her parents with translations, if needed, when an occasional American customer visited the store.

Voodoo priests and priestesses have a wide knowledge of pants, and their potential uses in healing. The ample-figured Mambo Clarke excelled at restorative rituals and the preparation of herbal remedies, amulets, and charms.

"She loved the brighter side of the craft. Momma learned to love it, too."

"Now, I never knew my grandfather, but Momma described him as gangly. Houngan Clarke preferred the darker aspects of Haitian Voodoo, and their bickering on the fundamental focus of the shop heightened as their approaches to managing the American store diverged." Although knowing their differences caused them to separate, "I must admit, it pleased me to know both the Mambo and Momma preferred the lighter aspects of voodoo."

When their differences became untenable, the lanky Houngan left the shop and moved to a musty cabin somewhere in the deep swamps of Louisiana to practice his hedonistic version of religion. The Houngan dealt in Baka, or malevolent animal spirits, and organized periodic feasts for his outlying congregation, where they made ceremonial animal sacrifices. His life darkened.

Momma told me she never knew the location of his cabin.

"Denny, I don't think she wanted to know."

After her parent's separation, Momma Clarke saw little of her priest father. As she grew older, Houngan Clarke came back to the shop on rare occasions to leave portions of his licentious profits behind to support his only child. Mambo Clarke sent her daughter upstairs to her room during most of these visits. "I could hear them argue and shout at each other whenever he returned," momma told me. "When those visits dwindled, and he stopped coming around, her father began turning into a memory, and thoughts about him faded."

When Mambo Clarke died, she had owned the old apothecary building, containing the shop and apartment, and a small neighborhood grocer, for several years. Momma Clarke continued to operate the profitable boutique offering healing oils, dolls, trinkets, as well as other spiritual practices and spells. She operated it both the way Mambo did and how she wanted.

"Momma's reputation grew."

***

Momma took her turn to pass on all she knew about herbs, oils, scents, and the accompanying rituals she used for healing and enlightenment or protection. I touched Denny's knee.

"I became her student. She taught me amazing things and almost made me believe in magic."

"When she didn't know I listened, I heard her telling people she had an exceptional and intuitive student who absorbed everything," I laughed. "Having my mother's excellent Caliste family memory helped. She told me all the women from her maternal grandmother's family had remarkable memories." I took a breath, considering. "This no doubt came about by generations of Caliste women passing their knowledge and traditions from daughter to daughter through oral tales.

Momma Clarke talked about and taught me many things, though never about the relationships between men and women, other than echoing her own Mambo. "Men are no good. Stay away from them." Momma said. "Serve only women."

Momma warned.

***

My father, a white businessman from New York, handsome and tall, with a full head of brown hair and a thin mustache above a dimpled chin, came to the shop one day. As he stood, standing, and shivering in the entry of Momma's shop, water droplets puddled on the floor. Had his appearance been the result of a hurricane rather than a minor tropical storm, she might have recognized the omen.

"This started my understanding of Momma's feelings about men."

The man came back several times over the dreary week. Momma explained how he tried to pressure her into a business venture with a chain of stores. "He wanted to establish a Momma Clarke branded voodoo boutique on the other side of New Orleans, in a fashionable tourist area, and several other boutiques spread from Los Angeles to New York."

"Momma had no interest beyond her one store and told him so."

When his initial commercial overtures failed, the businessman changed his approach. Over numerous visits and several months, he brought her chocolates, cheeses, and chrysanthemums.

He hoped the chocolates would represent his appreciation of the historical development of cocoa drinks for more than just pleasure, but also for health remedies and its use by indigenous people for ceremonial purposes. He hoped to satisfy her sweet tooth, as well.

"It did."

Since cheeses are a food developed in ancient times, he intended them to show the longevity of the relationship he wanted to establish.

"I have to admit, he worked at it for a long time and did not give up."

For the trifecta, he chose chrysanthemum flowers to represent his understanding of her fervent connection to the environment and how nature's abundant botanical varieties provided a myriad of potential health benefits and other useful purposes.

He did his homework well. My father's attempt at seduction worked, and Momma came to believe she loved him, and he loved her and came close to giving up total control of her shop.

"Oops." I opened my eyes wide and smiled at Denny. "Then Momma became pregnant."

When confronted with the news of her pregnancy, my father encouraged Momma to abort the baby. "To abort me." He knew she had the knowledge and capability. Over the years, she helped hundreds of young women rid themselves of unwanted or unwelcome pregnancies through natural means.

The process is safe. The solution is easy. The suggestion is abhorrent.

"No! I keep baby." Momma said, exaggerating her heavy island accent. She welcomed her pregnancy.

Giving up on the potential boutique venture, my 'married-to-someone-else' father returned to New York and never showed his loathsome face in Momma's New Orleans shop again. He never contacted Momma and never provided any support for me, his daughter.

I grew up not knowing my father. I grew up not wanting to know my father. I grew up without my father's name.

I grew up watching Momma. I grew up learning from Momma. I grew up with Momma's name. I grew up as Panacaea Clarke.

***

"Momma personified the entertaining supernatural shop owner in New Orleans and cultivated a lucrative life of herbal health and fragrant mysticism. She regaled visitors with stories, songs of her own imagination, which only she understood, and colorful outfits in keeping with her shop's ambiance and exaggerating her generous figure. Many of her songs and stories had elements of the oral family tales she taught to me."

Numerous visitors and customers would come to her shop at various times each day. An affable and social woman, Mamma looked forward to interacting with everyone, whether they were buying customers (new or regular) or nosey, vacationing one-time window shoppers. It did not matter. No one left her shop ignored or untouched by her gregarious warmth and charming smile.

I teased Denny. "You've seen her singing and dancing. Do you remember?"

Denny nodded, smiling and laughing. "Yes. I do."

"Mamma tutored me about her craft and the importance of honoring our Haitian culture while living in America and living life in an American way." Shaking my head, I nodded to Denny. "She diverged from traditional voodoo training and its intrinsic initiation ceremonies. Mamma Clarke took a simple and daily approach to my mentoring and made it her purpose to raise me as an American, using an American educational process."

Closing my eyes, I breathed in, recalling those memories. "During the day, I attended public schools. After finishing my schoolwork, she tutored me on her unique processes during the evening. She ignored the typical Haitian voodoo ceremonial initiation rites, requiring witnesses to be present for me to complete my voodoo priestess education."

I laughed and patted Denny's knee. "She teased me and referred to me as her Mambo in training."

Denny looked up at me, eyes wide. "Will you teach me too?" He sighed. "I want to be like you and Momma."

CHAPTER 10

BILLY

The witch hummed to herself while standing at the kitchen counter, slicing potatoes and carrots on her cutting board, pushing them to the side in neat rows. The veggies must be for a roast or something she planned for Thanksgiving dinner tomorrow as meaty aromas already filled the kitchen. A pot with tonight's dinner simmered on the stove; the lid rattled as steam escaped.

I'll be sure to keep her away from that pot.

As she focused on chopping, on again, off again, shadows soaked through the cracked window. Unaware. She faced away from me as I entered. The vestibule floor creaked, announcing my arrival.

"Back already? What did you bring us for dinner?"

She must think dog-boy caught some fish. The retard isn't capable of anything else.

She spun around, hands flailing when I answered, "Smells like dinner is already cooking."

Her knife spun in the air and landed point first, missing the toe of her shoe by inches. It stuck upright, wobbling, in the worn linoleum at the point where two opposing sets of black and white squares met. Her chest heaved, and I could almost hear her heart pounding from across the room. She raised her fractured voice.

"What are you doing here? Get out! Get out now," she backed up and braced her hands on the counter behind her.

Leaning inside the kitchen doorway, I held back an internal laugh with a flinch. She glanced down at my clothing, and her mouth fell open. I wore a paint-spattered pair of worn coveralls, old sneakers, and the retard's flannel shirt, buttoned to my neck, and gloves pulled up over the sleeves. I charged her and yelled. "Payback!" With one quick blow, I punched the left side of her head, knocking her to the floor. She landed on her back, dazed and moaning. She rolled her head, eyes blinking, tearing.

"Feels good. Don't it?"

I plopped down and straddled her, pinning both of her wrists under my knees. Snatching the kitchen knife from the floor, I yanked up on her apron and sliced its strap from her neck. She began to whimper as I pulled the apron down and shoved the top between my legs. In a quick and steady move with both hands, I yanked on her blouse, ripping it apart. Buttons popped and flew around the kitchen. Tiny patters sounded as they bounced on the linoleum. I took a moment to scrutinize the fullness of her exposed, faded, and threadbare Formfit brassiere.

My right cheek twitched. How can she look so good? I hate this woman. The satisfaction left as fast as it arrived.

Getting some of her wits back, the witch struggled and attempted to cry out. I leaned forward to cover her mouth with one gloved hand and pressed the knife against her neck. A first trickle of blood oozed. I could smell her trembling and wanted more. She whimpered with my full weight on her wrists. I shifted back and heard and felt a snap under my left knee. She squirmed with a moan and began to cry out. I moved to cover her mouth again and stifle her scream.

"Call out for dog-boy and I'll slice your neck and kill him too." My jaw hurt as I wheezed the words and realized I had clenched my teeth. Opening my mouth, I wobbled my jaw, loosening the tightness. Removing my hand from her mouth, I lifted the bra between her breasts and cut through it with one swift slice. "Sharp knife. How convenient," she sobbed and shook her head. She's worried about me exposing and touching her chest. With these gloves on, there is no way for me to feel the warmth of her flesh. There is no way for her to know, and it is too late to matter. I am only here for one thing.

The witch's eyes went wide, tearing. Whimpering from the pain of her crushed wrist.

"What do you want?"

I want to scare you to death, came to mind as I curled my lips.

"I told you." Still up on my knees, I put my left hand around her throat, pointed the knife toward her face, and growled. "Payback." My bark sprayed her with spittle. She blinked as it hit her face. I felt drool dripping down my chin. "You ruined my life, Pansy," she blinked as I sprayed her face again. "Now, I'm going to ruin yours."

The damn witch moved the only thing she could, her legs. When I raised my knife hand to wipe my chin with my forearm, one knee rushed up and caught me in my groin. Wincing, I toppled forward and banged my forehead on an open cabinet drawer. It slammed closed.

Damn.

With her wrists free, she rolled over and tried to brace herself. She pushed up, fighting to stand, and cried out as her wrist gave way. She fell. Before she could make a second attempt, I jumped on her back, my cheek flinching when I heard her umph.

"You're gonna pay for that witch!"

I dragged the knife across her back, crisscross cutting through the fabric of her blouse. Blood began soaking through, spreading. While ripping blouse remnants apart with one hand, I exposed her ruined skin and kept slicing flesh. When she cried out. I reached down, grabbed her broken wrist, pulled her over, and drew the knife down her cheek and chest. Whatever dark God the witch worshipped must have answered her prayer. She went limp and stopped struggling. She would no longer feel any pain as her life drained away.

For several minutes, I continued to cut and mutilate her chest and face, slowing my cuts as fatigue started to set in, my strength failing. Gripping the knife with both hands, I raised and plunged it into the dead witch's chest as hard as I could, once, twice, and three times. I could feel the knife penetrate the floor through her body.

A wet plop grabbed my attention. I looked up, and the overhead light came on. The witch always burned candles, and I never noticed the kitchen light before. The sudden brightness surprised and blinded me, and I released the embedded knife to shield my eyes. The action flew blood across my face when my glove smacked my forehead. I tasted an old penny on my tongue.

Disoriented by the bright light, I tried to focus on the noise and could make out what looked like a plucked goose on the floor just inside the kitchen door. Dog-boy stood there, his forehead peaked and mouth open. He shook his head as if in disbelief.

The useless tub of spit can believe it now.

I pointed at him and screamed. "You!" Again, a whip of blood swung through the room as my finger shot out. As time slowed, I watched individual droplets flying across the room, splattering against the cabinet doors. Needing to get to him, I jumped up and slipped into an expanding pool of blood. Of all places, I landed on top of the witch's damn lifeless body and felt a pain in my belly. The handle on the knife pressed into my stomach. There will be a dark bruise there tomorrow. I glanced up to see an empty kitchen doorway.

Shit.

Where did he go? I did see him, right? Yes, he left evidence: the goose lying on the floor, the light turned on, and the outer porch screen door bouncing against the frame, its metal hook rattling with each rebound. The sound hurt my ears. I rolled off the body to get up and chase him. When I tried to stand, my foot stepped on one of the errant blouse buttons, and when I pushed to stand, I slipped again and fell to my hands and knees.

Crap!

I gained my feet on the third attempt, leaving two red-gloved handprints on the floor. Moving through the kitchen into the vestibule, careful to avoid another fall, I kicked open the screen door. It swung wide, smacked against the porch siding, and jammed in place at an angle, hanging from the lower hinge while three corroded and stripped screws dangled from the upper.

At least the damn rattle stopped.

Standing on the top step, I shaded my eyes from the barn's floodlight and scanned the area surrounding the workshop, wondering where the retard had gone. Dog-boy must be hiding somewhere. Then I saw him. Even at a distance, through the glare, I could tell he looked back at me. He stood still, unmoving, one foot in the snow and one on the back of his sled.

"Wait! Come back," I gestured for him to return.

I heard the retard say one word. "Mush!" After he vanished in the darkness, I turned and shuffled back into the kitchen.

Damn!

The visit to the dark enchantress took a messier tack than planned. Good thing I wore gloves, no fingerprints. Stepping through the kitchen, I entered the washroom and looked in the mirror. Blood had splattered across my face, and streaked patches of it covered my shirt and coveralls. I turned on the water and removed my gloves, careful to avoid touching any smooth surface.

I took off the bloody flannel shirt, revealing an old sweatshirt, turned inside out, its frayed shirtsleeves cut off. I saw an actor in a recent beach movie wearing a sweatshirt inside out and liked the look. In the movie, the actor said he wore the outside in to put the clean side out. I dropped the bloody shirt under the sink.

After washing blood from my face and neck, I dried it with a towel. Examining myself in the mirror, I could see no more evidence of blood on my skin. Using the towel, I turned off the water and put my gloves back on. Back in the kitchen, I let out a breath while analyzing the bloody handprints and sneaker prints crossing the floor.

"I know what to do," I chuckled and went back to the washroom and picked up the blood-soaked shirt.

Still wearing the sneakers, I strode through the blood and walked out to the workshop, stepping in tracks left behind by dog-boy. With the bloody gloves, I unlatched and pushed open the workshop door, entered, and tossed the shirt in a corner.

"That should seal the deal."

Making sure to leave bloody sneaker prints, I stepped on the threshold of the workshop door and inside on the floor, stomping my feet several times. Even though I had walked through the snow, enough blood remained to be found by the police. Leaving blood on the door handle and frame removed all doubt. As I returned to the farmhouse, I made sure to leave a deep and clear set of tracks going both ways.

Back at the porch, my eyes recovering from the bright yard light, I scanned the kitchen. The goose carcass on the floor kept the kitchen door from closing. I remembered the knife and entered one last time and squatted next to the body. It took a healthy tug to extract it from the floor. I wiped off most of the blood on her apron, and using a larger remnant of the witch's blouse, I wrapped the knife and walked out of the kitchen.

On my way, I grabbed the old broom and headed to the porch steps. I chuckled, "One thing's certain. The witch no longer needs her broom." The ground scrunched and crackled as I walked to my new black Oldsmobile. Once there, I had second thoughts and turned to the old truck sitting next to one of the outbuildings. Flickers of snowflakes began floating through the arc of the area light.

That should take care of any footprints in the gravel. Any disturbance in this compacted area will be covered soon.

The truck's tailgate squeaked as I lowered it for easy access to the gas can in its bed. Next to the can sat an old milk crate, several of its slats cracked, empty except for an oily old rag, stiff with frost. Lifting the can, I smiled at the weighty slosh.

Nice.

After opening my car trunk, I set the blouse-wrapped knife behind the spare tire and pulled out my boots. When I leaned my weight on the open trunk to remove my sneakers, I heard a tinny ting.

It must be the car joints complaining about being cold.

Standing again, I dropped the coveralls. Under them, I wore jeans folded up at the ankles. My body began a violent shiver, so I shoved my feet into my boots and put on my heavy jacket.

Moving to the truck, I took out the rag and dropped the sneakers into the worn wooden crate, followed by my coveralls and bloody gloves, leaving it all on the tailgate of the truck. Using the rag, I lifted the gas can and poured fuel on the soiled clothing, box, and tailgate. I dribbled some on the brushes of the broom, as well, and set the open can next to the gas-soaked box.

Perfect!

As a precaution, I backed up, smearing the broom over my slight boot prints between the truck and my car. Despite fresh, wet snow on the bristles, it flashed bright yellow when lit with my pocket lighter. Still stepping back, I launched the broom onto the truck's tailgate, and with a brilliant whoosh, the box ignited.

Sudden heat hit my face, and I turned my head, giving me a clear view of the witch's body lying on the floor through the open door. Confident with the evidence left behind, I began to lower myself into the front seat of my car when the back of my neck prickled. Standing again, I turned to survey the area, seeing no one.

Dog-boy is history.

Satisfied, I got in and started my car. With no reason to hurry, I did a slow backup turn-around and idled down the drive to the road. I watched the burning box in my rearview mirror until the can burst, spewing flames out on the driveway. Pleased with the results, I pressed on the gas pedal, turned onto the country road, and headed toward the highway.

Hmmm, before I get to town, I better do something with the knife.

My parents have an old rental home on the outskirts of town. Although the place is more of a mountain cabin than a home, they let me move in during my senior year in high school. My mother wagged her finger.

"So long as you keep up your grades and pay utilities."

Before arriving in town, I stopped at the place to hide the knife. I didn't want the damn thing to fall out if I ever had to change a tire.

The rental has a small garage and lean to, filled with cut firewood, off the driveway. I removed the knife and slipped it into my tackle box, sitting on a small garage workbench. Inside the house, I headed to the bathroom. With the better light in my bathroom, I double checked to make sure no blood remained on my face and neck and noticed a drop of blood on my forehead.

This must be from when the witch toppled me with her knee. I also found a small amount on my sweatshirt. Using my styptic pencil, I stemmed the forehead nick and after changing my sweatshirt, headed out again.

An hour and ten minutes after leaving the farmhouse, I pulled in front of the Whitefish police station and charged in. The front door banged open as if straight armed by a running back. It was. The startled officer on watch jumped and almost fell out of his chair. Having consumed his share of police officer donuts, the deputy's pudgy fingers brushed the latest glazed old-fashioned crumbs from the protruding front of his uniform as he regained himself and stood. He had pock marks on his large nose, with reddening splotches on his face and a dirty blond horseshoe of hair bristling around his shiny pate.

"What's the emergency, Billy?" Deputy Steve Daniels asked.

While giving a bit of a gasp, I sniffed and blubbered and fell to my knees.

"I … I need to report a murder," I said, putting my hands to my face as I started to cry.

CHAPTER 11

DENNY

The morning before Thanksgiving, I finished all my chores around the homestead and let Pan know I wanted to bring home some fresh game for the holiday dinner and planned to go out for a few hours. With no mess in evidence, she smiled and handed me a chicken sandwich to take on my big game hunting trip. She tried to conceal a chuckle as I turned to leave the kitchen. I smiled back at her, and her wink confirmed she knew I caught her humorous moment.

Turning again, I headed out to my workshop and kennel to assemble my sled team for the afternoon. A team of three or five dogs would be fine for the short trip I planned, but the whole pack needed the exercise, and I hate to disappoint the ones left behind. They know I give in when feeling guilty.

They have trained me well.

Two hours later, we pulled to a stop near a small clearing. I released my lead dog from her harness. Pixie, an Alaskan Malamute, had a white underbelly, grayish sides, and a mix of dark gray and black from the top of her head down to her white tail. She shook her body, ears flopping against her head. She looked up at me, and I swear she smiled and nodded, indicating she stood ready for the hunt.

Never having owned dogs before this team, I had no idea they could be so attentive, expressive, and vocal, aside from barking. She tipped her head, side to side, and popped her jaw open and shut, making a sound half smack and half bop. I have learned this means she is ready for whatever event is about to take place and waits for me.

Pixie walked beside me as we headed toward the pond. We left the sled and the other dogs behind. Too many with me during the actual hunt could alert anything I would want to shoot. If I failed to get a rabbit or something bigger on the walk to the pond, I hoped for a passing duck or goose. As we approached the pond, Pixie became alert. Her ears turned forward, and her steps slow and deliberate. Following Pixie's clue, I hunched over and readied my old. 30-06 Winchester rifle and followed my girl.

***

My refurbished rifle had been left in the back of the workshop by its previous owners. I found the rifle and a small single-shot, 410 Champion, break-open shotgun in the back of the workshop after Pan bought the old farmstead and we moved in. I figured we should return the weapons to the sellers, but she told me anything left behind became our property.

She smiled and said, "Welcome the prosperity. We don't need to buy a rifle or shotgun now."

Our little family did fine in the money department; Pan paid cash for the farm. Momma left her with a considerable amount of funds, several gold coins, and one gold bar when she died. With no bank account, Pan had no idea Momma's cash box held so much. Still, she taught me to conserve funds whenever and wherever possible and never to flaunt our wealth.

With no other relations in New Orleans, Pan felt it best for us to relocate closer to my extended family. My Kootenai father came from the Flathead Indian Reservation, south of Kalispell, Montana. His sister married a member of the Upper Kootenai Indian Band and lived near Grasmere, British Columbia. Although I have cousins in both areas, Pan felt the area between Whitefish and Eureka provided a reasonable distance to either location. We found the little homestead on a hill near Stryker, Montana, to be perfect for our needs.

Pan had me pack up the two weapons for one of our early trips to Eureka. We took them to a hardware store, where they sold and serviced weapons. A nice young man who worked at the store said the weapons were in decent condition, and we left with plenty of ammunition. He taught me how to clean and maintain both the rifle and the shotgun. With practice, I became proficient with both weapons and soon began providing fresh fowl and games for our meals. Coupled with the occasional fish from a local stream and vegetables from our garden, we ate well.

***

Disappointed by the hunt so far, I began to worry. Then Pixie let me know our luck had changed. I looked up to see several transiting snow geese dipping their heads, causing ripples in the pond water. They must be spending the day here on their trip south. I kneeled and considered which one to shoot. Because those out in the center of the pond would be difficult to recover, I chose a big one on the far side. My hunting companion glanced at me, tilted her head, and shifted her attention back to the goose.

Pixie is terrific, but she is no retriever. The word fetch means nothing to her. She had better things to do than go chasing after something I threw. If I wanted whatever I tossed, I should not have hurled the thing away in the first place. At least, this is how I interpreted the look she gave me when I tried to teach her to fetch. Pixie would not stoop so low. Several other members of the team will fetch a ball or stick, but not fowl. They were consumers, not retrievers, and if I wanted a whole goose, I'd better be prepared to get it myself.

The large goose rooted through some dried-out cattails opposite of where we squatted. Pixie sat at attention as I prepared to catch the goose when its head popped back up. Her body sat rock solid, her eyes locked on the goose.

Squeezing the trigger of the old rifle, I watched the head of the chosen goose vaporize. Half a growl and half a whimper got my attention. Pixie shook her head, her ears flopping side to side for several seconds before stopping. She tilted her head to the right, raised her forehead, and blinked, mocking me. I swear her look conveyed a "What the hell was that?" feeling.

I got the message. "A bit overkill, I know." I rubbed Pixie's jaw. "The goose swam too far away for my 410, and I'm supposed to bring home dinner for tomorrow." I chuckled. "Besides, Pan doesn't like little metal pellets in her meal. No matter how hard I try, I never get them all cleaned out."

Raising my hand, I scratched behind her ears. "I'll be sure to save some for you guys." Her mouth opened wide as if smiling, and her tail swished a fan pattern in the snow. "Sorry. No pumpkin pie, though." I stood up from the marsh edge and found my legs cramped from squatting. I stretched for a moment while Pixie remained on her haunches, unfazed by the frigid ground.

She tipped her head toward the pond. One eyebrow went up. I knew the look.

"I'm a sled dog. Get your own damn goose."

Nodding, I rubbed her shoulders. "You're a good girl, Pixie."

Pixie continued sitting on her haunches and watched me struggle around the pond, my sloshing and slushing echoing from the trees. No worries. With a series of flaps and squawks, the other geese departed in a flurry after my shot. Only the headless goose remained, and when I got back, a large wet snowflake landed on Pixie's nose. Her tongue whipped out to snag it. I noticed a cloud of Pixie's breath and reflections on the pond getting darker. I gave Pixie another rub.

"We better get this cleaned up and head home."

Rather than cleaning the goose at the pond, I decided to head back to my favorite fishing hole by the stream. We moved to my special spot, over halfway back to the house. I prefer to use water in the moving stream over the rigid pond to rinse away the goose's innards. Access to the water is easier, and besides, the entrails might get caught in some of the reeds and rocks and encourage fish to hang around. I might get a chance later to come back and try to hook some trout. With luck, the stream will carry away all the plucked feathers and down.

I knew the cleaning would take a bit of time, and my team had already been harnessed for a while, so I released them from the sled and put them all on long leads so they could move around and drink water while I worked.

Upstream of my goose cleaning, of course. I had no problem cleaning the goose, but plucking the darn thing was something else, especially as the sky darkened. Every time I have plucked some type of fowl, the exercise turned into another example, demonstrating I have tons of room for improvement.

I am grateful that, so far, Pixie has yet to share her critique.

When we pulled around the back side of the workshop, I noticed the shiny black Oldsmobile parked across from the kitchen door. Under normal conditions, I would avoid bothering Pan when she had a customer. But I wanted to get the goose into the kitchen, and the sight of the Oldsmobile bothered me. The last time I saw the vehicle parked here, its driver attacked Pan. I decided to leave my team harnessed to the sled and set the snow hook. I rubbed Pixie's head.

"I'll be right back, girl. You guys hang loose for a minute."

I grabbed the goose and headed to the house.

When my feet hit the porch landing, I heard the first of three thuds. Stepping through the kitchen door, I heard another thud and saw a man straddling something red and messy on the floor. He raised a knife and thrust it into … oh no, it can't be? No, no, not her. I dropped the goose, reached for the light switch, and flipped it down.

The switch has been wired backward, and when you flip it up, the light turns off. We had no experience in fixing electrical things, so we never got around to trying to rewire the switch. After about a year, I began teasing her about how she used the backward switch as an excuse to burn candles for illumination instead of the overhead dome light.

My eyes rolled over a horrible, bloody red mess, my Pan. Part of her apron spread across the lap of a man straddling her. She lay motionless. He looked up, and I got a solid look at his face. The same man who attacked her before. He had a snotty sneer, and his dripping sweat merged with the snot as it slimmed down his chin.

When I dropped the goose, his head jerked up, and he swung his hand up to shield his eyes. Blood flew. Pan's blood. After the initial shock of seeing me, recognition set in, and his face contorted, and he pointed at me. With his chin tucked, his cheeks began billowing. I thought he might vomit, but he yelled and started to get up.

I had no intention of letting him get to me and turned to run back to my waiting team. They sensed something awry and pawed the snow, anxious to move. Pixie growled; her hackles raised. Several of the others followed her lead. I lifted the snow hook, took a step onto the sled, and turned my head when I heard a loud noise from the porch. The man stood there, tittering on the stoop, shading his eyes. When he saw me, he motioned with his hands, trying to encourage me to come back.

Like hell.

Shaking my head, I turned to my team and brought my other foot up. Just for the bastard who killed my mother, I called out loud enough for him to hear, "Mush." We took off and, within seconds, passed behind our shed and moved into the trees. I looped around a cleared path surrounding the old pasture, my sled and team concealed behind an overgrown fence. During the day, my head could be seen over the top rail, but Pan's killer stood in the parking area under a bright mercury lamp situated high up on the front face of the barn, its hood casting light to the porch; it concealed me in the darkness.

Pixie led the team down to the end of the pasture, and we turned back toward the house and stopped at the edge of the garden behind the windmill. It creaked on one side, and branches of the trees opposite groaned. Her hackles stood in a row, and her grumbling growl continued to spread among the other dogs. I stepped off and stroked her neck and rubbed her ears. I gave attention to each dog with its ears on alert. We all watched the house and waited.

He came out of the house, moved between his car and our truck, and stuffed something into the box we used to contain groceries on our trips to Eureka. Moments later, I heard the flash of flames shooting up. Then, his headlights swept across the barn and the trees beyond. Seconds later, the truck exploded. Although my ears echoed, I heard his engine gunning toward the road.

"Well, Pixie, I guess we no longer have a truck."

Her entire body shook, spraying me with icy drops.

Under normal conditions, the drive to Whitefish or Eureka could take about thirty minutes, a little longer on snowy roads. It would take authorities at least an hour to get here, and then only if he notified the police.

Why would he? He could blame this on me. It would be my word against his, and since I am supposed to be a challenged individual, I would have to admit Pan and I have been living a lie. Can a good defense start by admitting several years of a fabricated relationship? Goodness no. I'll head north to my cousin's house. In a few days, my bus for boot camp leaves from Eureka. Between now and then, I'll decide what to do. The prudent thing to do now is leave.

Stepping back onto my sled, I directed my team out of the trees and moved them around to stop at the front of the house. Always unlocked, I entered through the front door. It screeched and made me wonder if we ever used the entrance. Moving through the parlor, or waiting room, I hesitated in the short hallway and caught a glimpse of Pan in the kitchen to the right. In front of me, the washroom basin and floor showed smears of blood.

I turned left into the doors leading to Pan's lab and the stairs to the second floor. The stair treads creaked as I went up to her bedroom. Folded into a neat square on top of her bureau, I picked up the prayer shawl Momma had given Pan in the weeks before she gave birth to me. Back in the hallway, I shook the shawl out, placed it over my shoulder, and entered the kitchen. Skirting the edge of the blood pool and bloody sneaker prints throughout the room, I bent down on one knee and covered my mother.

"I love you, Pan. I'm so sorry I didn't get here in time."

While touching her forehead and her heart through the shawl with my fingertips, I caught the aroma of overcooked food. The stew pot on the stove boiled to a dry paste, its heat threatening a fire. I moved it to the kitchen counter to cool. Turning back to the oven, I closed the stove vents and shifted the firebox slide from stove to chimney, hoping the fire would soon burn itself out. Scanning the kitchen, I noticed the goose sitting where I dropped it earlier.

"Oh dear. I can't leave the door open. Who knows what critters could wander in after I'm gone."

Goodness. I'm talking to myself. Have you answered yet?

"No."

I walked around all the blood, grabbed the goose's legs, and plopped it in the sink. I went to close off the kitchen and remembered the coat hanging under Pan's extra apron in the vestibule. It hung on one of the many coat hooks lining the wall to the right when entering the house. Only the shattered screen door remained on the porch; its outer door was still missing after many years. Even if functional, a determined animal could easily get through the screen, so I latched the kitchen door shut.

Back through the kitchen, I walked past the washroom and entered Pan's herbal lab. On the floor next to her working table, I opened the chest we brought from New Orleans. The cash box still sat at its bottom. I picked up her shoulder bag and added all the papers she kept in her work desk drawer.

I'm not sure what's important, and I can sort through them later.

With the papers, I slipped Momma's diary in the bag. It included notes from my mother about things she created since Momma's death and her comments on successes or failures when working on Momma's old tinctures. The diary dates to my great-grandmother, Mambo's mother, and is the most important artifact I have left of her family. It all went in the chest.

On top, I pressed the coat from the vestibule into voids between items in the chest to hold them in place. Picking up the chest, I carried it out and put it in the basket of the sled. Before leaving, I checked the lab for anything else of importance and stuffed several jars of my mother's tinctures into my pockets or in her medicine bag.

These could come in handy.

I slung the bag strap over my shoulder and left through the front door, closing it, and put the medicine bag in the basket next to the chest. I covered both with a blanket and canvas cover and secured them with several short leather straps.

With one last look at the house, I gave a final nod and directed my team over to the workshop, where I loaded some food for the trip. We took the access road north. Following a series of forest roads, deer trails, clearings, and snowed-over creeks, I headed for Canada.

CHAPTER 12

BILLY

The deputy looked at his notes. The crime scene pictures he took would be developed later. My dad is a tall man with short, dirty blond hair. His husky, muscled frame broached no nonsense. I learned not to give him back talk years ago. However, I am no longer a little snot nose. Chuckling to myself, I am a big one now.

Dad spent a lot of time at the farmhouse, returning a short while ago. His eyes squeezed shut, and his lips pursed. By the wrinkle of his forehead and sigh, I wondered how much of the witch's death scene remained on his mind. He looked at me, his eyes open to a squint.

"Where did you get the bruise on your forehead?"

"At the park, after the game."

He closed his eyes and harrumphed.

"Okay, tell me, why did you go out to the old farm?"

"Dad. I already told Steve. I heard the old witch could heal people and hoped she could give me something to keep the blisters on my arm from scarring. When I drove up the drive to the place, I saw something burning in the back of an old pick-up truck and Musher Man leaving on a dog sled. I rolled down my window and called to him."

"Why do you refer to him as Musher Man?"

"I remembered they call people on a dogsled mushers. So, Musher Man."

"What did you say to him when you called out?"

"I just said, Hey!"

"Did he answer?"

I took a deep breath and pretended to be thinking and trying to recall.

"Yes! He called "mush" to his dogs, then they took off."

I scratched my chin.

"That's when I turned my head and saw the witch's body on the floor through the kitchen door."

"Through the door?"

I nodded. "Yes. I had a straight line of sight through the open door."

"Did you go into the kitchen? Did you touch anything?"

"No, Dad." I shook my head. "I'm not an idiot. I never got out of my car. I hightailed out of there and drove to the station as fast as I could."

"You sure looked like an idiot on the field when those scouts came to the game," Deputy Jacobson said. "You been smoking something? It sure would explain your game behavior, that bump, too. Besides, how else could you get yourself burned like that?"

"Dad! No. Jeeze. I told you. Me and Becky had a fight. I was thinking about her and worried about how to apologize. I was also unprepared and preoccupied about a big test coming up. And yes, I was way nervous about the scouts being there. Until the last game, my season had not been what it should be. The whole thing had me rattled."

I huffed and looked up, rolling my head, hands up.

"I screwed up. Okay?"

"After we got back from the game, I went down to the park and started a bonfire." I wanted to stress the point, so I slowed my words into a steady rhythm. "I might have had a beer or two down there." Now, speeding up my tale. "Anyway, I got lighter fluid on my jacket, and my sleeve caught fire. By the time I noticed and got the damn thing off, it got ruined, and I got burned. It was an accident. Cripes! Leave me alone."

DOC DENNY

CHAPTER 13

DENNY

November 1967

Two days after leaving my mother covered on the kitchen floor, I gave the disturbing news of her death to my Aunt Diane and Uncle John and confirmed arrangements for leaving my dog team with them during my enlistment in military service. Pala looked forward to spending time with my team and promised to keep them well cared for. I had one day left to get to Eureka and board a contracted Greyhound bus to take me to San Diego and Recruit Training Command. I would spend the holidays in boot camp.

***

I gave final hugs and rubs to Pixie and the team. She bobbed her head several times and placed her paw on my foot. "Woof." She either understood I would be gone for a while or wanted to keep me from leaving.

Rather than taking another bus from Grasmere, Uncle John and Cousin Pala drove me down from their ranch to Eureka. We arrived early, and before going to the bus depot, I asked them to drive me down to our Attorney's office.

"This is the office of Abe Williams. We have him on retainer for the farm as our …" I closed my eyes and sighed … "my lawyer for all my legal requirements."

When I asked to see Mr. Williams, the receptionist shook her head.

"Sorry. He left earlier for a client in a legal case down in Kalispell. I don't expect him back until late."

With no time to wait to see him and still meet my bus, I asked if I could leave an important message. She gave me a yellow notepad, like Abe used during my other visits, a pen, and an envelope. The envelope had the law office address printed in the upper left corner. She noticed my raised eyebrows.

"Use the envelope to seal your note to Mr. Williams. Since he became your family attorney, all communications are deemed private, and the sealed envelope ensures no one else will see the note until he reviews the information after opening it," she smiled and chuckled. "The requirement for privacy includes me."

Having prepared a little speech for him, I knew what I wanted to say and sat back to begin writing. Putting everything I could remember in the note took a short ten minutes. I did not include the killer's name.

If she knew, it died with Pan.

I folded the paper, slipped it into the envelope, and winced at the bitter taste of the envelope flap. I brought it back to her and stood there, staring at the envelope. It seemed silly to put his name and address on it.

"Here, let me."

She took the envelope. Setting the pad and pen down, I watched her write "From Denali Darkcloud" on the envelope and underlined it twice. I thanked her and returned to my uncle's truck. They drove me to the Greyhound bus stop, and we said our goodbyes. Thirty minutes later, I sat in a window seat of a Greyhound Bus, five rows back. I waved at Pala, standing on the sidewalk, as the bus departed. His right hand hit his chest.

***

After several quick stops for other recruits, the route took us through Butte, Montana, where we stopped for an hour. Here, we met several additional waiting recruits. They lined the group of us up under an outside awning-covered area next to the bus, in front of an erected folding table. We all raised our right hands while taking our oaths and signed paperwork before the entire group got on the bus again.

Late the following day, and two additional bus drivers later, my cramped and stiff body waddled off the bus at the Greyhound Depot in San Diego. A Navy bus and a Chief Petty Officer with a uniformed driver waited a few yards away from where I yawned and stretched. The Chief greeted me and the twenty-four other volunteers we picked up along the way. His warm reception and welcome turned out to be the kindest words we would hear for the next nine weeks.

The following morning, my long hair, tied back in a tail, lay on the floor of a bootcamp barber shop. I rubbed the sides of my head and felt stubble. On top, the quarter-inch hair bristled as my fingers brushed through. My haircut took 20 seconds. Sigh!

CHAPTER 14

ABE

When I got back from Kalispell, my receptionist Sally had closed the office. I unlocked the door and entered, turning on lights as I walked through the lobby into my inner office. I needed to make a few notes about my Kalispell case and put away its files before going home. Sally had laid out new mail and several papers on my desk for review, including the Panacaea Clarke file folder. It lay there with its flap open. Some papers peeked out.

Sally's getting sloppy. The file popped open when she plopped it here.

Each client had their own brown accordion folder. The first section contained wills, followed by powers of attorney, other legal documents, and then my personal notes. The last slot in the folder held client correspondence.

Why would Sally have brought out the Clarke folder?

My stomach rumbled, reminding me my dinner would be waiting with my wife tapping her toes. So, I picked it up, shook the file to settle all the papers inside, and placed it back on the corner of my desk. After making my notes from the day's activities, I put all my other files away. The few letters remaining on my desk and the Clarke folder could wait.

The next morning, the local newspaper published an article about the death of Panacaea Clarke. She had been murdered a couple of days ago. News travels like flowing molasses.

Now I know why Sally had the file out.

Someone must have called the office asking about Ms. Clarke's will, so I knew why Sally had pulled it from the file drawer. Aware of the recent will, I saw no need to review it now. It can wait until Denali returns from the military. I made a mental note to call Sheriff Robert Hastings and let him know I represented the family.

Sally greeted me when I walked into the office.

"Did you see the Clarke file last night?"

"Yes. Thank you."

After pouring a cup of coffee, I entered my office, sorted through all my mail from the day before, and placed the Clarke folder in the filing cabinet.

When lunchtime rolled around, I decided to drive down to the local café, hoping to find the sheriff. Sure enough, he sat in his normal spot, and as I approached, he pointed to the bench opposite. "Hi, Abe. What brings you to the café?"

"You." I went on to explain how I represented Panacaea Clarke and read in the papers she had been murdered. "I have her will and power of attorney on file, with other notes and instructions."

"Sheriff Jacobson, from Whitefish, has jurisdiction on the Stryker case," Sheriff Hastings said. "He might give you a call."

Later in the day, the Whitefish sheriff called, and after confirming I represented Ms. Clarke, he asked me about a simple-minded boy named Denny, who worked at the Clarke farmhouse and had sled dogs.

"He is a potential material witness in the murder."

"I'm sorry, sheriff, I don't know anything about a boy named Denny working for Ms. Clarke. She does have relations up in British Columbia, including the executor of her estate." The sheriff confirmed they still considered the farmhouse a crime scene. "Can you tell me when it will be released to the family?"

"In a few weeks," he said, and before I could offer information about Panacaea Clarke's son, Denali Darkcloud, he thanked me and ended the call.

Although worried about informing the young man about his mother and the family in Grasmere, I called Mrs. Whitehorse. She let me know Denali knew about the murder and had gone on to fulfill his military service. She gave me his fleet post office mailing address in the event I needed to contact him for any legal reason.

CHAPTER 15

DENNY

Dear mental diary,

Bootcamp is an interesting experience. One might assume the nine weeks of preparation the Navy gives you prior to going into its service would focus on teaching you about the Navy. I'm not so sure. Although there are a few classes of instruction on various naval subjects, those topics are general and scattered. A class on naval rank structure could be followed by marching to a dingy building and running into a small, enclosed, and windowless room, 90 seconds of instruction on donning gas masks, followed by the instructor activating a tear gas canister and rushing out. Two days later, your eyes cleared up.

On another day, you could spend an hour in a pool, trying to remove your trousers, tie the pant legs into knots, and flop them over your head to fill the pant legs with air, making a personal floatation device. Marching to the next class of instruction in a wet uniform with wrinkled ankles made little sense to me. Well. The march did help the pants dry.

In the next class, you might be introduced to types of ships and shown pictures of their dark silhouettes. Instruction touched on dozens of topics, all giving a quick overview, with the subject never visited again.

We only got to see, hear, or try most topics of instruction once.

On any given day, we could be marched, in a rush, to a medical facility and lined up in a corridor, heel to toe, between the person in front of us and the one behind. There we stand, trying not to think about our personal space being squeezed. “Heel toe, heel toe, hurry up and wait” became our mantra. More than once, someone fell asleep or fainted during the many waiting periods.

These intervals of waiting could be for haircuts, immunizations, uniform measurements, eye or dental exams, weigh-ins, or a brief doctor examination. There is nothing like standing next to dozens of other naked men and being ordered to bend over for an exam. A bunch of naked men standing in heel-toe formation in a hallway takes on a different facet altogether.

We marched to breakfast. We marched to class. We marched to lunch. We marched to a quick firefighting exercise on a mock-up of a naval ship. We marched to dinner and then marched back to the barracks. More than anything, we marched to the parade ground and learned to twirl a fake rifle. I could twirl it over my head like nobody’s business after a few weeks. I had doubts about the importance and purpose of this skill. Do sailors need to twirl rifles aboard ships, aircraft, or submarines?

Dear diary, Did I mention we marched a lot?

I began to believe the real purpose for all the marching was to break in our new boondock footwear. Navy socks are made of a thin, stretchy black material and provide little chafing protection. Before the sailors in my company could break into their shoes, the shoes broke into their feet. Blisters developed blisters, and the phrase ‘down in the boondocks’ developed a new meaning.

When we arrived at boot camp, they assigned pairs of us to bunks in the barracks with an upper and lower bed with small standing lockers. The open lockers had upper and lower shelves, as well, and one small drawer for each bunkmate. The locker had room to accommodate our initial issue of uniforms, including a few sets of underwear (tee shirts and boxers), socks, handkerchiefs, washcloths, and bath towels. We also got work coats and raincoats. Although our coats hung on hooks, everything else had a specific place in the locker, and folding them and stacking them in proper order became one of our biggest early challenges, other than blistering marches and trying to stay awake in class.

We received a padlock for the locker drawer and could keep any personal item we brought with us, so long as it fits in the closed drawer; little fit. All items in the barracks, our lockers, our clothing, and our bedding are subject to daily inspection, except our locked drawer. Individuals had to be in big trouble for their personal drawers to be inspected. Of course, none of our civilian clothing fit in the drawer. Most everything we brought with us had to be shipped back home in the bags or suitcases we used to transport them on the bus. I managed to keep two of Pan's short jars of healing ointments. Although a tight fit, with a little push or tug, the drawer opened and closed with the short, fat jars inside.

Before we figured out the secret of wearing two pairs of socks to protect our feet from chaffing, I began administering ointment to blistered toes and heels. With a limited supply, bad cases of blisters had to be seen by a corpsman in the medical clinic. However, most instances of breakout and irritation cleared up from one or two uses of Pan's ointment. Coupled with other occasional sweat rashes in my armpits and areas I would prefer to forget. I became a popular recruit in the company.

We had little money to spend and few opportunities to spend it, so thankful sailors would offer to polish my shoes, bring me cookies, or whatever other goodies they received when their families sent them things as payment for their relief. Except for the cookies and shoe shining, for which I needed lots of help, I would not accept any recompense. Remembering Pan's words, "We help anyone who needs medical assistance when they cannot help themselves, even if they do not deserve it," I felt caring for my fellow recruits was my duty.

Besides, they all needed my help. Even my bully of a bunkmate. Once he relaxed and became friendly, he asked me if the ointment came from my Native American mother. He dropped his jaw when I told him, "No. My father is Kootenai. My mother is a Haitian voodoo priestess."

He never bothered me again and became my biggest supporter.

***

Days ran together, repeating the same mind-numbing routines. I lost track until one morning when we fast-marched to an unfamiliar building. It contained an overlarge room set up with rows and rows of one-person desk chairs spaced evenly apart. Today is assessment day, they told us. A Navy Lieutenant stood up front and explained the importance of the test and how its results would be used to determine what Navy career paths we could expect to be assigned to and what command locations we might be eligible to request.

I did a quiet and slow shake of my head. We should all be eligible for positions requiring rifle twirls. For weeks, we had near-daily twirling exercise drills, marching with and whirling our fake rifles. As far as we understood, twirling is only used at our graduation ceremony, still weeks away, and anything else. No one understood why. Time well spent, I guessed and changed my mind.

No, just time spent.

The Lieutenant called the exam the Armed Services Vocational Aptitude Battery test, or ASVAB. After finishing the exam, I found the daunting name and its acronym confusing. The test had more general knowledge questions than armed services questions, or Navy, in our case. I gave a prayer to Pan for her years of tutelage in reading, writing, and arithmetic as the old tune danced through my head.

The hickory stick aspect only applied to my training here in boot camp.

Those of us who had a decent education before boot camp and who could also manage to pay attention in classes where they gave us a quick introductory exposure to a broad naval topic did well. Most recruits wound up eligible for deck gangs on various naval ships upon leaving boot camp. Their immediate futures would evolve around brooms and mops or swabs. A few, like me, would go on to advanced training for specialized rates of our choosing or to fill needed critical rate shortages based on our individual skills or education and test scores.

Following boot camp, most of the new Navy Airman, Fireman, Hospitalman, or Seaman, depending on their chosen or assigned paths, took the usual two weeks of vacation or leave we recruits received upon graduation. With nine quick weeks in the Navy, none of us saved up enough leave to take a two-week vacation. Doing so puts you 'in the hole,' and it would take several months before you earn enough leave to regain a positive balance.

Starting out with a negative leave balance did not bother me but did not enter my decision-making process, either. I had no place to go and no one to visit, and a better reason to conserve my meager leave balance. I chose to stay in San Diego and reported directly to the U.S. Naval Hospital Corps School. Had I taken the normal two weeks of vacation, I would have missed the start of the next corpsman course and needed to wait several weeks or months, no doubt in a work division, before beginning a later training session. Six days early for the start of the next session, I killed time by working at the Naval Medical Center in San Diego.

Not certified to do anything medical in the hospital, also known as 'Balboa Hospital,' due to its location within Balboa Park, I wound up in a work division swabbing, waxing, and buffing floors (decks in the Navy) and cleaning bathrooms (excuse me, heads). Why do sailors call bathrooms heads? I would have to find an "old salt" and ask him. At least, I can imagine how the term "old salt" came about.

On my second day in the work division, one of my future instructors, Hospital Corpsman First Class (HM1) Henry Moyer, found out a new Hospitalman Apprentice had arrived early, just out of boot camp, and volunteered to work at the hospital. After pulling me from the work crew, he told me he appreciated my initiative.

During the day, HM1 Moyer gave me the opportunity to study some of the school materials. The bulk of the basics came to me like second nature; I had been under Pan's tutoring for years. However, some of the processes or procedures had quite different names from what she taught me. Identifying those differences came easy.

Henry Moyer and I spent hours talking. He preferred being called Hank, and he wanted to know why a young man from Eureka, Montana, would sign up to become a Hospital Corpsman and to understand what motivated me to want to be a medic in a unit of Marines in Vietnam. I reached for my wallet and pulled out a folded and tattered piece of newspaper. After unfolding the clipping, I handed it to HM1 Moyer (to Hank).

"I never met my father, and all of his official paperwork, what little I have, remains back home," I told him.

The clipping from a New Orleans paper is all I brought with me. Hank Moyer looked at the article and saw a black-and-white likeness of a Marine heading up the column. He looked at me and remarked about the resemblance to the Marine in the article.

He read the cold and impersonal news report.

Staff Sergeant Denali (Denny) Joseph Darkcloud served in the 1st Marine Division's X Corps, combating the Korean People's Army (KPA) as well as the People's Volunteer Army (PVA) after China entered the Korean War in October 1950. When they were forced to withdraw from Northeast Korea, X Corps repositioned to bolster the depleted UN forces near the 38th Parallel as part of the 8th Army, operating under the command of Lieutenant General Matthew Ridgeway. Staff Sergeant Darkcloud participated in the defense of Seoul during the Chinese New Year's Offensive, which started on New Year's Eve, 1950/51, initiated by the combined forces of the PVA and KPA. The Chinese and North Korean attacks overwhelmed the UN defenses, and the joint enemy forces captured Seoul for the second time. It would take another three months before the 8th Army, with Staff Sergeant Darkcloud and UN forces, retook Seoul, now in ruins.

Staff Sergeant Darkcloud survived all five major Chinese offensives, only to be killed during one of the stalemate battles in the 1951 Battle of Bloody Ridge. During the battle, the 1st Marine Division moved on the northeast rim of the Haean Basin (referred to by the Marines as 'The Punchbowl'). The Marines met little opposition on 31 August 1951 and pressed on with confidence the following day. During the night, KPA forces stiffened their resistance, and Staff Sergeant Denali Darkcloud fell to enemy fire on 1 September. He received the Silver Star for actions during the war, posthumously.

Staff Sergeant Darkcloud has two surviving family members: his sister, Dyani Whitehorse of Grasmere, British Columbia, Canada, and his son, Denali Joseph Darkcloud Jr. of New Orleans.

After Hank finished reading, he handed the newspaper clipping back to me. Glancing at it, my eyes misted before folding it and slipping it back into my wallet.

"There's something else you should know." I took a breath. "After we moved to Montana, my mother homeschooled me. She became a marvelous nurse and taught me about basic first aid, amongst lots of other things. She and my grandmother both delved into old-fashioned home medicinal remedies, as well." Otherwise known as voodoo or black magic. "So, I have 'helping people' in my blood."

I went on to explain both my mother and grandmother had passed, my mother just months ago, and joining the Navy to become a medic with the Marines answered the call left by both of my parents.

"I'm so sorry. Your losses are much more than most of us have to endure this early in life." He rubbed his chin. "I can understand your motivation and appreciate your willingness to put in the extra effort, even when that effort started out with you swabbing decks in the work division."

Hank explained getting accepted into the Special Amphibious Reconnaissance Corpsman program, SARC for short, is a simple matter of volunteering during initial Hospital Corpsman 'A' School.

"I'll help prepare the paperwork for you to sign. You can move straight into special operations training after this course ends."

I closed my eyes, remembering some despondent sailor's attempt at humor in a drawing I saw on the side of a toilet stall in the barracks. Above a stick-figure sailor holding a broom, the artist wrote 'N.A.V.Y. Never Again Volunteer Yourself.' I brushed aside the thought and nodded with an internal smile.

"In the past," Hank said, "corpsmen had to spend time in the fleet after completing 'A' School before they could apply and be accepted into the SARC course pipeline." He rolled his head. I heard his neck pop. "The Vietnam War has changed priorities and loosened many limitations. Due to the growing need for additional field support, they lifted the fleet requirement to get into the program."

"And FYI, select personnel with advanced medical training and knowledge can be fast-tracked through the program. They only needed a command recommendation." He bumped up his eyebrows. "I can get you the Commanding Officer's endorsement. You just need to keep your coursework grades up."

"I will."

Through conversations with instructors during training, I found out the full SARC curriculum included passing three different physical fitness assessments. Those requirements only applied to someone attending the entire series.

Hank regarded me. "Most people specialize in one primary area, Army Airborne, Combatant Diver, Amphibious Reconnaissance, or Combat Medic." He tipped his head. "I don't think anyone has attended all the courses."

With no clue knowing which of the courses had which physical requirements, I decided to be prepared. To make sure I could pass whatever physical requirements we faced, I began exercising in the base gymnasium and alternated either swimming in the pool or running and then finished each evening by studying course materials. Somewhere in the mix, I found time to eat and sleep.

Demanding work, little sleep, concentration, patience, and determination turned out to be a combination of skills useful in my near future.

***

When we completed the initial corpsman program course, they

advanced all of us to Hospitalman Third Class (HM3). With a new one-chevron patch on my arm, I left hospital corpsman school and packed to leave for my next assignment. On Saturday morning, I checked out of the barracks and climbed aboard another Navy bus with my new seabag to take a short drive to the San Diego airport. From there, I boarded a Trans World Airlines flight to Atlanta, Georgia, destined for Camp Lejeune, North Carolina.

I had never been on a plane before, and an attractive Stewardess noticed my tight grip on the armrest.

"Would you like a complimentary glass of Cold Duck?"

"Sure," I said, wondering why they didn't serve duck on a plate. She handed me a glass filled with an amber bubbling liquid.

"What's this?"

"Cold Duck."

I peered at the glass with a wrinkling forehead.

She smiled. "It's a kind of champagne."

Although I scrunched my lips at the first sip, each swallow tasted better than the last, and somehow, my glass always had fluid in it. The Stewardess never asked my age, and I realized she must have allowed me to drink the alcoholic drink because I traveled in uniform. I felt much better by the time we arrived in Georgia, and my knuckles had returned to their normal color.

During a three-hour layover in Atlanta, I ate a quick meal consisting of a dry turkey sandwich. Later, I found out they had condiments to the side, so people could add their own mayonnaise or mustard to their sandwich.

Who knew? Pan's sandwiches always had them added.

The effect of the Cold Duck began to wear off, and an ache in the back of my head began to wear on. Somewhere during a throbbing ache, I arrived at the departing gate for my next flight. An appealing woman in an airline uniform received me and checked my ticket. The effect of the Cold Duck still cluttered my head, and I had difficulty focusing on what she said, but a sign behind the counter indicated a one-hour wait before the flight would begin boarding.

Action at the counter slowed down from a crawl to a stop, and I stood to stretch my legs, still sore from my earlier flight. Only two other passengers had checked into the flight, both wearing Marine uniforms. At the waiting area window, I gazed out at our little plane and noticed the ticket agent moving luggage from carts and stowing them into the baggage compartment of the plane. I could see her breath billowing under bright security lights.

Back in the terminal, the ticket agent returned and checked our tickets as we prepared to walk to the plane. Since the flight had only three passengers, she told us to sit anywhere we wanted. I boarded the small twin-engine craft and sat in a window seat on the left side. One side of the craft had two seats in the row, while the other had one. The two Marines took their seats, and I buckled myself in for the ride. Moments later, the agent boarded the plane and asked one of the Marines to change sides to even out the weight distribution. I closed my eyes.

They do not pay this woman enough. If she steps into the cockpit and flies the plane, I would not be surprised.

She turned and talked to one of the two pilots, who came out and closed the plane door as she left. Several minutes later, we began to move, and my bladder endured a bumpy flight to Wilmington, North Carolina. After the flight, duffle bag in hand, I shuffled to the ground transportation area and waited again before boarding another bus.

It took the entire day for me to reach Camp Lejeune. A large Marine greeted me at the gatehouse. "Greeted" might be a generous term.

On Monday morning, I joined the Field Medical Training Battalion and began the first of two accelerated SARC schools. The first, Field Medical Service School (FMSS), would take eight weeks. The second Special Operations Combat Medic (SOCM) course at Fort Bragg, North Carolina, would require a short four months.

***

By the end of 1967, the 1st Marine Division managed to maintain a solid hold on much of the northernmost region of an important zone in South Vietnam. In the early months of 1968, the communist and North Vietnamese forces launched their massive Tet Offensive and besieged the old capital city, Huế. Along with other U.S. forces and South Vietnamese units, components of the 1st Marines fought to reclaim the city. The ensuing 'Battle for Huế' became one of the longest and bloodiest single battles of the Vietnam War.

I finished the nine-week field training course at the top of my class and received the opportunity to go directly to SOCM and complete the additional training. The need for medical support in Vietnam remained high as the Tet Offensive had taken its toll. In support of my new family, I elected to defer the SOCM course and deploy to South Vietnam.

After nineteen years, a 'Darkcloud' returned to the 1st Marine Division.

When in-country, I joined a Marine platoon headed by a young First Lieutenant, Michael Hastings. I saluted the officer. "Hospital Corpsman Third Class Darkcloud, reporting for duty."

With a raspy whistle, Lieutenant Hastings exhaled and looked at me up and down. "Don't do that." When I blinked, he added. "Don't salute. Not here in country." For a moment, relief relaxed his face before his eyes began staring off into the distance, and a slight crease tightened his forehead. "Welcome to Vietnam."

He led me out to where several men prepared for a new operation. They moved around in a busy, systematic process. The Lieutenant introduced me to platoon sergeant Gunny Sawyer, who told me the operation started in two days. He might have added, "Get your shit together," but I remember it as getting my medical supplies in order.

Then Gunny took me around to introduce me to the other men. The platoon had been through several skirmishes under Lieutenant Hastings.

"LT's a good man. He's earned our respect," Gunny said. "We have a tight unit, and everyone plays a key role."

I stepped into one of those roles.

Sitting with the men at dinner, between grouses, they started asking questions about my background, and I let them know about my mother and her medical tutoring. Although interested in those stories and pleased to know I'm not just any other rookie medic, they listened with greater attention when I talked about my father.

It's a good thing Aunt Diane told me so much about him.

An appreciation of my place among them grew from those few stories I knew. At the time, I failed to grasp its importance. With little familiarity with people outside my family, I had no understanding of the male bonding experience.

Wondering how much action the platoon faced, I asked a simple question.

"Do you guys see much action?"

"We're the vanguard," one of the Marines said.

"We're what?"

"The tip of the spear," another said.

Gunny answered my simple question. "It means we're in the thick of every skirmish."

The men told stories too, some true, some tall tales. They laughed, joked, and passed around a few beers. They told me I could have a beer or four tonight but none tomorrow. In between long skirmishes, they just wanted to get numb. As a group, though, they agreed to avoid partaking in any alcohol the day before a known campaign. One of them started joking about beer commercials and how advertisers always lied.

Gunny joined the conversation. “Some commercials tell the truth.” Heads turned toward him. “I know the Schlitz beer commercial is true.” The men laughed and argued it couldn’t be possible. “No, it’s true.” He did a little jig. “The jingle says, ‘When you’re out of Schlitz, you’re out of beer.’ This is true. It’s true because Schlitz is the last fucking beer you would ever want to drink.”

The men laughed until they cried. I laughed with them but did not finish my beer. After my experience with Cold Duck, the idea of drinking beer or any other alcoholic drink held little appeal. I preferred to avoid its headaches.

CHAPTER 16

MICHAEL

Go Noi Island had been a stronghold of the People's Army of Vietnam (PAVN) for some time and one of our many desired target areas. The island is jumbled with low hills and snaking waterways. It's difficult to go ten steps without getting your feet wet or worse. Hidden within the lush jungle's darkness are villages and concealed trails offering the People's Army easy opportunities to provide a rugged resistance and elude our infiltration attempts. Earlier operations resulted in little success. The 1st Marine Division commanders decided we needed a more thorough offensive code named Operation Allen Brook.

Here we go again.

Always ready to engage with little notice, my experienced platoon geared up for the operation. Platoons from our company joined one another, and the combined companies prepared for combat.

Besides the obvious difficulties and danger of combat, my latest personnel concern showed up two days before our operation started a new medic, HM3 Darkcloud. Hoping the mainland knew what they were doing by sending a rookie to the war, I introduced him to Gunny and reported to the command tent for an operation briefing. While there, I let them know my replacement medic arrived. My last one had been injured and evacuated back to the States. With little time to orient the young medic into my team, I asked Gunny to keep an eye on him. With Allen Brook starting in two days, we would know soon enough how well he fits into our little dance group.

Early on May 4th, my platoon led the Marines across Liberty Bridge onto the island. The bridge, a temporary structure, allowed us to move heavy vehicles, trucks, tanks, and men in a hurry across the island. I say temporary, as it had to be rebuilt several times. The bridge and anything crossing on it were easy targets.

The presence of leading tanks caused the enemy to be circumspect, and we faced little opposition. This changed three days later as skirmishes became more rigorous. I lost my first man on the third day and another the following day as fighting intensified. Although we continued clearing hidden pockets of enemy soldiers and caches of their supplies, internally, I questioned whether the cost of those successes outweighed the gains. A few hours after my second man fell, they called us back to Liberty.

Time for a breather.

We retreated across the bridge as the command group airlifted from the island. The idea, the plan, the hope, is to cause the PAVN to believe our operations concluded, and we left the island for good. Not so much. Before dawn the next morning, we recrossed the bridge and struggled to continue our incursion of the hellish island.

As each Marine in the platoon fell during those first days or those near us from other platoons, HM3 Darkcloud appeared, giving aid. Enemy fire had no bearing on his willingness or ability to aid the wounded. The colloquial form of address for a hospital corpsman is "Doc." In the United States Marine Corps, Marines use this term as a sign of respect. As we prepared to return to the island, Doc Darkcloud walked and talked among my men.

We moved back across Liberty before the first light and found a quiet island. Too quiet. Heavy combat engulfed us when we encountered a PAVN battalion. Unable to outflank the regrouped and bolstered enemy, our company major called for air support. By evening, the enemy had withdrawn, leaving over two dozen Marines dead and more than half wounded.

At the leading edge of the skirmish, my platoon swept the area. Now, with four dead and six wounded, we endeavored to find our way back to the main force. In the process, I received a career-ending wound to my left leg. Whatever hit me came from nowhere and severed most of my leg below the knee. Under heavy fire, Doc Darkcloud rendered aid to stop the bleeding and pulled me undercover.

Gunny Sawyer appeared next to him. "Orders, LT?"

I told him to continue maneuvering our wounded from the area and attempt to rejoin the main force back at the bridge.

The Doc stopped one of the other wounded Marines, who could still walk, and handed him my weapon. "Walk with us," he said and pulled me up and laid me over his right shoulder. At least, people told me that's what he did. I passed out about the time he lifted me. While we withdrew, a wild shot pierced Doc Darkcloud's left arm. While several Marines took out the sniper, he ignored his injury and continued to carry me. We merged with another group of Marines, and without further losses, the two platoons managed to get all our injured out of the heavy combat area to a location where we could wait for an airlift. As we waited, Doc did little more than tie a handkerchief around his arm.

Because of his injury, Doc Darkcloud accompanied all the injured back to the relative safety of a field hospital. During the transport, he continued to provide aid to any injured Marines being relocated to relative safety. At the hospital, he relented to receiving treatment.

Termed a success, Operation Allen Brook resulted in the routing of a PAVN battalion. In the wake of their departure, the Marines found the enemy headquarters and substantial supplies, believed to be the motivation for their fierce resistance. The short 'successful' campaign came with 25 dead Marines and 38 wounded. Although remnant clashes from the earlier offensive remain and the 1st Marine Division continues intense fighting, they are doing it without me and nine of my men.

***

I get my medical evacuation tomorrow, joining several other Marines on our trip back to the States. Doc Darkcloud stopped by to see about my treatment and sat on a stool next to my comfortable cot.

"How's your pain?" He asked.

Although part of me wished he had left me behind. I opened my eyes. "Fine. I could use an actual mattress," he laughed. "I owe you my life, Doc." I went on to explain how, after the war, I had hoped to join the police force back home. "My dad runs the department, and I wanted to join." A flash of pain hit me; my leg reminded me I left most of it in the jungle. Wincing and blinking the pain away, I continued. "Guess I can't be a policeman now."

Doc Darkcloud shook his head. "You can do plenty of things when you get back, Lieutenant," he told me. "Being a policeman might be out of the question, but they must have other jobs in the department. Someone answers the phone and talks on the radio. You won't be immobile, just less … versatile."

He winked and smiled.

"I suppose, but I know myself. Nothing else in the police department would be challenging or fulfilling. I would go crazy knowing I should be out there being a real policeman. Hopefully, I can get my old job back."

"Of course, you can. Where are you from, Lieutenant?"

"A little place you probably never heard of, Eureka, Montana."

He laughed again and gave me a big, toothy smile with a shake of his head. "Not only have I heard of it, but that's where I boarded the bus when I left for boot camp. I lived with my mother near Stryker." He lowered his eyes, shoulders slumping.

"Lived with your mother. You're not planning to go back?"

The Doc almost whispered. "My mother passed. Murdered. Just before I left for boot camp."

"I'm sorry." I watched him until he looked up again. "Do you know who did it?" He nodded. "So, they caught him?"

His hands went up. "No idea, but I'm sure they must have by now. I expected to hear from the authorities while still in boot camp." He shook his head. "Nothing."

I squinted my eyes a bit and reached out to touch his knee. "I'll make a deal with you. When I get back, I'll ask my dad about your mom. If he doesn't know off hand, I'll get him to check. He knows the police chief in Whitefish. One of them must know." He nodded again. "In return, you come back to the States with us and complete the SOCM course at Fort Bragg."

His hand popped up, and he rumpled his forehead. I countered his reaction.

"I am aware you finished top of your class at Field Medical School and chose to come here first. I am grateful for your decision. More than you know. But the Marines need you, and SOCM will help."

He hesitated, rolled his head, and scratched across his chest.

"Look, you need a few weeks for your arm to heal before you're at full strength anyway. Why not spend part of the time in a classroom?"

He squinted his eyes, thinking.

I took the moment and went on to say, "With a little luck in timing, you could be back here by Thanksgiving, in better shape and more capable of helping other Marines."

He nodded again and closed his eyes. "Okay."

CHAPTER 17

DENNY

Pan would have lectured me for hours about ignoring my arm injury for as long as I did, but she would also have praised me for delaying the inevitable until after saving the life of Lieutenant Hastings and providing critical aid to several other Marines. The wound did not feel as bad as it turned out to be. As a student, I learned about battlefield fight-or-flight responses. Now, I've experienced how adrenalin can shield the depth of an injury. The stress-produced chemical can be as good as morphine. Its effect just does not last as long. When the combat stress clears, the temporary shield dissipates, too. The pain remains.

I arrived at Fort Bragg with my arm in a sling, missing the first week of the SOCM course. Under the circumstances and recommendations from the 1st Marines, they authorized my late entry. By the second month of the course, my arm had recovered, and through late hours of uncomfortable physical therapy, most of my strength had returned.

Unlike Field Medical School, I graduated SOCM second in my class. One of my instructors indicated the difference in our class standing played into the first week of coursework, which I missed at the beginning. I let him know class standing had no impact on my motivation. I wanted to be the best medic possible to support the Marines in my charge and hoped to go back to the 1st Marines as soon as possible. He smiled and nodded his head.

***

As Lieutenant Hastings predicted, I rejoined the 1st Marines Division before Thanksgiving, joining Operation Meade River, two weeks in process and amid intense combat. The operation intended to clear the area beyond the now familiar Go Noi Island and included a similar stream-scattered terrain.

Wet feet again.

The area also hosted another PAVN stronghold. The operation concluded on 9 December with about ten enemy dead for every Marine killed. Even so, a month later, the Vietcong and the PAVN returned. Closing my eyes, I shivered with the feeling we danced a dangerous foxtrot consisting of one step forward, one step back, and a lot of shifting side to side.

Damn the music.

Damn the dance.

THE MUSHER MAN

CHAPTER 18

AMBER

Whitefish Lake, Montana, December 1969

My best friend Nancy Adams and I sat with Rebecca Daniels and her older sister Jeanine, at a large picnic table. Laying old towels on the bench, we all sat on one side, facing a small campfire. Each of us held a can of beer, taking small sips as we chatted and laughed about all sorts of things: boys, school, clothes, everything pure nonsense.

Following a group of friends, we drove out to East Lakeshore to get away from the Whitefish holiday bustle. The popular secluded area, midway up Whitefish Lake, became crowded during the summer with older kids swimming, picnics, and many large family gatherings. Little used during winter, the remote location grew to be a popular hangout for high school kids.

"Nancy, tell those kids to put a couple of logs on the fire. I'm cold," Jeanine said.

Nancy snickered.

"We could move closer, you know."

"Closer to the smoke?" She shook her head and chuckled. "Besides, if we get too close to the other kids, we can't talk about secret stuff."

Snickering, Nancy walked over to the fire.

Nancy and I will graduate from Whitefish High this summer. Home from the University of Montana for the holidays, Rebecca and Jeanine sat next to me. We gathered with a group of eight other young people crouched on logs near the campfire.

Satisfied with their efforts, Nancy left the campfire and came back to snuggle next to me. When the added log caught fire, moments of heat kissed my face as occasional flashes of bright yellow danced yards away. A slow swirl of embers wafted upward, and my eyes watered whenever smoke drifted in our direction.

We continued to sip our beers. We sipped because none of us liked beer. We only drank it to be accepted in the crowd. I hate the taste. Never liked it, but drinking beer is the thing we do. Numerous pull-tabs, tossed around the area, provided evidence of the tradition. However, most will remain covered in snow until the spring thaw. So, I sat here taking tiny sips. As always, I will pour most of the bitter crap on the ground later, creating another kind of yellow snow. I never finished my beers, and no one ever noticed or complained. If you add up all the sips I have taken through high school, you might get one full can of beer.

But I doubt it.

Later in the evening, when the high school varsity boys arrive, the small campfire will turn into more of a bonfire, and the gathering will turn rowdy. There will be beer-guzzling and both laughter and testosterone-based shenanigans. Becky knew. She and Jeanine had spent enough time at the hangout during their heydays. They often had to drive their boyfriend's home when they drank too much.

Becky has long blond hair. Her curlicue locks smush out from her stocking cap and spread across the back of her white fuzzy coat. She wore matching white gloves. Maintaining her slender and petite high school cheerleader figure, she looked striking as yellow shimmers reflected from her coat.

"We better leave," Becky said, more decree than suggestion. "It's getting late, and the team boys will be showing up soon." Her breath billowed. "Billy doesn't like me out here with the varsity crowd. Now that he's a police officer, he has to be respectable and can't carouse with the naughty boys anymore." She laughed. "Especially since he's working with both my dad," she chortled again, "and his. Besides, my butt's cold and getting numb."

Jeanine stood up. Her dark hair, pitch black, flickered with red and yellow bursts. Pleasing to the boys, her buxom figure filled her goose-down jacket. I often marveled at how she managed to get it zipped. Of course, the boys liked the look, and she knew it.

"Yeah, my butt too. Besides, my glasses keep fogging up. Let's go, Nancy. You too, Amber."

Nancy got up, rubbed her bottom, and shook her legs out one at a time. "Damn bench." She started gathering the towels. Rather than a younger sister, she could have been a twin to Jeanine. They looked so much alike.

Although Jeanine's glasses are dark with angled rims, Nancy prefers rounded frames.

She looked at me as I stood up and caught me shaking my head. I folded my arms across my chest and tucked my hands under my armpits while leaning side to side from one shimmying foot to the other.

"I'm gonna stay." I dropped my arms and smiled. "I'm meeting Tom tonight. I think he might propose."

As the self-proclaimed fashion setter of the foursome, I wear different colored socks and bright contrasting colors or designs. Sometimes, I mix checkers and polka dots or leopard stripes with paisley swirls. As a rule, I always wear contrasting color combinations. Tonight, I wore a dark green winter coat and a bright yellow stocking hat, with a light blue glove on my left hand and red on the other. Because of my snow boots, no one could appreciate my mismatched green Christmas and orange Halloween socks.

A few of the undergraduate girls began imitating my example and started mixing up their color choices too, though I admit, few of my classmate friends ever followed suit. I hear occasional jokes about my choice of colors and combinations, but always at a distance, never to my face, mind you. I know I get away with being distinctive because I'm in the popular crowd, beautiful, and dating a varsity boy. The idea of this being the main reason I get away with my atypical fashion sense is okay with me. Someday, the trend will catch on.

My three friends began tittering, jumping, and clapping their gloved hands. "Quiet." I pointed to the kids around the campfire. "I don't want the others to know in case Tom loses his nerve tonight." We all laughed. "You know Tom. He'd be embarrassed if they knew and heard it from me. He might never ask." I shivered. "I'll walk with you to the car. I need to stretch my legs." We continued to giggle as we stepped over snow drifts to the car.

Becky glanced at the sky. "Looks like more snow tonight."

We giggled and wiggled all the way to the car and said our goodbyes. Deputy Billy patrolled out there somewhere, protecting the town, so Becky drove his car to the lake. Nancy asked if I wanted her to stay with me, and I let her know Tom would be too nervous if he saw her with me. She understood, and we grasped each other.

"Well, good luck, Ms. Batchelder."

We both looked up to see large flakes falling and stuck out our tongues to see who would catch the first one.

Laughing about our snowflake-catching contest, the three piled into the white-flaked black Oldsmobile, and I watched and waved as they left. Between the sips of beer and the cold walk, I needed to pee. On my way back from the parking area, I diverted to the outhouse toilets. I hate using them and dread the cold seat. At least, in the frigid air, the smell should be tolerable, and during winter, there is no bothersome fly problem. Opening the potty door, I stepped in. Struggling to see anything, I laid out strips of toilet paper on the cold seat, grateful the toilet had tissues. Sitting down, I took care to keep my pants from falling to the floor. Who knows what might be down there?

With my business done, I hopped up, bringing bits of toilet tissue with me stuck to my backside. Of course. Sigh. With my gloves on, I could not feel well enough to remove the paper from my bottom and took one off by pulling and holding the back of the middle finger of the glove between my teeth. The cold fingers of my right hand had more luck as I fumbled in the darkness and managed to remove all the pieces of toilet paper.

At least, I think I got them all.

Turning, I started to pull up my pants and, in the darkness, began fussing with my pants buttons; part of my shirt covered the buttonhole. Hoping for a campfire glow or moonlight, I opened the door, stepped out of the potty, and looked down to fasten my pants. I heard a crunch of snow and felt a painful blow to my left temple. My face became cold and wet, and one thought came to me as darkness overtook me.

Why couldn't I get my pants zipped before my face hit the snow?

CHAPTER 19

BILLY

Passing the turn to the lake picnic area, I parked my cruiser in a turnaround and got out. Walking the short distance down to the lake, I could see the picnic tables and early partiers illuminated by the campfire. My girlfriend Becky sat with three friends, one a real fox. A colorful fox. I worked my way close enough to hear some of their conversation but stayed back so no one would notice me.

They sat there sipping beers. Who is Becky trying to fool? She hates beer and should be drinking soda pop when driving my car. I ought to follow her and give her a ticket when she leaves. Of course, then her dad would kill me. Or mine.

I watched for a while and wondered if Becky would be leaving soon. As if hearing my thoughts, they got up shivering, rubbing their hands together, and shaking their legs. Laughing on the way to my car, they stopped, and Nancy hugged the fox. The other three got it, and Becky drove off.

Hello, opportunity. I have an itch, and the fox didn't leave.

She wandered in my direction. I prepared to take her there, but she turned to the outhouse and strode in. I approached. Around the back, I listened to the trickling splash until it stopped and moved to the side. Feet shuffled. The door opened, and she stepped out, looking down.

My footfall scrunched, and as her head came up, I popped her hard on her temple. Her head flopped to the side, and she toppled face down into the snow. No muss and no fuss. Yes, there would be a shallow half-snow angel on the ground near the toilet, but the impression will disappear with the falling snow. I grabbed the little fox and lifted her to my shoulder without any difficulty. I have hauled and tossed bales of hay heavier than her. Linebackers too.

Before any of the others left the campfire or anyone else arrived, I carried the slack bundle back to my cruiser. I set her down against a tree and opened the trunk. Unfolding an old tarp, I spread it across the bottom of the trunk. When I plopped her on the tarp, I folded up its edges to make sure nothing from the fox transferred into the trunk.

***

Three days after reports of her disappearance, search volunteers found the body of Amber Batchelder at Brush Creek, northeast of Whitefish Lake, near a small pond. I read the report Sheriff Boyer filed. Amber's naked body had been sliced, crisscrossed, front and back, from neck to waist. Her chest had three deep knife wounds. Because of mutilation and some animal scavenging, identification came from dental impressions. Except for a red glove, found in the snow by kids near the parking area where she had last been seen, searchers never found Amber's clothing. The medical examiner determined the disturbing mutilations and stab wounds were postmortem. Amber died from a severe blow to her left temple.

***

A 31 December 1969 article in the Whitefish Sentinel, attributed to an anonymous source, indicated the police had been searching for a suspect in the murder of a young local woman in the area north of Whitefish, Montana. The suspect is also linked to the scene of a similar grisly murder near Stryker, Montana, by an unknown person two years ago. A witness saw the so-called "Musher Man" leaving the area of the Stryker murder on a dog sled. There has been no sign of him since then.

When contacted for comment, the Whitefish City Police Department would confirm only there had been a person of interest in the Stryker murder of two years ago. The investigation into the older case had gone cold until the recent murder of the Whitefish woman. The similarities between the two murders indicate a strong possibility they are related, renewing interest in the earlier killing.

CHAPTER 20

KEITH

December 1970

It took us about two hours to make a loop around downtown, strolling from 1st Street to 3rd and Center Avenue and back. We focused on open stores or businesses, and in particular, when they displayed Christmas decorations, the more, the better. We stopped at any business with employees or patrons visible through windows, a barber shop, a hardware store, and a restaurant. The more people and attention we received at a location, the more songs we played.

The five-member ensemble played our last Christmas carol at the corner of Central Avenue and East Second Street. Most stores closed early during the holidays, and the few late-hour customers began returning to their homes for their family Christmas Eve festivities. We finished near Peter's parked car, half a block away, across from a popular restaurant.

The small group consisted of me on trumpet, Peter Reynolds on trombone, Vicky Tisdale on French horn, Bruce Miller on Baritone, and Phillip Thornapple, the only non-brass instrument player on tenor saxophone. We completed our round of downtown holiday caroling with a rendition of *Good King Wenceslas.*

Steaming for over an hour, Vicky glared at me, tears in her eyes.

***

I began playing trumpet in fourth grade and grew up with two other trumpet players, the three of us learning together. We first caroled on Christmas Eve in fifth grade and continued the next holiday season. Although we thought our performances were marvelous at the time, our novice ears failed to realize how discordant we sounded. Our innocent holiday intentions came through in a wonderful fashion, though. Spreading Christmas cheer at friends' and family's homes tended to lead to cookies, hot chocolate, and other holiday treats. After our first year, the treats became our main motivation for continuing the tradition.

It surprised and pleased the three of us when the first of those houses we visited brought out treats for us. My mother, who drove us around from one location to another, had planned the route ahead of time. She told us she wanted to make sure people would be home so we did not spend time caroling at houses where the occupants had left on Christmas vacation. Both years, the holiday caroling ended at our band director's house, where treats included seasonal soups, sliced meats, warm breads, cheeses, and hot chocolate. We never left his home hungry.

***

As we grew, I lost contact with my two former carolers, and when my family moved to Whitefish, Montana, I carried fond memories of the trio and longed to recreate the holiday event. It took me two years to muster up a brass ensemble, and in my junior year of high school, I found three fellow band members willing to go holiday caroling. Without Vicky joining the group, I doubt I would have managed to gain enough interest. As one of the most popular band members, Vicky had sway over most others, and when she agreed to play in the ensemble, Bruce and Peter lost all apprehension and decided to join, as well.

I will admit the four of us sounded a lot better than my old trumpet trio. I shivered thinking about how young we were back then and was pleased how no one threw tomatoes at us.

After having so much fun during our junior year, we four looked forward to repeating the event as seniors. Phil joined the brass ensemble for this season's excursion. As in the year before, and per my old holiday tradition visits, we planned to finish our Christmas caroling by performing in front of our high school band director's house.

Standing at five foot ten and average build, I am your typical high school band geek and have no clue what I want to do with the rest of my life. Although a consistently above-average student, much to my parents' dismay, math is the only subject I excel at in school. I know they are frustrated by my lack of serious interest in schooling. My parents, both educators, believe they have failed me in some way. I hear them complaining to each other in the evening sometimes when they think I am asleep.

I heard them in agreement several times. "Education should be more important to Keith," one would start and the other finish with, "and a bigger focus."

We packed up and moved to Whitefish when my parents both took positions at the local high school. We live a comfortable life, but on teacher's salaries, I knew they could not afford to send me to college. With little to no possibility of obtaining a scholarship, I would have to work to pay my tuition and expenses, and I knew myself well enough to acknowledge the struggle of working to support myself while also attending college and studying for classes. If I tried to do both at the same time, I would fail at one or both endeavors.

As a child, I liked watching *Victory at Sea* documentaries and many other war movies. One of my favorites, *Run Silent, Run Deep,* kindled my interest in submarines and launched a lingering desire to join the Navy.

I am in the early months of my senior year in high school and turned 17 a couple of months ago. As soon as I turn 18 next summer, I must register for the draft. Even so, getting drafted into the Army and going to Vietnam has no appeal. Joining the Navy is a better route, a safer route. By the time my enlistment ends, I should know what I want to do with the rest of my life.

A rare female French horn player, Vicky, stood as tall as me. Because of her height, she seldom wore shoes with high heels. A practical young woman, she wore her blond hair in a ponytail to keep it from falling into her face when she played music or studied. She only arranges her hair forward when dressing up.

For the cold evening of caroling tonight, she wore her favorite red Christmas sweater above black wool pants and matching red earmuffs, although her black overcoat hides the holiday designs on her sweater. She prefers to wear fuzzy gloves during the winter, but when playing her French horn, she puts on black leather gloves to keep the horn from slipping from her grasp.

By far the sharpest quill in our ensemble's calligraphy suite, Vicky's grades dipped to a B only once in high school. Of all things, Home Economics became her one blemish. She plans to go into law school and argues she has little need to learn how to can peaches or bake pies from scratch.

"It's not anything I will ever do. What's the point?"

The biggest member of the group, Peter, stands six foot three inches. You can tell he is nowhere near an athlete by looking at his profile. Due to his size and shape, he tends to look rumpled, his shirt becoming untucked and his belly pushing down on his waistline. Peter never looks comfortable in anything he wears, and no clothing looks fashionable on him. He finds obtaining proper fitting sizes in the small local stores a challenge and places special orders for most of his pants, shirts, and coats.

Although always disheveled, only a few of the other kids tease Peter about his looks and weight. Towering over almost everyone, after rolling his neck with a pop and offering a quick snarl, kids left him alone. He kept his blond hair cut short, with a thin tuft of longer hair along the ridge of his forehead. Stiffened by butch wax, it sticks half an inch straight up. He is a funny-looking but lovable bear.

Bruce stood tall, as well, six feet one inch, but thin and slight. His mother always encouraged him to eat more, afraid the whoosh from a passing truck would blow him over as he walked down the street. I sometimes chuckled at Bruce's slight frame and questioned how he had the strength to carry his baritone horn. Even with his heavy dark blue pea coat, he created only a slender silhouette from overhead streetlights. Skinny legs protrude below his coat, ending in boots fit for feet larger than Peter's.

His enormous feet must have anchored him in the wind.

Unusual for a kid in high school, Bruce has a splash of white hair spreading from his right temple and streaking back through his dark and slick-combed hair. He blames it on Brylcreem. "A little dab too much." He would say with a chuckle when asked. Bruce wears wireframe glasses wrapped around his ears.

To offset Peter and Bruce, tiny Phil completed our little ensemble. He carries his tenor saxophone on his right side, connected to a support strap around his neck, and its generous size forces him to lean to his left. When looking at him, I cannot help but think about a picture I saw in a National Geographic Magazine article. The growth of some old trees had permanent bends from years of blowing winds, stunting their normal growth.

Because of its larger size, Phil seldom chose to walk around with his tenor saxophone. In marching band, he played the easier-to-carry alto sax. For this caroling group, though, he opted to haul the tenor around as he wanted to provide a deeper sound to compliment the trombone and baritone instruments in the group.

Phil has on a nice pair of brown wool slacks under a long chestnut brown overcoat. Always debonair, he topped his outfit off with a white woolen ascot tucked into the top of his coat. Phil's hair curled into tight brown springs like a thick and fuzzy woolen stocking cap. His hair could be several inches long, and you would never know with it coiling so close to his scalp.

The five of us groused and teased each other between stops as we wandered downtown, passing shop after shop. People's heads turned as we performed, and many stopped to smile, wave, or clap. As the evening waned, stores began turning off their inside lights and flipping over their 'closed' signs. I lowered my trumpet.

"That's it, guys. Time to go."

With our last carol completed, we headed back to Peter's car in a festive and marvelous holiday mood. Well, not everyone.

Vicky fumed.

High school sweethearts for years, Vicky has distinct ideas about our future together. Since I mentioned to her about considering an alternative course of action earlier, she has given me nothing but scowls. Intimidated by her grades, determination, goals, and financial resources, I have come to worry about my ability to contribute to our future relationship.

I was also facing the draft even though some news reports said the Vietnam War might be winding down. We have heard 'The War Is Ending' story before, and I do not want to take the chance things could escalate again and see just four ways to avoid going there.

One. I can delay the draft if I'm enrolled in college. Nope. It's not a financial possibility.

Two. I could avoid the draft if I get married and have a baby. Oh boy. Nope. It's not going to happen, and neither marriage nor babies fit into Vicky's planned timeline. I am not sure I would survive the suggestion.

Three. I could avoid the draft if found unfit due to medical or mental reasons. Hmm. Peter and Bruce could put up several good arguments about my mental fitness. I chuckled to myself. Nope. Then again, I could try to learn to drool on command.

Four. I could avoid the Army draft if I enlisted in another service. Check! Yes, my only real choice. I need to join the Navy.

With all the thick winter coats cladding our bodies, it took extra effort for us to squeeze into Peter's car. The five of us headed several blocks over to the high school band director's house. Rekindling my earlier caroling tradition, I wanted to surprise our director. It should have been no revelation; my mother gave heads up to our band leader, Mr. Young.

Knowing we planned to go caroling one night, my mother let the director know. Unsure we would choose Christmas Eve to venture out, a Thursday this year, or wait for Christmas day, she gave him several days advance notice to prepare. Of course, he might remember our caroling invasion last year. When Peter picked me up on Christmas Eve, Mom called Mr. Young and confirmed the ensemble would arrive sometime later in the evening.

Peter parked his car one house down the block from the director's house to conceal our approach. The house on Park Avenue sat quietly a couple blocks from the high school. We walked to the front of the director's house and began to play a medley of *Jingle Bells*, *Silent Night*, and *White Christmas*. Mr. Young and his wife came out and stood on their porch, arm in arm, swaying in time to the music. The couple joined in and sang along with the holiday tunes. When the songs finished, the Youngs applauded, as did neighbors on both sides and across the street, who also came out to listen to the holiday tunes. They waved hello to all the spectators, and Mrs. Young walked out to the street to invite us inside. She called the neighbors, as well, inviting everyone to join the not-so-impromptu gathering.

Vicky shared a few words with me as we packed away our instruments. Tears streaming down her cheeks, she pulled out a tissue, blew her nose, and blubbered.

"Well! If that's your wonderful idea, you can just go on with the boys without me."

She turned and started to march off up the street. Vicky lived several blocks down Park Avenue, beyond Memorial Park and over on First.

"Wait!" I said. "Aren't you worried about the Musher Man? It's winter. It's snowing. You shouldn't be out in the dark, alone. Come inside with us. Please."

"Don't be ridiculous!"

She rolled her head and exhaled, and a large cloud of breath vapors through a groan.

"That's just a winter fairy tale; varsity boys tell their girlfriends to scare them into staying in their cars when they're parked at the lake. There is no such thing as a Musher Man or any other sort of boogeyman."

She saw my face contort and knew I had begun formulating an argument. Vicky rolled her eyes, nodded, and plopped her hands to her sides. "Yes, yes, I am aware there have been a couple of mysterious and unsolved murders a long time ago. But those victims have all been way north of town or around the lake. I'll be fine," she turned to Peter. "Will you bring my horn by sometime tomorrow?" she asked, inviting no argument.

Not wanting to get between the two of us, Peter looked up, the edges of his mouth tweaked down. His brow furrowed. "I can't tomorrow, Vic. It's Christmas, and my gram and gramps will be here." His head moved back and forth between me and Vicky. "Can I bring it the day after?"

She stomped her foot.

"Fine!"

She turned away and took quick, long steps toward the corner of Second Street, her arms swinging outward in an exaggerated march.

Peter looked confused and turned to me. "What did I say?"

"What's going on?" Bruce asked while rubbing his hands together.

I let out a breath, billowing in the crisp air, like Vicky's. "Back when we walked between caroling stops downtown, I told her I'd decided to join the Navy after graduation." I turned to look where Vicky rounded the corner, hoping to see her coming back. "She's upset with me and has been getting angrier as the night got darker and colder." Much of the temperature drop came from her, I'm sure. I shook my head and let out another foggy breath. "I guess she wants me to remain the good little boyfriend, working at the Five and Dime and waiting for her to get back from law school."

Peter snorted and patted me on the shoulder.

"That means you'd have to get a job at the Five and Dime."

Phil and Bruce joined in laughter. The gap in Bruce's teeth showed through his wide guffaw.

"Very funny, guys. Hah, hah." I started snickering with them. "I'm thirsty, hungry, and getting damn cold. Come on. Let's go inside, warm up, and get something to eat. The way Vicky clomped off, no doubt she's already home."

The four of us headed into the director's house, still chuckling, with Bruce smacking me on my shoulder.

"It'll be okay. Just give her time. Vic will come around."

"Or YOU will," Phil said, starting another round of laughter.

As we laughed our way into the front room of the house, I saw my parents chatting and holding drinks, my dad eating a large, frosted snowman. I stopped short and put the heel of my hand to my forehead. At last, the realization of past caroling gatherings hit me like a rubber dart smacking our fridge door.

As I watched the slow descent of a crumb from my dad's cookie fall to the living room carpet, all the other holiday treats we received when caroling came to mind in a series of flashes. I always wondered how folk always seemed to be prepared with holiday goodies when we 'surprised' them with unannounced holiday caroling visits. I am such an idiot. From the outset, my devious mother gave them advanced warning. I pushed my arms out into a lazy 'T,' fingers spread wide, nodded, smiled at my mother, and mouthed a silent, "Thank you."

She stood and walked over to greet me. We hugged, and she

whispered in my ear.

"I suppose it's time for us to tell you there isn't a Santa Clause, either."

She leaned back and gave me a misty grin. She placed both of her hands on the sides of my face and smiled. The warmth from her fingers felt wonderful.

"I knew that one," I started to chuckle. "Just don't spoil the Easter Bunny for me, okay."

As we both teared up, we laughed and hugged again.

Swallowing the last of his snowman, my dad got up and joined our hug.

"Okay, you two. Why so emotional?"

"We're just acknowledging to each other how our boy is becoming a man."

The three of us hugged for a few more seconds, and she let go.

"You best grab something to eat before Peter gets it all."

She looked over at Bruce, taking off his coat. She tapped my arm as he turned away.

"Make sure Bruce eats something. He needs it."

I snickered.

"You've been talking to his mom?"

"No. But I am a mom, you know. And observant." She pointed to the tall, slender boy who had difficulty casting a sideways shadow. "I've seen little girls with beefier arms." She looked around. "Speaking of which, where's Vicky?"

"She left for home. I told her I planned to join the Navy after high school." I closed my eyes and took a breath. "She got mad and stomped off."

"Oh, don't worry. She will understand. You can enlist, do your service, and be out and going to college using the GI Bill long before she finishes college and law school. Don't dwell on it too much." She smiled again and patted my arm. "You'll be in a much better situation after doing some military service than you will by moping around here and trying to get by with a low-paying job at the hardware store or a restaurant. With luck, you'll come out of the service with some useful skills, too."

CHAPTER 21

VICKY

Keith can be so infuriating. How could he even think about going into the military with the war still raging? What if he gets killed? I thought he loved me. How could he do this to me? My dad could give him a job at the bank after he graduates from high school. He can always wait to go to college. What is so wrong with working for my dad? And, of course, of all places, he just had to tell me about his new grandiose plan across from my dad's bank.

Squished between Keith and Phil, I had difficulty waiting my turn to jump out of the car when we pulled up to Mr. Young's house. My hands shook, and not from the cold, as I glared at him. While we played our last set of songs, my eyes watered, and my ears clogged so much my horn sounded flat. After we finished, I found a tissue in my pocket to blow my nose.

Keith did not expect me to leave before the party, and his eyes went wide when I told him. It sure got his attention. He seemed more agitated than I expected, which is good, and ragged on about the boogeyman myth. Of course, I am glad of his concern for my safety, but he should have thought this whole thing through. If he cared enough for me, he would change his mind.

He is getting what he deserves, and with a silent chuckle, I let him know how ridiculous he sounded. The idea of him thinking of me as a silly girl falling for scary stories simply because of winter snow angers me.

Besides, I like snowy weather.

Not wanting to give Keith a chance to say anything else, I headed to the end of the street. He can stew all night. I will talk sense into him tomorrow when he comes over to exchange Christmas gifts. But for now, I turned and walked away from the corner streetlight and sat down on the curb under the shadow of an old oak tree at the edge of Memorial Park to finish crying.

With perfect timing, my tissue soaked through to a disgusting wet ball as my tears began to wane. I saw lights first and then heard the crunch of tires. A car slowed to a shadowy stop, and the driver reached across and lowered the passenger window. It took me a moment to recognize Deputy Jacobson. He smiled and leaned toward the open window.

"You alright, miss?"

"Deputy Jacobson. It's me. Vicky Tisdale."

"Oh. I wondered who might be sitting in the shadows." He scanned the surroundings and looked back at me. "Why are you sitting all alone in the dark?"

I sniffled and wiped my nose again.

"I had a disagreement with my boyfriend when we finished caroling downtown."

He got out and leaned against the car with his arms crossed on top.

"I listened to you guys down on 1st Street. You're pretty good."

"Thank you. But Keith, my boyfriend, told me he planned to enlist in the Navy after high school."

"I would think him joining the Navy would make you proud," he said as he walked around the back of the car. He leaned back against the trunk fender, a couple steps away.

"Well, yes. I suppose it does. It's just not how I saw our future developing."

His cheek flinched into a grin. "One thing I have learned is things change, and youthful plans turn into dreams and often never come to pass." He pointed to the passenger door of his car. "It's cold and snowing. I know you live close by, but can I offer you a ride home?" He smiled, and the streetlights cast fluttering shadows of naked tree branches across his face.

"Sure."

I leaned forward to get up, and something hard smacked the side of my head. A flash of thought passed.

Damn. That really hurt.

Everything went dark when the back of my head hit something harder.

CHAPTER 22

BILLY

No surprise, Whitefish started to get quiet on Christmas Eve. Shops and stores began closing, and the busy sidewalks shifted from a bustling foray of last-minute shoppers to an empty gray slate framed in dirty, dark, sandy snow. Most people had already gone home to their various evening activities, kids anxious for Santa's visit and parents wrapping last-minute presents and deciding when to fill stockings. With luck, I could catch someone walking home when parties begin to wind down.

Christmas Eve turned out to be a rare opportunity for me to wander around without anyone knowing, caring, or wondering where I was. Becky went to Helena to spend the holidays with her parents. They moved last summer. I stayed behind, preferring to get some overtime and hoping to ease the growing itch. Tonight, I got to be alone and pick up a little extra pay.

At this hour, the only people still strolling around were five musicians who had been caroling downtown. For some unknown reason, when they reached their car, I followed.

No. I needed to follow.

They stopped and walked down to one of the houses and began to carol again. I kept my distance as several people left their homes to listen to the group. I recognized they chose to play in front of the band director's house.

The musicians played for several minutes before finishing. The crowd applauded, and the director's wife waved everyone into their house. Disappointed and assuming the group would all head in, I rolled up my window and thought about calling it an evening.

Tomorrow is another day. The itch will have to wait.

Then, I noticed the girl rushing away from the group. She strutted up the street, so I rolled around the block and headed her way. Turning the corner, I slowed and scanned the sidewalks, thinking I missed her since she took off in such a hurry. Something moved, a pair of shoes protruding from behind an oak tree at the edge of the park. I pulled up and stopped.

She raised her head from her hands and blinked with red, drippy eyes. Her eyes went wide when she recognized me, and I pretended not to know her until she identified herself. Getting out of the car, I made sure she sat alone. She told me why she left the party.

For my benefit, of course.

Walking around to her side of the car, we talked for a moment before I asked if I could save her from a cold walk home and gave her my winning grin.

As she leaned forward to get up, I stepped up and kicked the side of her head. She flew back, her head hitting a tree root. I opened the trunk, spread out an old painting cloth, and picked her up with one hand. After flopping her in, I closed the trunk and took a quick glance at the area. No one in sight.

Playing it safe, I continued down Second Street until it crossed the railroad tracks and turned left to head back to the lake.

CHAPTER 23

DEPUTY DANIELS

Making several worried calls to her friends, the parents of Vicky Tisdale managed to connect with Keith after he got home from his holiday ensemble evening. The four boys spent an hour or two at Phil's house before they ended their holiday fun, and all went home. Keith explained how Vicky became upset with him and clomped off from their director's house earlier in the evening after they finished caroling.

When I interviewed the other boys, they all confirmed Keith had pleaded with her to stay at the party. Since the group finished playing a few blocks from her home, and Vicky left in such a huff, Keith told her parents she should have been home in minutes. I confirmed she disappeared while all four boys attended a gathering at the band director's house.

After the Tisdale's heard Keith's rendition of the events and knowing their daughter left the boys hours earlier, they called to report her missing. Although Keith and Peter drove around the neighborhood after Vicky's parents called, by procedure, official missing persons efforts did not move into action until the following day.

Not another one.

Teams began to search along the stretch of East Second Street from Park Avenue and extended beyond Memorial Park and over to East First. Searchers looked behind buildings, in alleys, into backyards, the park, and down foot and bike paths toward the railroad tracks. They knocked on doors, asking if anyone saw Vicky walking home or if they saw any suspicious persons, vehicles, or anything out of the ordinary. The search expanded further away from Second Street and Park Avenue over successive days.

I turned to Sheriff Boyer. "Damn. Fewer volunteers today than yesterday. We lose more each day."

"I know, it bothers me too," he said. "Like everyone everywhere, they have their own holiday priorities, visiting relatives, getting ready to depart the area after Christmas, or family obligations in preparation for the New Year." He shook his head and sighed. "How would they feel if their daughter or sister disappeared?"

I nodded. "I know how I would feel if my Rebecca went missing."

Hoping to solve the string of winter murders before he retired and worried Miss Tisdale could be the latest victim, Sheriff Boyer encouraged everyone to begin searching the wooded areas along East Lakeshore Drive and near the railroad tracks. A handful of searchers continued through the weekend. They included high school band members.

As night began to fall on the fourth evening of the search, I tapped on the sheriff's office door. He sat in his office chair, one arm across his chest and the other rubbing his forehead.

"I'm gonna make one more trip out along Whitefish Lake before heading home."

He nodded, flipped his hand, and went back to rubbing.

Taking my time, I crept up the undermaintained Lakeshore Drive. The potholes got worse as the paving ended, and my cruiser rattled in complaint. I pushed on as my snow chains thumped over a lengthy stretch of snow and ice packed over washboard furrows. Moving as slowly as practical to help keep the focus on my searching and holding a cup of coffee in my steering hand, I shifted my spotlight back and forth, left down toward the lake and right up the slope into the trees.

I hope she turns up okay.

At the extreme end of the lake, before the lake road veered away to the northwest, it came closer to the lake, about as close as anywhere along the route. The incline to the lake eased in this section and gave me a reasonable view down the slope. In my spotlight, the edge of the lake came into brief periodic view. When the light beam made it through all the shrubs and undergrowth, I could make out the distinct transition where the dark, deeper water met the shallow, white, frozen edge. I began to move the spotlight back to the right when I noticed something about fifty yards down the slope.

"What's that?"

In the distance, the object looked out of place, like a chewed-on piece of two-by-four or the broken end of a baseball bat protruding from a thicket of shrubs and small pine trees.

Paying more attention to following the spotlight than my driving, the cruiser began sliding toward the ditch on the lake side of the road. My arm floundered, knocking the spotlight lever; it flipped directly toward the windshield. I struggled to get better control of my steering and winced as the bright light flashed into my eyes. My efforts to turn off the light and gain control of the vehicle had mixed results. Although I managed to get control of the vehicle, I also splashed coffee on my lap.

"Crud!"

Looking back at the lake, I could no longer see the protrusion. After the flare of light, I couldn't see anything and knew I had to hike down the slope for a closer look.

First, I needed a safe place to stop. A few moments later, the road widened, and I pulled over to the right against the upward slope into the trees, grabbed my flashlight, and got out.

Walking back toward where I spotted the anomaly, I found the slushy tire tracks where I began to slide toward the ditch. Recognizing this as the correct area, I stepped down from the road and through the small ditch. My foot sank into the slush, and on my way up to the other side ditch, I slipped to my knees.

Damn. Just what I needed: cold, wet knees.

Getting back up, I brushed off the sloppy snow from my hands and knees and began walking and scanning from one brushy copse to another down toward the lake. Knowing what I had seen before and now looked for, it took me only a couple of minutes to zero in on my target.

As I got close, the odd form took on the shape of a pale foot, its toes missing. Pushing through the brush, I found the body of a naked and mutilated woman. She had no face, and her upper body had cuts and tears and animal scratches everywhere. Turning, I lurched toward a larger tree, fell to my knees again, and vomited.

CHAPTER 24

DENNY

The Return

The dance of war continued through 1970, and we participated in numerous additional skirmishes, with the heaviest action occurring during Operations Taylor Common and Oklahoma Hills. Although the ratio of enemy to Marine dead continued to indicate our side would win a war of attrition, our efforts seemed more of an exercise in raking leaves in a hellish windstorm.

With no fanfare, the 1st Marine Division began to withdraw from Vietnam in 1970, marking the inevitable end to our dance in hell. Replete with a cluster of medals, including two Purple Hearts, I left Vietnam in June 1971 as part of the last Marine infantry unit to depart.

The music stopped.

During the trip back to the States, I took time to review my bible. Pan gave it to me a few days after I asked her about black magic and spells to cure Momma. She thought I should have another perspective on good and evil. On the blank pages at the front of the bible, I read the names and ranks of all the Marines and Corpsmen I had helped save or treat. Every evening after a skirmish, I would jot down names from the day. No doubt, my Caliste family bloodline helped me recall those names.

Reading the dates by the names struck me when I grasped how many times I helped multiple Marines on the same day. I found Lieutenant

Hastings's name twenty-third on my list. While making entries, I ran out of room on the blank pages at the front of the bible and began using outer margins, one name per page. The notion pleased me as I realized how the names of saved Marines covered so many pages.

I turned to the back of the bible. There, I found a similar list of names, the ones I could not save. I toyed fondling the pages containing one list in my left hand and the other in my right as if the joy and light of one list would outweigh the disheartening heaviness and darkness of the other. My eyes blinked away a sudden mist. Maybe. I did know both of my parents watched me, helped me, and protected me. Without their ever-present support, all the pages would be blank, and a lot of brave men would be lost.

***

Back in the United States, at Camp Pendleton, California, I addressed a letter to Aunt Diane in Grasmere, Canada. I used her given name, Dyani, and told her I would be getting discharged in August and begin a trip back to see them and reunite with my dogs. Knowing the probability that this could be my last chance, I mentioned my plans to visit New Orleans before heading North. I wanted to see what, if anything, had happened to Momma's old shop.

Preferring to avoid air travel, I traveled by bus. Although the federal government provided the cost of a ticket for me to return to my home of record, Eureka, Montana, I had to pay for the trip to New Orleans out of pocket. I chose to exchange the original Greyhound Bus ticket, paid cash for the difference and diverted my trip through Louisiana. Still, traveling by bus would minimize my costs. Pan's frugal nature remains a part of me.

Unknown to us in our Stryker farmhouse, with little outside-world communications, Pan and I knew nothing about Hurricane Betsy in 1965. The storm devastated New Orleans, and the old apothecary building became one of its many casualties. The city never acted to preserve the building, and the shop has been idle since our departure. Doing anything at the site fell low in priority. After the severe damage from the storm, the grocery store closed, and the city lost all interest in renovation. The building remained an obscene derelict until a new developer purchased the property. They wound up destroying and replacing it the year Pan died.

I had a nice chicken dinner at a new restaurant built where Momma and Pan spent so much of their time in New Orleans. In honor of the original structure, the new owners named the restaurant "The Apothecary." An archival picture of the former building showing its apothecary signage hung on the wall behind the restaurant's cash register. I saw no evidence of Momma's shop anywhere. It's as if it never existed. Pan would be disappointed with the changes in New Orleans. I took a respite in the idea she did not live to see the loss of Momma's building.

A day and a half later, my Greyhound bus stopped in Eureka. The scheduled break would only last thirty minutes, providing time for those of us traveling on to Canada to stretch and change buses. Without enough time to reach out to Abe Williams, talking to him had to wait. I needed to see my dogs. While thinking of them, I took the opportunity to find a payphone and call Aunt Diane to let her know my scheduled arrival time in Grasmere.

THE WINTER CABIN

CHAPTER 25

KEITH

December 1971

Now I can admit that the end of my senior year sucked, big time. On rare occasions, okay, maybe not so rare, I would lose patience and bark at people for being idiots and getting in my way. Or because they simply existed near my personal space. Okay. So maybe … just maybe … people only asked me if I wanted to come over for a game of cards or Monopoly or to watch the television. Whatever. The nerve.

In time, I realized I blamed myself for Vicky's death. If only I had waited to tell her about the Navy. I damn sure should have made her stay at the holiday party.

As if I could have stopped her from leaving.

Much later, much, much later, I realized my parents had recognized the signs of my distress and intervened on my behalf. Still, at the point when they convinced me of this obvious fact, I did acknowledge what they said and realized I had been blaming myself. So, give me a little credit. At last, I faced the truth.

Yes, it took a while.

Okay, a long while.

Mom and Dad helped with my ongoing mental anguish.

"Why don't you honor Vicky's memory by focusing on your studies," Dad said.

My mom would follow. "It would be what she'd want."

Although reluctant to give in to their parental and/or educator trickery, I did find it easier to get through the days when concentrating on homework and study rather than thinking about Vicky's death.

Before the summer break, visits from my internal demons became more manageable, and my mood continued to improve as the end of school approached. I started hanging out with Peter, Bruce, and Phil again.

"I want you guys to know I appreciate you remaining my friends after me being such a jerk."

"No problem," Bruce said. "Vicky was our friend, too."

Peter chuckled.

"You're one of us. We understand. But I will admit, you only had about three minutes left on the friendship timer before we cut you off forever."

Everyone chuckled.

"We're the Quads," Phil said. "We need you to be the fourth." His forehead popped as he looked up. "Otherwise, we'd have to call ourselves the trips." He sighed. "I, for one, think the term stinks."

***

I turned 18 the month after graduating from high school and registered for the draft the next day. My mother convinced me to have one more Christmas at home, so I waited and played draft board roulette until my nerves got the better of me.

Without Mom and Dad knowing, the Quad drove down to Kalispell, and on the 9th of November, I signed enlistment papers with a three-month delayed entry into the Navy. For mom, I would be home through the holidays and could wait until Tuesday, the 8th of February 1972, before reporting to the city town hall.

In a surprising move, my friend Peter did the same thing while little Phillip enlisted in the Marines. Although Bruce accompanied us on the drive and picked up some recruiting pamphlets, he elected to take his chances and did not enlist with the three of us.

My excitement about the special occasion could not be contained, and I told my parents over dinner on the evening I returned from Kalispell. My mother cried, and my father shook my hand and patted my shoulder. Anticipating the likelihood of me entering one of the services sometime next year, either by draft or enlistment, my father had already made plans for a special winter treat.

"We've been talking about it for years and never taken the opportunity," my dad said. "As a special Christmas present, your mom and I arranged for a winter hunting trip by ski plane. The two of us will fly up, land in a snow field, make camp, and hunt for one to three days, depending on how long it takes." He bounced his eyebrows. "We could leave early if successful if we want, or empty-handed on the fourth morning."

***

Late on Monday morning after Christmas, my dad and I drove to the Kalispell airstrip to meet Dave Springer, our charter pilot and hunting guide. He flew in from Missoula earlier in the morning. By the time we reached the airfield, dirty snow and ice from the road had covered the sides of my dad's 1968 Chevy Blazer, almost obscuring the bright color of the vehicle. Dad loved the red Blazer with a white top, a rare splurge for the Brown family.

"I'm gonna need to wash it when we get back," he said.

"Won't the water freeze?"

He chuckled. "At least the ice would be clean." I joined his laughter.

Dave had been operating out of Missoula for years and recently upgraded to a 1967 Helio Courier. "It's a reliable utility aircraft. I've converted it for use in winter by adding snow skis."

Listening to Dave's description, I had to ask, "So, you don't need an airstrip?"

"No," he explained.

The Courier's 295 hp engine, combined with a large three-bladed propeller, allowed it to take off within a short distance and could climb in altitude at steep angles, higher and quicker than most similar aircraft.

"This makes the plane perfect for landing and taking off on short runways, small fields," and he popped his eyebrows up and down, "or mountainous snow-covered meadows."

We unloaded our gear and sat down with our guide in a small corner office within an open airplane hangar. Dave had a grizzled face and dark long hair with splashes of gray. He had a full, uneven beard of coarse red hair, also in the process of going gray. The beard tried to cover his smile, but his wide grin could not be constrained, exposing a jagged tooth in its center. Smiling, wrinkles spread across his face, and his eyes twinkled in the hangar lights.

"Welcome," Dave said, issuing a cloud of breath. "Coffee?"

I declined, but Dad took a steaming cup. The pilot unfolded a map, laying it across a table stained with paint and several dried coffee cup rings. He held down the corners of the map with several old, recently rinsed, and dingy-looking cups threatening to dampen the map.

He pointed to a shallow valley within the Flathead National Forest between two mountain ranges. "This is where we're going, near the foothills of Mount Locke," he told us. The site offers a safe place to land and take off and provides a location generous with wildlife. "I've flown in there many times with hunters over the seasons."

"Here's the thing."

He lifted his cup and took a sip of coffee. The map began to coil.

"The current forecast indicates we're in for mild weather until late Thursday evening. So, at the latest, we must leave the valley by noon on Thursday, whether you have a successful hunt or not. This is a safety issue, not a success determination." He arched his eyebrows again. "Amongst other things, leaving on Thursday will get us home in time for New Year's Eve." He looked at us and back at the Courier. "With the two of you, my plane can manage two average deer, or one large and a portion of another, or if we are lucky, one bull elk, depending on its size. Please keep that in mind."

My dad wobbled his head and waved his free hand, careful to avoid spilling the coffee held in the other.

"No worries, we are only interested in deer, and one will do. An elk is too much of an animal for our first hunting trip." He took a breath. "We might think about it in the future. If ever." He looked at me and back at Dave, tipping his head toward me. "Keith enlisted in the Navy and will leave in a few weeks. Who knows when we'll get a chance to do this again?"

Their guide nodded, stood up, rolled up his map, and tapped my shoulder. "Good for you, Keith. You two head out to the plane with your gear." He pointed to a plane about halfway between the hangar and the runway. "It's the white one with a red tail." He turned back and waved his hand toward a sign behind him. "Men's room. You might want to drain your radiators before we leave. It'll be a bumpy trip." He winked. "I'm going to file our flight plan and will be out in a few minutes."

He turned and scuttled off, humming an awkward rendition of Jingle Bells. His rhythm followed the holiday classic, while his painful melody revealed how little he could carry a tune. As we headed out, passing several covered, open-air plane hangars with a variety of other personal aircraft, Dave called to us.

"Wait for me before loading anything."

When our pilot joined us at the plane, he examined our gear, gauged the weight, and asked us what we weighed, too.

"We want an even load distribution."

He directed where we should place our gear and where to sit.

"Frank, you sit up front in the co-pilot seat."

He turned to me. "You get the back seat over there."

Dave got the plane engines started and communicated with the flight tower at the little airstrip. He received quick clearance to take off and moved out on the ice and snow-packed runway.

Scooting down the airstrip, I was surprised at how fast the plane lifted from the ground. The last time my stomach lurched like this, I threw up on a roller coaster. Dave accelerated upward at such a sharp angle I tasted bile in the back of my mouth before managing to regain composure and overcome the sudden urge to puke.

Vomiting on my first flight in an airplane had little appeal to me as something I wanted to live with. My Quad buddies would never let me forget it.

If nothing else, the realization they would carry the embarrassing reminder for years, if not decades, gave me sufficient motivation to overcome any queasiness. I inhaled, held several deep breaths, and managed to calm down. With one last soothing breath, I swallowed and looked out a small window and watched buildings get smaller and fall behind. Within minutes, I could see only trees, snow, mountains, lakes, and an occasional distant road or stream.

The quick gain in altitude caused me to yawn several times, and I realized how tired I had become. We left home late in the morning, allowing me to sleep in, but the excitement of the upcoming trip left me unable to get a good night's rest. Leaning onto the side of the plane, my head began to sink to my chest, and before long, sleep overtook me.

Dave interrupted my nap when he called out over the sound of the engines. "There we go. We'll land down in the meadow over there." He tipped his head toward his window. "I'll circle as we lower to search for any obvious obstructions and pick the best approach."

I leaned forward so he could hear me.

"I thought you'd been here before?"

Dave bobbed his head.

"I have. Still, things happen. Someone could already be there. Trees fall in the winter and during storms. One could be down and blocking where I landed last time. Also, for some reason, the darn things keep getting bigger. I have to account for taller trees each year."

My dad turned to grin at me, and I pursed my lips and gave him a silent nod.

As the plane continued to circle, I peeked out the window and caught my first glance at the landing area. The clearing looked so small. The thought of us landing in it brought the taste of bile back. The area, or meadow, bordered a curved stream and looked flat from above. Extending east from the bend in the stream, the clearing approximated the shape of a rough isosceles triangle.

"We'll be in the meadow in a few minutes."

As we descended, I caught intermittent glimpses of the area, and with each look, the snow field became larger, and with each pass, my lurching tummy unwound.

"I'll make my usual approach from the west side of the stream. It provides the longest approximate straight line for landing."

Along the hypotenuse, I mused. My math education is good for something.

Within minutes, the plane bounded down, and I could hear scattered pattering on both of its sides. Davee lowered his flaps to slow down. I yawned to clear my ears. Before stopping and cutting the engines, he maneuvered the plane around to face the opposite direction from our landing approach.

"This allows for an easy and quick take-off in the event we need to leave in a hurry." He released his seat belt. "Safety first."

To the southern edge of the meadow, most of the dry snow had drifted clear. The tree line on the opposite side glistened with an uneven white winter berm.

Dave examined the ground on the wind-shadowed edge of the clearing. "This site has several good locations for a tent." He pointed to four small rock piles, marking a square of ground. "We'll put the tent here. I've cleared most obstructions here during earlier trips." He looked at the sky.

"The slope allows for drainage in the case of rain or melting snow, but it shouldn't be a problem this trip."

Just off the clearing, in the trees, my dad pointed at a horizontal trimmed log suspended about 12 feet in the air. The beam looked to be a good five or six inches in diameter and rested between the top of an older split pine tree and a pronounced bend in the branch of another large pine several yards away. The center of the log had wear marks around its girth.

Dave noticed our gaze. "Like I mentioned earlier. I've used this place before. The crooked tree and broken snag over there provided a perfect place to hoist a deer. I've got a gambrel and a rope in the plane." He grinned when I turned to him with raised eyebrows. "A gambrel is a curved frame used to hang a deer by its hind legs." He scrunched his eyes closed, opened them again, and continued. "It looks like a hooked coat hanger and provides a center point for attaching a line to hoist game animals off the ground."

He turned and pointed at the arrangement. "Once I got this setup, I didn't have to carry as much gear on the plane. Until then, I had to haul a tripod frame up here to lift the animals off the ground." Wearing a snarl, I'm not sure he meant to express, he shook his head. "The bulky thing took a lot of room in the plane and only allowed me to get smaller deer clear of the ground. This arrangement works much better." He grinned. "Besides, less weight and gear on the plane allows for carrying more deer on the return trip."

Remembering what the pilot had said before the journey began, I had to ask.

"What happens if you get too much deer or elk?"

"We quarter the animal, take the best parts, and leave everything else behind." He gestured to the east side of the meadow. "We drag the extra stuff over there and toss it in the woods. It'll be an easy meal for some passing critters."

"Keith, start gathering some firewood for a campfire. You should be able to find plenty of dryer wood under the tree canopy. Although we gather wood every trip, new stuff falls all the time. Gather what you can and put it over there." He tossed a stick near a circle of rocks. "Although hidden under a bit of snow, we have a ready-made fire pit." He smiled and tilted his head. "We'll shovel out the bulk of it, and the fire will melt anything left over. While you gather the wood, your dad and I will set up the tent."

With the firewood, tent, and sleeping bags situated, the two men focused on an evening meal. Dad worked on the fire, and Dave walked over to the crooked tree and came back with a three-legged iron grate, its short legs ending in bent angled footers. He banged it on a log and worked a wire brush to clean off any residual debris.

"All the conveniences of home." He chuckled to himself as he carried it to the campfire. "With this, we can cook without our pots and pans tipping over in the fire. I made two trips up here before thinking about bringing this along. It's a bit heavy, so I just leave the cumbersome thing here."

He gave another big smile.

Dave grilled hotdogs while heating up some pork and beans for dinner. In a separate pan, Dad stirred some creamed peas. While the peas warmed, he separated out several slices of bread and butter and placed them on a small cutting board to the side of the fire. I broke out the camping plates and utensils, and we began to portion out the meal. While we ate, Dave and Dad talked about hunting plans for the morning.

After we finished our dinner, Dave heated a pot full of water. He spooned healthy portions of hot chocolate mix into three metal camping cups and added the hot water. The cups let off billowing steam, catching shadowy glimmers from the fire. While I stirred the chocolate with my fork, I noticed Dave pouring something into his and my dad's cups. Dad smiled, and they clinked their cups together. We all enjoyed the warmth of the chocolate drinks and had a second cup. I am not sure what additional merriment Dave added to their beverages, but I heard "Cheers" echoing as they clinked their metal cups together again.

After cleaning up from dinner, we watched the fire burn down before turning in. Although the hot water had gone cold and the chocolate mix had been put away, Dave and my dad continued to take sips from their metal cups. Dave told us stories of some of his more memorable hunting trips to the area, most of them successful, though not all.

One failed excursion turned out to be a simple drinking trip. He told us about when he brought up two old college friends who wanted to celebrate a business venture, and all day long, he watched them drink, eat, drink, play cards, drink, and sleep. They did spend one afternoon plunking empty cans with their rifles. Dave took care of watching them to make sure they did not shoot each other by accident, or him, or his plane.

With the fire turning into glowing coals and the air getting colder,

Dave called for us to retire for the evening. A kerosine lamp hanging inside the tent provided our interior illumination. Outside, the effect provided a muted yellow glow through the tent fabric. Although each of us had a flashlight to use if needed during the night, in the darkness, we had little else to do until morning. As I fell asleep, the two men talked a bit longer. When they ran out of things to chat about, Dave turned the lamp down low, providing minimal light yet adding a small amount of heat to the tent.

A small amount.

Not accustomed to sleeping on the ground, I struggled to get comfortable and stay asleep. I woke on several occasions needing to shift positions and pull my sleeping bag tight around my neck to retain body heat. During one of those wakeful shifts, I had to pee.

I thought about getting out of the relative warmth of the sleeping bag to get dressed, just to run out of the tent for a few moments. Knowing it would take me longer to get dressed than to pee, I decided to hold it. As a result, I had a fitful sleep, dreaming of a lengthy search for a bathroom in a large building built by a drunken maze master.

In the dream, I never found a toilet.

I woke up to the sound of my dad and Dave talking and the smells of bacon frying and coffee brewing. Although torn by the priorities of what to do first, when I crawled out of the sleeping bag, the morning chill greeted me with its priority. I dressed and stumbled out of the tent, running for the trees. I could hear the two men chuckling as I dashed. The repeated crunching of my steps hid their continuing laughter.

Walking back, my dad waved me over to the campfire. Dave stirred a pan of scrambled eggs to go with the bacon, and my dad frowned at his blackened bread. "Guess I need some practice." He shook his head in disappointment. "I'll call it toast, only because it started out as bread." He laughed and scraped off some of the worst burnt scorches. "Now it looks better."

Our guide smiled. "It'll go down just the same. And we have plenty of butter, my wife's blackberry jam, and these eggs and bacon. We can disguise the taste if needed." He lifted his coffee cup. "And we can always wash it down." He smiled and chuckled to himself.

Sating my hunger, I ate two slices of Dad's scorched toast. I spread scrambled eggs on one slice, added strips of bacon, and folded it in half. The stiff bread split apart, and the halves took both hands to eat while keeping egg drippings from falling on the ground or my lap. I put butter and extra jam on the second slice. "Perfect Dad." I said with an added "hmm" and licked my lips, trying to catch escaping goo.

Not a normal coffee drinker, I poured a cup and added two cubes of sugar. Swirling The hot drink with my fork, I sat back in a folding chair to take careful sips. I scrunched up my face at the taste but kept sipping. The bittersweet coffee tasted better with each sip, and I found the warmth welcoming, wrapping my fingers around the mug. Surprising my dad, I got up for a second cup.

Dad chuckled and gestured with his own cup.

"Be careful, or you could become a regular coffee drinker by the time we finish this hunting trip."

Dave joined the musings.

"Well, to be a 'regular' coffee drinker," stressing the word, "Keith needs to hold off on the sugar." He smiled while winking and holding up his own cup. "Black and bitter."

Dad and I cleaned up the plates, utensils, and cooking materials and picked up the empty tin can and other trash. Dave put all the open food away. He kept everything in a large airtight cooler in the plane, where passing animals could not smell or have easy access to it.

"A grizzly bear could do a whomping bit of damage to the plane if motivated," he said. As a precaution, Dave pulled out a watering can and poured some reddish mixture into it. He began to sprinkle the concoction around the circumference of the plane and campsite.

He noticed me watching. "It's an old family recipe: some red pepper and garlic mixed with some vinegar and a few other secret tidbits. It provides a little bit of a deterrent for any wandering critters." He smiled, then got serious. "It might smell like salad dressing, but don't get it on your fingers and rub your eyes. You'll be sorry." He turned and continued sprinkling.

CHAPTER 26

SANDY

You can find the First Presbyterian Church in Whitefish at the corner of Central Avenue and East 3rd Street. On most Tuesday evenings, I can be found in a youth bible study group meeting from 7:30 to 8:30 in a classroom toward the back of the church.

"Goodness. Look at the time. It's already 9:00," I said and closed my bible. "We better head home."

Most of the eight kids lived on the south side of town, a few blocks from the church, and would leave on foot. Three of us lived across the railroad tracks, northwest of town, nearer to Whitefish Lake. Although an easy mile away, we all chose to drive to church, as the mile could be a long walk on a frosty night. Samuel and his sweetheart Katie left in their car.

I held back for a few minutes with my two girlfriends, chatting about welcoming 1972 at the New Year's Eve party. We intended to drive down to the lake together and celebrate with another group of kids. Still three nights away, we giggled with excitement about our plans.

"Let's meet at my house around 9:00 on Friday. I'll drive to the lake."

The three of us would take snacks, and the boys would bring drinks, fireworks, and a variety of seasonal noisemakers. First, though, we needed to coordinate our outfits to include festive hats and flags.

Last to leave the church, I followed Roberta out to the sidewalk by the church and waited for Brenda, who turned out the lights and locked the door. We said our goodbyes, and they waved and headed off down East 3rd Street toward their homes.

"See you Friday."

I crossed over Third and walked to my car, a few parking spaces down Central, to drive the short distance home. After opening the door, I got in and struggled in the cold to find my keys; they settled somewhere near the bottom of my purse. I pulled off one woolen mitten to find the key.

"There you are, you little stinker."

Once in the ignition, I turned the key. Silence. Nothing happened. Trying a second time, my car failed to start, and I sat there quivering. Facing a long, miserable walk home, I got out of the car, slammed the door, and leaned against the door frame. With my ungloved hand, I rubbed my face and jumped, nearly poking my eye, when a voice interrupted my irritation.

"Car trouble, Ms. Morris?"

A male voice said. Looking across the street, I saw a police car in the shadows between streetlights and a familiar face. Deputy Jacobson stood, leaning against his patrol car, one leg crossed over the other.

When did he get there?

He had one arm wrapped low across his body and the second arm positioned so his hand scratched the opposite elbow. Smiling, I let out a shivering, relaxing breath.

"Yes. My little darling won't start. Can you help?"

"Of course. Let me look."

Deputy Jacobson broke into a charming smile as his footsteps crunched ruts crossing the street.

He's not wearing a coat; he must have just arrived when I struggled with my car.

"Can you pop the hood?"

Nodding, I opened and leaned in the driver's door and released the hood latch. Standing back up, I moved beside the deputy as he lifted the hood. He braced it open and looked around.

"How come you're parked over there?"

"Oh, I'm about to finish my shift and decided to drive through downtown on my way back to the station."

"Lucky for me."

"There's your problem. Look here." He pointed. "The battery cable came off. No juice to start. It must have bounced loose. These ice and snow ruts can be quite a problem." He took a glove off and pulled some car keys from his pocket.

Gloves, no coat, sweaty brow. Strange.

"Okay. I'll put the cable back on, but I need to tighten the fitting down, so it won't slip off again. We wouldn't want you stranded somewhere else." He held out his keys. "Here. I have a small tool bag in my trunk. Would you be so kind as to get it from my cruiser while I work on this?"

"Sure."

Wobbling over to his car, I took careful crackling steps in the valleys between slushy tire rut peaks and unlocked the trunk of the police car. I leaned forward to pick up the toolkit and, in the shadow, had difficulty seeing anything other than an old blanket lying spread across the bottom of the trunk.

Blanket, no trunk lights. Strange.

Stopping my search, I began to turn back to the deputy.

"Is it under the bla …" I never finished asking the question. A heavy blow to my left temple left me with but one thought.

Poop. Hope this doesn't leave a bruise. I have a party in a couple of days.

CHAPTER 27

BILLY

There was no circumventing her compulsion. This I had learned. I did not know why she held the impulse until the big snow nor why her command was impossible for me not to heed. She left me each winter after I succumbed to her rage, and when the snow fell the following year, the sweaty, itchy urge grew again until I could not contain her anymore. My skin wept, and she could not be ignored. It got unbearable when I tried. This I knew. Somehow, the snow unleashed her fury or gave it a way to dominate me. In any case, I had come to recognize the signs, and they were hot and vivid. My sticky skin crawled and stung like fire ants trying to devour me, outside in and inside out. My only respite came from submission to the urge to the rage. It was not my fault. She left me no choice.

***

From the shadowed vantage of the front seat of my cruiser, I watched as most of the study group kids left for the evening. A few minutes later, Sandy and two other girls came walking out of the church. The two girls walked off, skipping in their giddiness while laughing and holding hands. Sandy crossed over to her car. As she got in, I got out and leaned against my car door.

After a few moments, she shook the wheel. Her shoulders remained slumped until she got out. She spun around with a jump when I spoke. Her face relaxed after recognizing me, and she let out a billowing breath of air before asking for my help.

Oh yes. I would be happy to help. I need to help you.

When she stood next to me at the engine, a brief aroma of jasmine wafted before my nose caught the indelible odors of motor oil. Pretending to examine her engine, I moved my flashlight around until its beam settled on her problem. She agreed to fetch my tool bag, and with her attention elsewhere, I turned the light off to keep the flickering from giving me away as I followed. She reached my cruiser, opened the trunk, and leaned in. Using the end of my flashlight, I smacked the side of her head. She collapsed, half in the trunk.

Nice. She made it easy.

Flipping her legs in, I bent her knees and wrapped the blanket around her to prevent any dirty snow from her shoes from dripping into the trunk fabric.

As I walked back to her car, I put my glove back on and pushed the cable on the battery. I closed the lid and did another careful survey of the area. Always quiet late in the evening, the downtown area becomes even more so during the holidays. I closed her car door and crossed the street again. Leaving the shadows, I made a quick right on Third. A block down, I turned right again on Baker Avenue and headed toward Whitefish Lake.

***

Volunteer searchers found the naked, mutilated body of Sandy Morris two days after she disappeared. Although her car sat near the church, with one glove on the front seat, searchers focused on the lake road area and found her body about fifty yards from where they found Vicky Tisdale the previous year.

CHAPTER 28

KEITH

The two best things to say about my first full day in the forest were after slipping off a log and filling my boots with frigid creek water. I did not freeze to death or drop my rifle and shoot myself. Although we had been hunting for a little over an hour, my dad and Dave Springer wasted no time, joining together to assist me back to camp.

"I can't believe I did that."

Dave built up the campfire to help get me warm, and Dad sorted through my duffle bag for a spare pair of dry socks. I put them on and stretched my feet toward the flames, wiggling my toes to warm them. My pant legs steamed. Dave forced two sticks into the ground near the fire by smacking them with a frying pan. He inverted my boots on the sticks and tipped the open tops toward the heat from the fire.

I sat near the fire, wriggling my extended feet and toes, and tried to remain warm and comfortable. I failed.

Both my dad and Dave chuckled while working around camp during the late afternoon.

"One thing's for sure," Dave said.

"What's that?" Dad asked with a big grin.

Dave sniggered and looked up to make sure he had my attention.

"His boots are watertight. They kept all the water in, no problem." He spread the words 'no problem' out longer than I thought necessary.

Dad nodded.

"I'll be sure to thank his mother for packing extra socks."

"Ha, ha. Very funny. Take advantage of the rookie camper."

Although embarrassed, I had to join in their laughter. Then my face blanked.

"I'm sorry I kept us from hunting and ruined the day."

We lost most of the day to my mishap.

No deer to show for our efforts.

My dad walked over and patted me on the shoulder. "No problem. Your health and safety are much more important than getting a deer, any time." He shook his head. "Besides, I wouldn't want to face your mother if you caught pneumonia," he laughed and winked, "or lost your toes to frostbite." He squatted near my boots to check for moisture and temperature. "And we don't want these to catch fire, either." He shivered and let out a deep, warbling breath.

Dave called out.

"And if this's the worst thing to happen, this'll be a fine trip."

Drying my boots took most of the evening. My toes toasted before I could put them back on.

After breakfast on Wednesday, we sat out with renewed spirits and determination in our hunt, knowing we had to leave by noon the following day. I did not expect we would be able to hunt on our last morning unless a volunteer deer happened to wander into camp for breakfast. So, if we failed to get a deer today, we would be flying home with simple stories of how I managed to slip into the creek and ruin the hunting trip.

I shivered and imagined the Quad humiliation.

Dave directed us South for about an hour, and then we headed East until we hooked back North. He planned for us to work our way back to camp for lunch and then do a similar loop North of camp in the afternoon. Our boots sunk and sloshed as we made slow progress. My feet began to get as cold as yesterday; dampness infiltrated my pant legs. The chill made me think the boots still contained creek water, though I'm sure my once sweaty feet provided the moisture supporting the chill this time.

I began to get tired and thought about calling it quits when Dave tapped me on the shoulder. He leaned in next to me, his bushy beard tickling my ear, and whispered, "Over there, a three-point."

I followed his calloused and crooked finger, pointing across a sloped ravine, where melting snow runoff would work its way down to Williams Creek next spring. A large deer meandered through the brush. I am unused to estimating long distances, but based on my years in marching band and practicing on football fields for halftime shows, I knew the deer had to be within eighty to one hundred yards from us. The wind must be disguising the sound of our trek as well as putting us downwind; the deer grazed, unaware of our presence.

My arm shook when I tried aiming my rifle; too much for a standing shot. My right knee smashed through thick snow, and I aimed again, my left arm supporting the rifle on my other knee. Continued shivering prevented any reasonable aim. Shaking my head, I held out my arm, showing Dad my shaking hand. Try as I might, I could not hold them still. Looking up, I whispered to my dad.

"You take the shot. Guess I'm still cold from yesterday and can't hold the rifle steady."

He arched his left brow and tipped his head.

"It's okay. I'll be happy to eat the deer. I don't need to shoot it, too."

My dad rubbed my shoulder and nodded. He braced himself, aimed, and fired. The deer fell. We sloshed our way down the side of the ravine. I only slipped to my butt once. Dave held up his hand as we approached the deer on the other side.

"We want to make sure it's dead before we get close. Injured animals are dangerous."

As we got closer, we could see no movement and no signs of breathing.

"We're okay."

Under Dave's tutelage, we field-dressed the deer. It took us forever, and the messy evolution convinced me to remove hunting from my list of desired future activities. Cleaning fish by a stream or a lake is one thing. Field dressing a deer in the snow is quite another. We had now experienced the hunt. I had no desire to revisit it again. I would let Dad know when we got back home. After we finished, I tried cleaning blood from my hands in the wet snow.

Yes, this was something to avoid in the future.

During the hunt, Dave had been carrying a canvas tarp slung over his shoulder. Before we finished, he had it spread on the ground. The three of us struggled to lift the deer and wound up rolling it onto the tarp. Dave pulled up and fastened the corners. Stretching and exhaling a deep breath, he turned to me.

"You get to carry the weapons."

With the deer secured within the canvas sling, the two men began to drag the bundle down the slope. With luck on our side, the ravine led to a point about a hundred yards from our Williams Creek camp. With more luck, most of the drag went downhill. I trudged behind the other two with three rifles over my shoulder.

Now, if I could only manage to keep from slipping again and dropping them into the snow or creek.

At camp, Dave taught us how to hang the deer using the gambrel and hoist. Once up, he explained how to skin the animal. Although he started with a short demonstration, he left the bulk of the skinning to us.

Perfect.

"I know a shop where they give you a big discount to process your deer meat if you give them the deerskin," he said, arching his forehead up and down several times. "They even give you a pair of deer-leather working gloves."

He returned to the plane and shifted things in his cooler, sorting through remnants from several blocks of dry ice held separate from our food by several folded sections of clean cloth.

When we finished skinning the deer, Dave showed us how to quarter the animal. We wrapped the best parts of the buck in the unrolled cloth and carried them to the plane, where Dave packed them in the cooler separated by other towels. I got the delightful chore of discarding the remnants.

Wonderful.

The last thing remaining of the deer, its head, rested near the hoist contraption. Dead eyes glared at me. With a bone saw, Dave removed the antlers. When done, he asked me to carry the head and toss it into the trees with the other parts.

Please, sir. May I have another?

This time, I heated up some water to wash my hands. With only three planned meals before departure, we had room to pack the deer in the cooler. Any food remaining unconsumed after breakfast could be turned into lunch before we left, assuming we had time.

Never knowing what would be left over on the last day, the final meal tended to be a mix of things, all cooked in one large pot.

"I call it, what-ta-ya-got stew." Dave chuckled. "Oftentimes, it's the tastiest meal of the hunt."

"As soon as we get back, we'll get the deer processed," he said. "The meat will be fine in the cooler until then. Shoot, it's cold enough, we could almost leave the wraps out in the snow."

Taking advantage of the last evening in camp, Dave arranged a special meal. He saved some of his wife's cornbread and warmed it in foil at the edge of the campfire while chili heated in a pot on the iron grate. He also had three New York steaks.

"It didn't seem right to leave these in the cooler when it's full of fresh venison." He slapped them on the grill. "Tonight, we eat like kings." Chuckling, he smiled and continued. "We'll have our normal breakfast tomorrow morning, then start packing up for the return trip. No need to hurry now. We can toss anything left over from lunch into the trees for our animal friends. I want to be out of here before the storm hits."

"You're right." My mouth began watering before my teeth bit into it. "Best steak ever."

***

Thursday morning arrived cold and damp, gray and blustery. The two men talking woke me. Although cramped and uncomfortable, I wanted to stay in bed. Unzipping my sleeping bag, I rolled over and got dressed. The moment I stepped out of the tent, my eyes watered, and when I exhaled, sent out a wispy cloud of breath. "Burr!" Six to eight inches of new snow greeted me.

As the two men prepared breakfast, Dave kept glancing at the mountains North and West, frowning.

"Me thinks the storm came early. We better eat fast and leave. I don't like the looks of that dark cloud."

My dad looked up.

"Come have breakfast, son. Eat whatever and as much as you want. Anything left goes back to Mother Nature."

After breakfast, Dave coiled his hoist line and stowed it with the gambrel in the back of the plane. He rolled up the soiled canvas tarp and packed it away, as well. He would have to clean the bloody mess later. I cleaned the pans, plates, and utensils.

We all returned to the tent, rolled up our sleeping bags, and packed whatever clothing and things we had lying around. I walked the bags over to the plane as Dad and Dave struggled with the tent. The lines had stiffened in the damp cold, the knots becoming difficult to untie. For the first time, I noticed my dad's beard growth.

Mom will love that.

By the time they had the tent stowed in the plane, Dave's forehead took on a dark, wavy line of furrows.

"Just one last look at the camp," he said. "I'll move the grate back to the trees. It's cooled off by now. Then we need to go. This storm is coming in way too fast."

***

During a typical year, snow geese migrate from September to October. Upon occasion, they would delay their migration until late

November. Their unusual late migration this year came in part due to a moderate El Niño keeping their summer breeding site warmer for a longer period. The weather provided ample natural reasoning to delay the arduous trek South to their non-breeding sites. Driven by a sudden winter bluster, the natural migration of this flock of geese kicked into gear. Passing across Montana, they moved South in quick and narrow lanes.

***

Dave went through a quick pre-flight checklist and started the engine, waiting until the heat started to enter the cabin and the foggy windshield cleared up. "Alright, everyone. Buckle up. We're leaving." He revved the courier's engine. The plane wobbled and stayed in its position. In the fresh, thick snow, the plane struggled to move, and then, with a vibrating groan, it scooted forward with a lurch. As advertised, the little craft left the ground after several plane lengths. We cleared the tree height well before the meadow ended. "It's all in the wrist." He chuckled, but I could see a darkening sky through my little side window, and I gave a silent prayer.

Sometimes, the wrist might need a little help.

The courier kept climbing as Dave checked the gauges and turned south. We continued climbing for several minutes. Visibility worsened, and I could hear the wipers whooshing at a fast tempo across the windshield. About ten minutes into the flight, my attention was alerted to the first of several rapid thumps and a splash of red smeared across the windshield. Over Dave's shoulder, I could see a mix of white feathers and entrails being pushed by the wipers. They struggled to clear the bloody detritus.

With another loud thud, the bulk of a snow goose cracked through the windshield, hitting Dave in the neck. His head whipped to the side, causing the radio headset to flip from his head. Glass, blood, and feathers splattered across the interior of the plane.

Time stalled.

The wipers stopped.

The courier began to shudder with the sound of one last thud. We had no way to know, but the three-bladed propeller now had two and a half blades. One broke in half with the impact of the second goose; only one remained straight after the last strike.

Dave yelled over the screeching wind.

"We have to land, and I can't see a damn thing."

Shielding my eyes from the sudden rush of air, I saw my dad in the process of wiping bloody debris from his face. Flying glass must have cut his forehead, causing heavy bleeding. When his face turned, I could see blood dripping from Dave's face, too. Well, I suppose the blood could be from the goose. The carcass lay somewhere up front.

Dave reached over and grabbed Dad's shoulder to get his attention and yelled again.

"Frank, we have to land. Open your side window and help me find a suitable clearing. Any open area."

My dad nodded and reached to open his window. Dave did the same, and with the two open windows, increased wind and noise coursed through the cabin. Dave noticed a potential landing spot and pointed down to the left. He began to circle, hoping to catch regular glimpses of the clearing as he descended. They both began shouting "there" or "over there" and pointed as the clearing came into view on one side or the other and passed out of sight again during our downward spiral. Dave caught sight again and yelled.

"Shit! This's more of a gliding freefall than a controlled descent." He struggled with the controls. "There must be damage to the propeller. We're losing airspeed."

He turned and called back to me.

"This is gonna get ugly. Grab a sleeping bag or something, and cover your head, and lean forward."

We had packed the bags in the back, out of reach, so I did the only option available and interlaced my fingers behind my neck and, as best as my stiff body could manage, tucked my face between my knees.

When he could see the clearing, I heard my dad call it out as we circled our way down. I lifted my head to peek through my window and hoped to see us passing over the clearing. With a quick glance at the trees, I knew we would be on the ground soon.

Dave yelled, "I need to slow our descent."

The engine screamed, and the sudden acceleration gave the courier enough lift to prevent a hard crash in the clearing and enough forward momentum to put us in the trees.

The plane made a violent twist, and cracking sounds came from both sides. Still leaning forward, I heard shattering glass, the crunch of metal, and splintering fiberglass. The rolled-up tent pushed across my back, pressing my head further down between my knees and pinning me in place.

Breathing became difficult.

Aware the plane hit something hard, I felt a wild shift sideways. The pilot's large white cooler, full of deer meat, slid forward and clipped my elbow as it passed, stopping with a loud whack. The force from the shifting plane pushed me to the right until a sudden stop slammed me back to the left, accompanied by a loud crack and a sharp pain in my leg. The tail of the plane dropped hard, and everything went dark.

Based on what I learned later, the courier tore through pine trees, well clear of the clearing. Both wings snapped off as the plane plunged deeper into the forest. The compromised propeller took turns shredding smaller branches and being sheared off by larger ones. Without its wings, the courier plowed through branches like a missile until a long-dead fallen tree crossed its path. The engine cleared the snag. The cabin of the plane did not. The right front edge of the engine smacked into a large pine tree. The plane twisted to its left, slamming to a halt against something solid.

CHAPTER 29

DENNY

With a couple more hours of work, the dusty old two-room cabin will be clean enough and ready for Cousin Paul's arrival in a few days. Bringing the bulk of our food supplies, he planned to stay for a week or so, with me, while we hunted for deer or elk. With both of our sled teams available, we hoped to get a larger animal. We would need both teams of dogs and Paul's toboggan-style sled to pull the extra weight of a big game animal. Tired from my trek to the cabin yesterday, I slept in, fed my dogs, and finished a late breakfast.

Before sweeping out the cabin, I took time to sit back, brooding about my mother and grandmother. I missed Pan and Momma the most during quiet, alone times like this. I didn't get much quiet time in Vietnam and never found myself alone. I poured a cup of coffee, moved out to the porch, and sat on a warped old pine bench. Although it creaked with my weight, its three legs provided a solid perch.

Looking across a large pond, I watched several large flakes flittering. The cabin's position offered a perfect view. Sighing, I watched the steam rise from my cup. Pixie came over and sat next to me, giving me some solace. I rubbed her head and worked her ears with my thumb.

"Snow's coming in heavy, Girl."

Satisfied with the affection and ignoring the snow, Pixie turned to lap water from a small trough at the corner of the cabin. A steady stream of water poured into the trough from a series of V-shaped gutters constructed by connecting hand-carved lengths of lodge poles, end to end. Long ago, someone carved each pole, removing part of one side and its center, down their entire lengths, allowing them to move water from one to another.

"At least I got the water flowing again, eh, Pixie?"

The gutter system extended behind the cabin, sloping up to a small handmade dam of larger rocks and smaller stones formed to divert water from a nearby spring to the cabin. The weakest part of the system turned out to be the points where two sets of pine gutters met. The junctures had short stacks of stones supporting the joint. Over time, they had collapsed or had been knocked over by weather or animals.

It took me most of the first day at the cabin to figure out the deconstructed gutter parts and how to piece them back together and clear the buildup of debris from the makeshift dam. Replacing the two piles of support stones took the most time. Through trial and error, I managed to stack them to proper heights, and spring water flowed.

Musing, I patted my own back. *Well done, Darkcloud.*

Overflow from the trough poured down through a hand-dug ditch to the spring's natural stream access to the pond. It needed clearing, too. Maintaining a constant, year-round temperature, the spring water in the gutter would not freeze. The further from the source, though, the more possible it could ice over.

Thinking about the ingenuity of the old timers who built this cabin, I had to chuckle. The cabin has running water, though it takes a few steps out the door to get it. The wood-burning stove provides easy heat for hot water and cooking and warmth.

"All the comforts of home. Too bad we don't have an interior toilet."

Pixie sneezed her disinterest and shook her entire body. I winced as wet flecks of snow hit my cheek and neck.

Glancing up at the darkening gray sky, I shook my head and looked down at Pixie.

"Good thing Paul isn't coming yet."

This time, Pixie nudged me in agreement.

"It would be a long and miserable trip in this weather."

Out in front of the cabin, Copper jumped up. Ears cocked forward. He liked to lay in the snow while chewing on a bone. The bone dropped. He did a quick hop toward me and the cabin, barked twice, and jumped back, facing northeast. Copper got his name from his mix of chocolate brown and gray fur, which gives him a coppery look when sunshine falls on his back.

Setting my coffee cup down, I followed Pixie out to where Copper stood at attention. The fur on his back bristled as he growled. Pixie huffed, and then I heard the sound, too. The engine of a plane struggled in the distance. It sounded wrong and clunky. The sputtering noise withered, came back, and disappeared again. The three of us jumped at the sound of the plane crashing into the trees. Although I could see nothing through the heavy snowfall, it did not sound like the plane crashed too far away.

Stepping back into the cabin, I took the waterpot off the stove, checked the fire level in the stove, and felt comfortable leaving it for a bit. Sensing a call to duty, the dogs gathered around the porch. Although I did not need to say it, I kept to their training and gave them the command.

"Let's go to work."

Just inside the cabin door, a series of alternating high and low pegs held all their harnesses. Although anxious to work, each of them pawing the porch or snow, the dogs trembled, waiting their turn. With their harness on, they hurried to the side of the cabin and sat, tails brushing back and forth.

My sled leaned against the porch, just under the overhang of the cabin roof. I lowered it to the snow, went back into the cabin, put on my coat and hat, and grabbed some gloves. Just in case, I picked up Pan's medicine bag. After strapping it in the sled basket, I covered it to keep it safe from excessive moisture.

Saving time, I chose to only hook up my wheel and swing dogs with Pixie in the lead and directed two of the team dogs into the basket and turned to the last two.

"Copper, Bingo. Follow!"

I stepped on the sled, grabbed the leads, and called out to the team.

"Marche!"

***

The dogs smelled it first, and then I recognized burning fuel, rubber, and pine. Through a swirl of snow, I could see intermittent white smoke off in the trees. Setting the brake, I stepped off, planted the snow hook, and moved to the front of the team. Releasing Pixie, I turned back to the two team dogs who had followed the sled.

"Copper. Bingo. Protect!"

Without knowing what might be needed, I uncovered the medicine bag and swung the strap over my left shoulder. Pixie nudged my leg, urging me to hurry. I called to her and the other two team dogs, who sat at attention in the sled basket.

"Loki. Odin. Come!" We followed Pixie.

On our way up a slope to the smoke, we passed wings on either side of a swath of broken trees and branches. Loki and Odin sniffed them. About 40 or 50 yards further into the trees, we found the plane hanging from a large fallen tree, which skewered the cockpit of the plane, and part of the plane's roof peeled back like a cereal box lid. The engine had smashed into a tree with no propellers in sight. The front end of the plane had been on fire until snow fell from the tree, extinguishing the flames. It still steamed. The body of the plane swung down to the left and rested against a large boulder at a precarious angle.

Hoping to find someone alive and conscious, I called out.

"Hello! Anyone hurt?"

I waited for an answer while listening to the sound of Pixie's breathing at my side and my heartbeat in my ears.

The side access to the plane stood about five feet above the ground.

I figured the possibility of me pulling myself up through the open side door would be a foolhardy move. And then only with an open door.

Poop!

I saw no need to embarrass myself in front of Pixie. The latch to the door waited beyond my reach. Taking a moment, I considered how best to reach the door handle.

"Got it."

I snapped my fingers, which did nothing but make slush fly from my gloves. Bits hit me in the face.

"Loki. Odin. Protect!"

The two dogs sat at attention as Pixie followed me back to one of the sheared-off wings. I managed to haul it back to the wreckage without difficulty. The process of stuffing the severed wing across a broken branch and wedging the other end between the plane and the boulder took me several minutes to find the sweet spot. I climbed up and took careful steps over to the plane. The stability of the sloped wing bridge surprised me.

After several yank attempts, the plane's door creaked open, and I leaned in. "Hello! Anyone alive!" I hopped up, ducked under the snag, and moved to where the pilot sat crumpled over. I reached for his neck and found it broken, with no pulse. The inside of the cockpit had bloody feathers scattered throughout. Blood also covered the passenger to the right. The tree snag rested where his head should be.

I turned back to the door and leaned out.

"They're both dead, Pixie."

Well damn, I thought and sat down to consider what I should or could do and let out a ripple through my lips. My legs dangled out the door.

Then I heard an "Umpff!" behind me. After moving debris, tent pieces, sleeping bags, coils of rope, and rifles, I managed to stretch over a large cooler and saw an arm hanging down across a leg. I kept moving things, tossing most of the stuff out the open door, "Look out below," and uncovered someone bent over in a rear seat. The arm rested at an unnatural angle.

The cooler blocked easy access, so I tried to move or slide the thing and found it too heavy. The top had popped open, so I reached in and pulled out pieces of wrapped meat. Once I could shift the cooler, I managed to jockey things around until it slid further back into the plane. With a careful touch, I leaned the limp body back in the seat and saw a boy. He had a young man's fuzzy beginnings of a beard. I reached in to disconnect his lap belt and heard another "Umpff!"

"Sorry." I examined the boy's arm through his coat. "I think you dislocated your elbow." He remained silent, his breathing shallow. I looked over and could see the side of the plane protruding into the cabin against his left leg. "Your leg might be injured, too." Sitting back on my heels, I considered how to get the boy out of the plane. "I sure could use the fire department right now."

Pixie barked. I realized I had been talking to an unconscious young man and myself out loud and unsettling her. Further self-discussions should be internalized.

"I'm okay, Pixie. There is a survivor."

I considered the good news. The unconscious boy should not notice any pain when I move him. I just need to make sure I don't cause any further injury by moving him.

But move him, I must.

Shifting to sit with my feet dangling out the open door again, I looked around at the items tossed out into the snow. An idea emerged. About thirty minutes later, I had the boy's leg braced with two halves of a tent pole. I tossed the rope over a sturdy branch above the plane and connected it to a gambrel found when I cleared space to shift the cooler. Its other end looped around the snag, giving me the ability to raise and lower the boy. Fashioning a sling from cut pieces of the tent, I tied its straps to the ends of the gambrel.

When I positioned the sling to hold the boy sitting upright, his head hung forward, slack. Checking, I determined the awkward angle had no impact on his airway. His chest had a normal in-and-out rhythm. Although he might wind up with a sore neck, it would be nothing compared to his other injuries. I noted the sling did nothing to support his damaged leg. To solve this, I looped one end of another piece of the tent line around the boy's boot and the other end through the gambrel's center loop, hoping tautness on the line would provide support by holding his leg out straight. I climbed back down to the ground.

"Okay. Hang on."

"Woof?"

"Not you, Pixie."

With slow and deliberate tension, I pulled on the hoist rope until the sling began to rise and stop. I needed to adjust the length of the line supporting the boy's leg to keep the lift from raising it too high and adding additional strain as the sling took his weight. Pulling on the hoist line a second time, the boy rose, and with a gentle pull, he swung out of the plane, swinging below the gambrel. Careful to keep from dropping him, I lowered him to within a few inches of the ground.

The three dogs examined him with interest. I managed to tie the hoist line to a branch, holding the boy in his sitting and swinging position, suspended several inches above the snow.

Back on the ground, I removed the fiberglass wing from its perch and sat it next to the boy. Taking another piece of rope, I tied a tight loop around the wide end of the wing, then laid out one of the sleeping bags on the wing.

Pixie yipped her approval.

Unzipping another bag, I spread it open across the wing, as well, and slid the entire wing assembly under the boy. Pulling up on the hoist line again, I released the tension on my knot and lowered the boy onto the makeshift stretcher.

With a tender touch, I unfastened the sling and lowered the boy until his head rested on the wing, cut all the lines, and set the gambrel aside. After folding the open sleeping bag over the boy, I zipped it closed. With several more lengths of rope, I secured the boy to the wing, hoping its strength and straightness would support the boy's leg while pulling him through the trees.

I struggled and failed, trying to get the makeshift sled moving. The weight of the boy prevented me from making progress.

Pixie bopped her jaws and shook her head.

Duh!

I had two harnessed team dogs at my disposal.

"You're so smart, Pixie."

"Woof!"

Using several other pieces of line, I added their strength to the pull. The wing began to move with the help of Loki and Odin, and the three of us pulled the wing through the brittle thicket surrounding the crash site. I even managed to remember the medicine bag. Pixie bounded around as if supervising the recovery. She was. We scooted ahead, ushering the way down to the dog sled.

Still concerned about adding injury to the boy's leg, I decided it best not to try shifting him to the sled's basket. Lifting him without causing further injury would be difficult, and there was no way the basket could support his leg. With his safety in mind and my back, I chose to keep the boy inclined on the wing tip, fastened to the back of the sled. With the extra weight, I placed the four-team dogs in their normal positions, and with Pixie in the lead, we pulled the boy back to the cabin. I kept a careful watch to make sure we didn't lose the wing and the boy didn't slide off.

Back on level ground, I managed to drag the wing into the cabin and kneeled to remove the lines holding the boy secured. Tipping the wing from its side, the boy and the sleeping bags slipped onto the floor. With him clear, I shoved the wing out of the cabin and closed the door.

After adding more logs to the stove, I unzipped the sleeping bag, removed the remaining pieces of the tent sling, and began to examine the boy. I removed the leg splint and sliced open his pant leg. After leaning in, I looked up at the unconscious boy. "Good news, this is not a compound fracture, but the leg is broken. Now, this is gonna hurt." His eyes remained closed. "On the count of three. One …" and I yanked hard on the leg, setting it back in place. I wrapped a towel around his leg, replaced the splints, and encircled everything with bandages to hold it safe and secure. Sitting the boy up, I pulled his good left arm from his coat and slid the coat down his injured arm.

"Okay, just dislocated."

A foul odor became evident, and I realized the boy's trousers and undershorts had been soiled. I cut them off and set them aside. Turning, I emptied the boy's pockets and moved the stinky clothing outside. While there, I took the opportunity and grabbed the medicine bag from the sled's basket and reentered the cabin.

"Let's set this arm." I squatted beside the boy and looked up at his closed eyes again. "Now, this will hurt too. On three." As I set the arm, I heard another "Umpff!"

Reaching into the medicine bag, I pulled out a bottle of painkiller and an olive-green-colored sling. I took two of the pills and pushed them into the boy's mouth, lifted his head, and tried to tip a small amount of water into his mouth. Although the boy sensed the water and swallowed, much of it dripped down his cheek. After folding the sling around the boy's arm, I tied the ends around his neck.

Satisfied with the initial treatment, I got up from the floor.

"Let me get ready to clean you up a bit."

I grabbed the pot from the stove, refilled it from the outside running spring source, and put it back on the stove to warm the water.

***

Tipping the boy side to side, I washed and dried him off and zipped up the sleeping bag. He laid there, his head tipped back at an awkward angle, shivering. So, I grabbed a pillow from the bed.

"Here. This should help your neck."

After checking the fire level in the stove, I added a couple of small logs. Remembering the boy's pocket items, I checked his wallet and discovered his name, Keith Brown.

I heard a whimper from outside and remembered the dogs, still harnessed to the sled. "I need to go back to the plane before it gets dark, Keith." Even though the unconscious boy had no way to respond, I added, "I'll try to find some extra clothes for you."

Believing the boy could manage a few minutes without further aid, I went out to my assembled team with a pan of water and gave them all a drink. Once again, I separated out the team dogs and left Loki and Odin at the cabin to 'protect' the boy. Copper and Bingo rode in the basket.

"Marche!"

Back at the crash site, I used the second wing to access the plane again. Searching through the plane's interior, I found two small duffle bags and a backpack. One of the bags had the initials KB on it. I searched the two bodies, pulled out their wallets, and placed them in Keith's bag. I removed three rifles, one of them damaged from the crash, a holster and pistol, and an ammunition bag, and took the items down to the basket sled.

Back at the plane, I rubbed Pixie's neck.

"What do you think, girl?"

She shook her head and body. Wet flakes flew.

"Yeah. Removing the bodies would be difficult."

It would take two trips to get them back to the cabin, and I had no place to keep them safe from wild animals. If I put them in the small bunk room, there would be less room for the dogs. We would need the space for Paul and his team when they arrive.

"Besides, Pixie. I am sure you'd be okay, but dead bodies in the bunk room would unsettle the other dogs," I rubbed her neck again, "They would unsettle me."

Given the circumstances and the fact the passenger's head was missing, it seemed best to leave them inside the plane. Up in this tree, the two bodies should be safe from most predators. Safer than on the ground, for sure. Nevertheless, determined to distract large predators from the bodies, I tossed all the contents of the cooler out into the snow and hopped out.

Although the door would no longer close all the way and latch, it would still prevent a large predator from jumping through an open door. To make access more difficult, I lowered the wing to the ground. Except for birds and squirrels, the bodies should be left alone. Hopefully, due to winter, no little critters are around to bother them. I paused as I turned to leave.

There was no reason to waste all this meat.

Assuming they had quartered a deer by the size of the wraps, I gathered the wrapped pieces of meat and took them back to the sled.

CHAPTER 30

KEITH

Waking up from the void. I opened my eyes and failed to see anything. I could hear a sizzle, as if water dripped on a hot skillet, then a hiss of steam. Then, the darkness returned. When I woke a second time, my body hurt; my right arm and left leg hurt the most. I tried to sit up. I could hear no sounds. The sizzling stopped. After a while, I felt movement, vibrations, shaking, and a voice calling. I am here. Why won't my mouth work? I needed to say something and managed a groan before blackness returned.

I dreamed of floating in an inner tube on a dark lake, everything still, cold, and quiet. The inner tube changed into a park swing, my legs kicking out to propel me forward and back. For some reason, only one leg moved. Strange. I wonder why. The swinging stopped when the pain returned and brought back the void. Emptiness came and left, came again, and left. I heard a sniffing sound and felt something cold and wet. I felt rocking and rolling and another period of emptiness. A light from a lantern hurt my eyes, causing me to blink as they watered. Movement stopped.

The voice came back. "…hurt on three," It said.

Umpff! I heard no three.

Bastard!

The darkness came like a circus strongman striking a tent stake with a sledgehammer.

NEW ORLEANS

CHAPTER 31

PANACAEA

Spring 1950

Before Denny came along, I attended nursing school and planned to become a nurse at one of the local hospitals. During school, I volunteered at the New Orleans VA Medical Center. Because of the type of hospital, I seldom had a woman patient and could not help but carry Momma's warning as a burden. "Serve only women." Even so, I melded into a full-time position at the VA Medical Center upon completion of my nurse's training.

"Your work ethic and natural bedside manner make you a natural fit," my supervisor said.

On Friday, I took a shift in the immunization ward. A host of young Marines lined up early in the day; the line trailed out through the doorway. They needed immunizations before heading overseas, destined for the Korean conflict. The end of the line disappeared down the hall. Many nervous young souls waited for their shots.

Oh my. My list had several pages of names.

This would be a long day.

Used to a line up for everything in their brief military career, the men stood quiet and waited for their inoculations. None of them wanted their buddies to know if they had any fear of getting injections. Even if afraid of needles, they stood rock hard and tall.

One at a time, they came to me, reported their names and ranks, and handed over their medical shot record. For each, I checked their names on my roster and, when done, annotated, initialed, and stamped their records. They exposed their arms, looked brave, and waited for their injections. Once I returned their records, they walked away, relieved to be done.

When my tummy began to growl, I looked up to see if the line still extended out of the room. I could see the last three Marines just inside my door. Sighing, I yawned, covering my mouth with the back of my hand.

“No worries, miss.”

The third Marine in line spoke up. We locked our eyes. He had a wide, natural smile under the squint of dark, dreamy eyes.

“I’m the last one,” Dreamy said.

Smiling back at the handsome Marine and blinking several times, I bobbed my head.

“Oh, good. I’m tired and hungry.”

After two more young men received their inoculations, Dreamy stood in front of me.

“Sergeant Denali Darkcloud, reporting for immunization.”

He snapped to attention and gave me a quick salute. He exposed a muscled upper arm, offering a howling wolf tattoo with a moon peeking out of a dark cloud in its background.

After studying his tattoo, I glanced up at his smile and felt my cheeks warming. Dreamy has a name. His name is not Dreamy. His name should be Dreamy.

"I'm sorry, what name did you say?"

I blinked twice, trying to clear the sight of Dreamy's eyes from my mind. They stayed. He gave me his name again, and I proceeded to give him his two injections, the second injection at the snout of the wolf.

"There. Done," I said, trying to hide the sudden shaking of my hands.

"Miss," Sergeant Dreamy said. "I'm only passing through New Orleans with my men and have never been to this VA center before. I heard you mention being hungry. I'm hungry, too. I'd be obliged if you would show me the cafeteria. Sitting and talking with someone other than my men would be a pleasant change." He smiled. "I'll even buy lunch."

It would be nice to sit and watch you eat. No, wait. I am sorry, my shift is over. I need to go home and take a cold shower.

"Um, sure. Give me a moment to put these things away."

I put the tray of equipment away, rattling it in the process, repositioned the table used for the injections, and placed the used needle container in a locked closet.

"There, follow me … um, Sergeant?"

"Sergeant Darkcloud," Dreamy said. "My first name is Denali, but everyone calls me Denny."

That's pretty close to Dreamy.

He glanced down at my name tag, making sure he did not appear to be ogling my chest.

"And you are Nurse Pana…"

"Panacaea." I began choking and had to repeat my name. "Panacaea."

He nodded, smiled, and repeated my name, enunciating the syllables. "Pan-ah-see-ah." Dreamy Denali Darkcloud smiled.

"Beautiful name."

As we walked, he asked the meaning of my name. I explained the answer differs depending on who you ask, but they were all similar. To some, Panacaea means a remedy for all difficulties, evils, or diseases or a cure for all. Some say it is the name of a goddess of healing. Others just say it means all-healing.

Sergeant Darkcloud listened as we walked, slowed to a stop, and touched my elbow with upturned fingers. He looked at me and smiled again. Hallway lights gleamed in his eyes.

"Beautiful!" he said again. "Your name is a perfect fit for you. It suits both you and your profession."

Did he just say I'm beautiful, or only my name, or my profession? I smiled back at him, standing there, head tipped to the side, grinning, his hand still holding my elbow.

Please keep your hand there.

I looked up into Dreamy's eyes.

"And your name? What does Denali mean?"

Dreamy Denali raised his hand from my elbow and fake coughed into his closed fist.

"It, um, it means the great one."

He scrunched his brow, shook his head, and looked to see my reaction.

Of course, it fits. It was a perfect fit.

I blinked three times, this time, and tried to keep my jaw from joining my feet on the floor. I failed.

"The gr-great one." I tried to say while suppressing a hysterical cackle. "Well, that … that certainly fits your profession too."

I turned my head, closed my eyes, and took a deep breath, trying to recover, and hoped my uncharacteristic gawkiness did not give away any obvious interest. It did. I took three steps down the hallway before breathing again. I looked back at him, walking toward me, and pointed at the next corner.

"The ca-cafeteria is just around here."

During lunch, we told each other several things about our lives. Denali was a Kootenai Indian from Northern Montana, near Kalispell. His parents both died in a car accident. I told him my mother immigrated from Haiti, and I never knew my white and absent biological father from New York. He had a sister. I had no siblings. He wanted to be a Marine and serve his country. I wanted to be a nurse and help people. He had a weekend pass in New Orleans. I had lived in New Orleans my entire life. He departed for Korea on Monday. I had nothing planned.

After spending a pleasant weekend with Sergeant Denali Darkcloud, he departed for the Korean War early Monday morning.

CHAPTER 32

DENNY

Growing up in New Orleans had its advantages and disadvantages. On the one hand, the area had a remarkable history and many incredible places to visit, and the sights and sounds provided a never-ending source of excitement and entertainment.

At the same time, living with my mother and grandmother above a store my friends refused to enter left me confused and torn between my interest in the good things I saw my generational parents doing, as opposed to the nefarious and evil voodoo spells my friends accused them of creating. Muddled about how to broach the subject, I settled on ignoring it.

***

During my formative years, I spent more time under the watchful eye of Momma than with my mother, who alternated working at the VA hospital and helping with the store. If I did not have homework to do, I would try to play with my friends. They often made excuses to avoid playing with me or simply became unavailable. On those days, oft-repeated days, I assisted Momma with the store. Of course, Momma would never admit my help tended to be more of a nuisance or distraction than assistance. Still, I learned a lot about responsibility and respect.

I learned responsibility from Momma, who could chastise my accidental messes and mistakes or correct my occasional and accidental or purposeful misbehavior in a way that left me feeling better about myself and learning rather than feeling like a failure.

"I'm sorry, Momma. I won't do it again."

I learned respect by observing the many repeat patrons who came to Momma for cures and life's other essentials and how she treated them. I watched how they acceded to her expertise and complimented her on the results of products they had purchased from her before. They always paid their regards to her and often hugged her or shook and kissed her hand.

"Momma. You're wonderful. I love you."

Momma's illness caused my mother to leave the veterans hospital and take over management of the store. I learned respect and responsibility from her, too. She left her nursing dream and took over Momma's shop without complaint, without hesitation, and without regret.

When things became clear Momma's condition would only get worse, I raised the issue my friends made me wonder about. "Why can't you do a spell to make her better?" I pulled at her hand. "My friends tell me you and Momma can create spells to raise the dead and do other evil things. They say you are evil voodoo medicine women. I've seen lots of people come into the store asking Momma for help with sickness. Can't you heal her?"

My mother tipped her head toward me and arched both of her eyebrows. "It does not work that way." She frowned. "And when have you ever seen either of us do anything evil?"

"But they say..." She cut me off with a wave of her hand.

"They don't know what they are saying." She kneeled, putting out her hands to hold my shoulders. "Denny, there is no good or evil voodoo. There are only good or evil people." She blinked and relaxed her face. "Do you think Momma is evil?"

"No."

"Do you think I am evil?"

I lost focus as my eyes began clouding.

"No."

She smiled at me and wiped a tear from my cheek with her thumb. "Denny. People, and in particular children, can be cruel when they don't understand things or if someone looks or acts different from them, or if other people believe in unusual ways of doing things." She shook her head and let out a breath. "It's unfortunate, but it's the way things are in the world."

She rubbed more dampness from my cheeks and handed me a tissue.

After blowing my nose, I looked at the most amazing woman in the world.

"Why are people so stupid?"

She took another deep breath and exhaled. "If people cannot explain why something is the way it is, they will make up a reason and often base the reason on fear or ignorance. Because they are afraid, they will claim someone or something evil or the work of the devil caused the unexplained thing." She raised the corner of her mouth and her eyebrow again. "It's the easiest way for them to overlook their ignorance."

She paused and held up a finger. “Ignorance, not stupidity. These are different things. Ignorance is a lack of education or awareness about something. Stupidity is knowing better and still believing it or doing it.” She smiled. “Remember, your friends are not stupid. They are just unaware of our beliefs and are not educated about the methods Momma teaches us about how to do things.”

Calming down, I turned around and pointed toward Momma’s bedroom.

“What do we do now?”

“For the moment, we take care of Momma and keep her comfortable. Make her last days as pleasant as possible. I will watch the store, and you go to school. Pay attention to your teachers.”

She stood up, putting her hands on her hips, and looked down at me with a grin.

“Pay less attention to your goofy friends.”

I heard a slight chuckle.

CHAPTER 33

PANACAEA

Momma passed away in April. After a few weeks, my interest in maintaining the store waned. I still had dreams of helping people, in particular women, and felt the current customers of Momma's shop were looking for more trinkets and baubles than elixirs and ointments or other medicinal support. Momma's former customers dwindled in numbers, moving on to other practitioners or passing away due to issues associated with advanced age.

My nursing training weighed on me, and I needed to move beyond the charm and bobbles aspect of the shop and the party atmosphere of New Orleans and into an area where I could make a real difference in women's lives. Women who needed help. New Orleans had enough bauble shops to support Momma's remaining clientele. After the school year ended, I sold the small building at a discount to the city of New Orleans, with a tacit agreement they would use Momma's shop as a tourist museum and maintain the store's ambiance.

"Okay, Denny. Pack your bags. We're going on an adventure and moving to Montana."

Using an old trunk, I packed Momma's medicine bag, her cash box, important papers, and her tincture diary. Denny and I began loading a wide selection of potions and ointments into the back of Momma's old green pick-up truck.

She got it from an aging widowed male client who could no longer drive. One of her few male clients he knew she needed a truck and wanted to give it to her in thanks for her help over the years. Momma refused the charity, and when he insisted, she agreed, but only if he would accept some payment for the truck. After squabbling for several minutes, they agreed to one dollar. In honor of the high-cost financial transaction, we gave the old truck its new name, One Buck.

Denny walked through Momma's work area.

"What about all of Momma's tools?"

With a sigh, I put my hand on his shoulder and surveyed the specialty tools Momma used in her craft.

"We'll pack up some of her newer things and anything personal and leave the older tools to the future museum."

Stuffing our clothing in empty milk crates, we lashed an old tarp over the packed contents and left New Orleans for Montana.

During the trip, Denny turned eleven.

When we arrived in Flathead Valley, we reached out to his father's family. Sergeant Denali Darkcloud hailed from the Flathead Reservation yet had no immediate relations remaining on the reservation, only distant cousins. His only sibling, Diane (Dyani Darkcloud) Whitehorse, lived in Grasmere, British Columbia, with her husband John Whitehorse and their son Pala.

"More adventure, let's visit Canada," I said.

When Denny met his Cousin Pala, they developed an immediate bond. Pala preferred using his common name, Paul, when dealing with non-Indians. The Whitehorse's bred, raised, and trained sled dogs for several mushers throughout Canada and the United States. Their business grew into a lucrative venture.

"We get a lot of interest in the months leading up to the Iditarod and the lesser-known American Dog Derby," Pala said. "The Derby is a short speed race held in Ashton, Idaho. It's in late February." Pala rubbed his hands together. "The big one, the Iditarod, is a 1000-mile endurance race from Anchorage to Nome, Alaska." He shook his head. "Although time is always important, the Iditarod starts on the first Saturday in March and can last from 8 days to 2 weeks." He sighed. "Just finishing the race is an accomplishment."

Although tempted to live in Canada, we chose to remain within the United States, and I worked with a Real Estate office in Eureka, Montana. We hoped to find a small ranch or farmhouse with outbuildings somewhere between Eureka and Whitefish. This would put us between and at a reasonable distance from both the Flathead Reservation and Denny's Canadian family. My first customers were native Americans and, for many months, my only customers. Just short of two years passed before non-Indian clientele began to come to visit me for help.

CHAPTER 34

DENNY

I started spending my high school summers with Cousin Pala, getting educated at their dog training compound. He taught me about dog sleds and dog teams and the component parts of the team.

"Each team has one or two lead dogs. The leads react to the musher's commands and will follow a trail and set the team's pace," Pala said. "It's important to have a smart lead. Then come the swing dogs."

"Swing dogs?"

"Yes, two swing dogs. They follow the lead dogs. They also help set the pace, but their main purpose is to help the team turn and move around corners or swing one way or another."

"Makes sense."

"The last pair of dogs in the line are wheel dogs. These dogs tend to be the strongest. They also need a good disposition because the sled rides so close to their hind legs."

"So, that's five or six dogs. But pictures in your living room show additional dogs."

Pala nodded.

"Between the swing and wheel dogs are one or more pairs of team dogs. The team dogs provide horsepower. Heavier sled loads require more team dogs."

"You mean like the old *20 Mule Team* advertisements?"

Pala chuckled.

"I suppose, but that would be a heck of a lot of team dogs. A small team pulling a light load could get away without any team dogs."

During the evenings, Aunt Diane told me about her brother. My father. She mused about how much I looked like him at my age. Pan only knew my father for one weekend and through a few letters. She had little to tell me. I'm sure my aunt looked forward to the end of summer, so I would no longer pester her for more tales.

"You know, listening to your stories makes me want to follow in my father's footsteps."

"That's interesting," she said. "Your mother says you want to be a voodoo nurse like her." She smiled at me and tipped her head. "Can you do both?"

Working among the dogs came naturally to me, and I took to mushing from the moment Uncle John walked me into the training pens. Although racing or competition provided no interest, I did value the utilitarian capability of the dogs and the freedom they provided. More important to me, I began to value their companionship. Because of this, the Whitehorse's promised to give me several of their less capable, slower, and difficult-to-sell dogs from among their pack. At best, these dogs would have been adopted by local families. Failing adoption, their futures were uncertain.

"All of our dogs are Siberian Huskies, Alaskan Huskies, Alaskan Malamutes, or a mix of what I prefer to call Malaskies or Huskymutes," Pala said.

I laughed. "Why not Siberskies or Alaserians?"

Pala grinned. "It doesn't roll off the tongue."

After trying them several times, I agreed. Like a shaking dog's head, they both flopped.

Midway through the first full summer with my cousin, Uncle John walked me through the 'second hand' dog pen to select a team, and I found them interesting, amusing, and surprising. Only a few dogs kept to themselves, wrestling, playing tug-of-war with short lengths of rope, or sleeping. After seeing me around the pens for weeks, most wanted to examine the strange new person and came up to sniff and greet me.

I did not pick my lead dog.

She picked me.

She leaned up against my legs and stopped my initial progression through the pen. She kept moving in front of me and leaning into me until I reached down and rubbed her ears.

"That's Pixie," Pala said. "She isn't fast, but she's the smartest dog in this enclosure and she is giving you a Malaskie hug."

"Excuse me?"

"Dog hugs. The way she leans into your legs. It's her way of hugging you."

I lowered to one knee, looked into the sweet dog's bright blue/steel-gray eyes, and rubbed her neck with both hands.

"Well, Pixie. Do you want to come home with me?"

As if in answer, Pixie wagged her tail as she sat and gave a crisp yippy bark. Smiling at her answer, I stood and turned to look through the other 15 or so dogs in the enclosure. Pixie moved by my side as we ambled among the slower, less saleable dogs. I rubbed heads and ears, scratched necks, and looked into hopeful eyes. Pixie shimmied through the dogs, as well.

After a few minutes of wandering, Pixie and I returned to where Paul stood. Uncle John sat on a bench with him, watching, smiling, shaking his head, and chuckling. A group of eight dogs separated from the others and trailed Pixie, tongues lolling and tails wagging. Most of the other non-Pixie-picked dogs wandered off and laid down in their individual kennels or sat busy chewing on lengths of knotted rope or old bones.

"Looks like you have your team," my uncle said. "You have enough for four team dogs." He rubbed his chin. "Maybe we should have given Pixie a closer look." Still laughing, he shook his head again. "You might have one of the best lead dogs we've raised in a long time." He smiled. "Still, racers want fast. Pixie's strong and smart, but she has only one steady and reliable speed and has shown reluctant interest in anything in the past." He raised his forehead and let out a breath, rumbling through his lips. "Now we know what, or rather who, she's been waiting for."

During the daytime, Paul and I labored with my new team, learning their strengths and weaknesses and determining the best position for each dog or pair of dogs. I learned the commands, how to control the team, and how to care for them.

"We don't use the term 'mush' to start your team," Paul said. "You hear 'mush' used in cartoons and people in silly Hollywood movies who don't know better. We use the proper term, 'Marche,' to begin the pull."

Pausing to reflect, I remembered Pan telling me about the difference between ignorant and stupid people.

She was right, as always.

In our late afternoon hours, Paul helped me renovate an old sled. Although worn in places, the old basket sled had good bones and remained in decent shape. Made of light ash, it needed several new lashes to tighten its supports and a new brake, with spring and a snow hook. Located on the back end of the sled and accessible to the musher, the spring-loaded brake was necessary to slow down or stop the sled. Both the brake and snow hook had been damaged or lost.

I hope they work better than the brakes on Pan's truck.

"The musher steps down on the brake, driving it into the snow, when stopped to hold the sled in place. When released, the spring raises the brake, allowing the sled to slide again." He chuckled. "The rusted old metal spring … lost its spring."

"We use the hook like a ship's anchor to hold the sled in position when the musher steps off the back end." Paul chuckled, waving an arm. "This can be important when stopping on a hill. Without the hook, on an uphill stop, the sled would put a constant strain on the harnessed dogs. Downhill, the sled could slide into the legs of the wheel dogs."

I nodded. "Well, we better make sure they work."

With fresh sanding and a coat of linseed oil, the renewed sled looked sharp and ready to go. To finish the project, we cut and stitched new canvas, with grommets to lace it to the basket. We finished the sled with a basket cover to protect any occupant or cargo from getting wet from rain or splashing snow. A short piece of bent ash below the front edge of the basket gave an occupant a place to rest their feet and keep them from interfering with the wheel dogs.

To accommodate the new team, we cut and fashioned harnesses and fit one to each dog. We also measured out several gang lines to connect the team together and to the sled. By the end of summer, we had a complete set of lines and harnesses for the sled team, with extra materials for repair or replacement. We arranged those in a canvas bag attached to the basket.

"Nice work. You have a complete dogsled outfit, ready to go," Paul said.

"You helped. Without you, I could never have completed this."

On Labor Day, the Whitehorse's took me into town to catch a bus back to Montana. Pan would pick me up in Eureka. I gave my goodbyes and thanked them for taking care of me and for their generosity and promised to return with the snow to bring my team home. All I needed to do now was to convince Pan.

"Mom, I found a dog. Can I keep her?"

And her eight friends.

CHAPTER 35

PANACAEA

Two weeks after Denny signed his enlistment papers, we returned to Eureka. In town, we stopped at the bank to complete our normal pecuniary business. While there, I asked the banker for his recommendation of a good lawyer. We stopped to ask the same question of the realtor who helped us buy the farmhouse. Abe Williams came recommended from both places.

After lunch, we drove to the downtown office of Abe Williams, Attorney at Law, and walked in. Without an appointment, we sat on cushioned chairs in the lobby. A small table to the side had a large glass jar full of an amber liquid with melting ice cubes and slivers of lemons. The cylindrical jug had a small spigot just above the bottom curve. Denny peered through the glass.

"It's sun tea," the receptionist said. "Go ahead."

Denny continued his examination. "How does the sun make tea?"

She chuckled. "I put tea bags in the water. They infuse as the sun shines through the glass, warming the liquid. It gives the tea a natural and less bitter taste."

Denny went over and poured himself a dixie cup full of the cool beverage. After a few minutes, he refilled his cup. Having chosen a good day, it took only 10 minutes before the receptionist spoke up.

"Mr. Williams is off the phone and can see you now."

She ushered us into an adjoining office. Denny snuck another cup of sun tea on his way.

In the office, we saw a jovial man with bushy, graying hair and wire-rimmed spectacles. Getting up from behind a large desk, he waddled to greet us. His glasses sat low on his damp nose. He had a wide smile separating his goatee from a thick mustache. He wore a brown tweed suit with a white shirt, a blue bowtie, and matching blue suspenders. He had no noticeable waist where a belt might have been, and his belly jiggled as he shook our hands.

"I'm Abe Williams. How can I be of assistance?"

He motioned to two cushioned chairs sitting across from him.

"Please sit."

He maneuvered himself back into his chair, interlacing his fingers atop his belly. His thumbs were tapping together.

"You come highly recommended from more than one source."

He chuckled. "Full Disclosure. I'm the only attorney in town." He gave a wide smile. "But it's nice to be appreciated."

I looked at Mr. Williams, then Denny, and back to Mr. Williams. "Mr. Williams …" I started to say before he waved a hand.

"Oh, please. Call me Abe."

"Abe," I smiled, "we're interested in several things. Wills, power of attorney, trusts, and a retainer for ongoing legal assistance."

Abe smiled and scooted as close to his desk as his belly allowed. He grabbed a long yellow notepad, a pen, and leaned in.

"Okay then. Let us start with who you are."

"I'm Panacaea Clarke, and this handsome young man is my son, Denali Darkcloud."

Abe's head tilted, and his left eyebrow bumped up. I told him about meeting Denali's father, a Marine Sergeant, at the veteran's hospital in New Orleans and how we had a brief romantic weekend together.

"We never married. The good sergeant left for Korea, and several weeks later, I discovered we would be parents. Although we sent a few letters back and forth, as time passed, he had difficulty finding time and available materials to write back. After Denali joined the world, I sent a copy of his birth certificate to Sergeant Darkcloud."

Shaking my head, I raised both hands, my palms forward.

"I was never looking for support; I didn't need support. I felt obligated to let him know he had a son named after him." Dropping my hands back into my lap, I smiled. "As things turned out, Sergeant Darkcloud arranged for Denali to be his primary beneficiary and had his records updated to include his son." I reached out to Denny and put my hand on his knee. "We found out when a Marine officer came to our home in New Orleans, looking for Denali. Since his father listed me as the mother and because of Denali's age, the officer talked to me."

By the time of his death, Sergeant Darkcloud had been field promoted. They told me, "Staff Sergeant Darkcloud died during a late skirmish in the Korean War."

Abe nodded. "I'm sorry for your loss." He let out a sigh. "So, wills, power of attorney, and trusts … where would you like to start?"

Rolling my eyes, I shook my head again.

"I'm not sure. We're hoping you can guide us."

"I can. First, tell me why you think you need these things?"

"Well. Denali just enlisted in the Navy; he wants to be a medical corpsman. He leaves after Thanksgiving. In case something happens to me while he is gone, I want to make sure we can take care of the house until he comes back. Also, I created a trust for him in New Orleans when he received his father's death benefit from the government. I held up the trust paperwork. I would appreciate your recommendation on how to manage this while he's in the Navy."

I handed him the documents.

Abe looked up and closed his eyes for a moment.

"Excuse me, but at the risk of appearing to be insensitive, we should account for things, like the trust, in the event something happens to Denali, as well."

Bobbing my head, I turned to look at my son, closed my eyes, offered a quick internal prayer, and whispered.

"Yes, I suppose."

Turning back to Abe.

"In case of an emergency, we'll need someone to manage the property until Denali gets back." I looked up to Abe. "Isn't that why we need a power of attorney?"

"I paid cash for our house and farm and keep the deed in a safe deposit box with other valuables, including several gold coins and bars."

I gave him the information.

"We have an old truck, oh, and Denali has an aunt, Dyani Whitehorse, in Grasmere, British Columbia. She has agreed to be identified as executor of my will."

After our next visit, we returned to our home with all our legal documents signed and secured and with Abe Williams on retainer as our family attorney.

BACK AT THE WINTER CABIN

CHAPTER 36

KEITH

December 1971

My head hurts. My back hurts. My hair hurts. Everything hurts, but nothing as bad as my left leg and my right elbow. If there had to be a pain winner and I had to choose between one or the other, the leg wins. I would open my eyes, but they hurt, too. I tried wiggling my toes and could feel them rubbing on some material. They seem to work okay. The pain is tolerable.

Oh good. I can wriggle the fingers of my left hand and even make a fist. Okay, not a fist, but I can close my hand. I doubt I could hold a fork, however. I tried wriggling my other fingers, and as they rubbed together, each finger felt like it brushed up against a fat sausage. They hurt too much for me to bend them.

I tried to remember the dream. As usual, the images slip from memory, and the bits and pieces once connected in a string of semi-coherent thoughts are now disjointed and separated. Nothing makes sense other than the pain. Although I can understand the pain, I cannot recall why I am in such pain. What happened?

I feel something cold sniffing my ear and a warm lick. It must be a dog. Wait, my family does not have a dog. After trying for several moments to open them, my eyes remained pasted shut. I cannot reach them with my hands and pry them open as my sore arms are refusing to answer the call. I try rolling my eyes to lubricate my eyelids while working my forehead to help separate the tops from the bottoms.

My right eye began to open first, and a blur of movement crossed my field of view, or something you could approximate as vision; fuzzy brown, black, and white movement greeted me, followed by hot breath, something cold and wet, and more warm licks. Although the licks helped me open my eyes, they did little to help clear my vision. Blinking several times, my right then left eye came into focus and two dogs, or wolves, sat back at attention, tails wagging and raising dust. They panted and then shook their heads.

Not wolves, then.

I realized I woke up on the floor. Dust made me sneeze.

"Hello there."

I tried to say. I discovered my voice made noise, though the crackle left a lot to be desired in clarity. I am sure no one would understand me through the sputter, but by the apparent smile and tilted heads, the two attentive animals understood.

"I don't suppose either of you two could fetch me some water?"

Their heads tilted the other way. Sigh. Too much to hope for. I'll try to sit up and search for something to drink.

"Where am I?"

One of the dogs leaned forward on its belly. The other shook his head, ears flopping.

"Fine. I'll figure it out."

Turning my head, I could see an old wooden door with a latch and the oldest stove I'd ever seen.

"Great. I'm in an old, dilapidated cabin. Wonderful. No sink, no water, no bathroom."

"Wait, where are my pants?" I could feel my bare butt cheek with my left hand. One of the dogs let out a deep breath. "No, I suppose you wouldn't know."

Still, how did I get naked in a sleeping bag? Now I know why my arms refused to move. Someone cinched my body in this thing with my good arm smushed against something solid. They zipped the bag to my shoulder, leaving my head exposed. If I can get my good arm free, I can try to unzip this damn thing.

The two dogs jumped up, and one of them ran out of my field of view. I heard something flapping and felt a rush of frigid air. The second dog paced back and forth next to me, and with each turn, its tail brushed across my face and kicked up more dust.

"Could you stop that, please?" I sneezed, and the pooch turned and licked my face again. "Great. Thank you."

From outside, I heard a commotion and someone talking among several barking dogs. I heard a man's voice. Over the next few minutes, more dogs came in and sniffed me. Many of them licked me, too. The flapping and swishes of tails across my face continued, and the room became crowded until footsteps stomped and a door opened, letting in a huge blast of colder air.

The man shivered at the door and hung up a series of leather strap contraptions on hooks extending from the door. Beside them, he took off his coat, hanging it on the first hook near the door. He looked over at me and smiled.

"So, you've come around. How do you feel?"

"Thirsty." I tried to say. My voice sputtered and scratched. He nodded and turned to a sideboard near the stove and poured water from a small pot into a metal cup. He came back to me, lifted my head, and I tried to sip the water. The room-temperature water tasted great, and I tried to drink as much as I could, and, in my haste, most of it ran down my neck.

"Hang on there, Keith. Let me help you sit up, and you can drink without taking a bath."

He knows my name.

He came to my right side, unzipped the sleeping bag to my waist, and helped me sit up. With my left arm free, I held myself upright while he reached down and pulled on a second sleeping bag, used as a makeshift mattress for me, and swiveled my legs toward the door. Then he reached up behind me and slid a couple of pillows behind my back.

"That's better. Now you can drink without spilling, and in a little while, I'll fix some dinner." He turned toward a couple of the dogs and rubbed some necks and ears. "First, though, I need to take care of my team. Without them, we would never survive this remote place in this weather, and you would still be up a tree." He kneeled and alternated, giving hugs and rubs to two dogs, sitting alert and attentive. "This is Pixie and Copper. Pixie is my lead dog and the brightest star in the sky. Aren't you, girl?" he continued rubbing the sides of her neck. She gave a little yip in response and smacked her jaw open and closed with a pop. Her tail swished dust.

"And Copper here alerted both Pixie and me to a plane struggling in the air." He gave Copper hugs and praises. "Without Copper, we would have missed hearing the plane. He shook his head. "Well, we would have heard the crash, in any case, but without the initial alert from Copper, we would not have known which way to search." He smiled and rubbed Copper again. I heard him say something to the effect he was thanking God and Copper they had a reasonable direction to start the initial search.

"Can you tell me the names of the two amazing dogs who stayed with me?"

"Loki and Odin."

I smiled and had to laugh, shaking my head.

"They were quite, um, attentive. Weren't you worried about them leaving or running after some wild animal?"

He shook his head and squatted down to give several other dogs hugs and rubs. "When given the command to protect, they will stay at the location and protect the person or property from anything threatening until released from duty. Of course, they will take turns to go potty outside, but one or both will stay with you until their work is complete." He stood back up. "Besides, with all the dog poop and other dog markings in the vicinity, there are enough dog smells out there to discourage most creatures."

The man sat down on one of two three-legged stools next to a small matching three-legged table and looked at me. "You are damn lucky the plane wound up near the base of the slope. If it crashed higher up in the trees, my team could not have maneuvered us as close. We are limited to open spaces like meadows, trails, stream beds, or anything solid that's flat and covered in snow or ice."

He refilled my water cup, which I managed to hold without dropping.

"Any higher up in the trees, and we might not have found you." He took a deep breath and exhaled before continuing. "At best, and assuming we found the site, we would have had to hike up slopes and climb through trees. At worst, we couldn't have pulled you out." He shook his head and continued. "With the plane stuck under a canopy of trees and fresh snowfall, even if the weather clears, I doubt an aerial search could find the site."

"Dave …" I tried to say and took another sip of water. "… our pilot searched for a clear area to make an emergency landing. I heard him and my dad yelling about how they found one. It must have been near the bottom of that slope." I closed my eyes, realizing my horrible dreams had been a reality. "He needed to land because something hit the plane and shattered the windshield. He had trouble seeing."

"A goose."

"A what?"

"The plane hit a snow goose, at least two. I found the bulk of one goose in his lap and parts all over the inside of the cockpit and evidence of more splattered across the nose of the plane."

At this point, I realized I could see no one else in the cabin and made a haphazard attempt to get up before the pain brought me back down. I scratched out another question.

"Where's my dad? Is he okay?"

"I'm sorry. Everyone else died in the crash." He lowered his head, closed his eyes, and breathed.

A heavy weight hit my chest. When I remembered to breathe again, I felt tears dripping from my chin. Breathing did not come easy. The man handed me a handkerchief, and I used it for several minutes.

He touched my shoulder. "I can tell you he died at the moment of impact and without feeling any pain." He stood back and began moving to a big bucket over in a corner. "We can talk more in a minute. I need to feed my sled team."

He picked up the bucket and moved outside, the frosty air making me shiver. All the dogs either followed him through the door or went through a flap in the wall in the other room. Sitting up, I could see it now. A rectangular hole had been cut into the wall, and a sliced piece of canvas had been fashioned over the opening. This allowed the dogs to go in and out while keeping out most of the frigid winter air. Later, I realized they had a second square of canvas fastened to the outside of the opening for extra protection against the weather.

I took his temporary absence as an opportunity to continue blowing my nose and wiping tears from my eyes.

CHAPTER 37

DENNY

When I got back to the cabin, Loki met me outside and vocalized his happiness to see us. His demeanor told me the boy remained safe. Without hesitation, he moved over to Pixie, and he sniffed and snuggled her in an obvious report to the one in command. Yes, I am quite grateful he came to me first and Pixie second and I have no doubt Pixie gave him instructions to let me believe I was in charge.

"See the nice man first, then come and give me a complete report."

Loki gave Pixie a lot more information than he gave me. I know where I stand in this pack and am proud to stand there.

After being harnessed for several hours, I chose to release the team before checking on the boy. I reached down and rubbed Loki's ears. "How's our patient?" He yipped, and several other members of the team joined as they went into the cabin and came back out, adding to his report. Only Odin remained with the boy. He waited to be released from duty.

I gathered up all the harnesses and entered the cabin, hanging everything in their respective spots, and closed the door. I turned and saw the boy alert, watching me.

His voice scraped out an unrecognizable word. After a few moments, I had him propped against a low cabinet built under one end of the main cabin bed and handed him a cup of water.

"That's better."

I watched him drink, his hands shaking. Realizing he could manage by himself, I got up to feed my dogs.

CHAPTER 38

KEITH

As the man stepped out, the thought hit me. He needs to feed his team, a dogsled team, which explains all the dogs.

Could it be him?

No. I shook my head. I set the cup of water down to rub my eyes with my open hand as one of the other dogs came back in through the flap. He (or she) came over and finished my water, then hurried out through the flap again.

The man did not appear to be the kind of person who would go around killing women. Still, I have never known anyone with a dogsled team before and have no clue who or what kind of person controls them. This could be a coincidence. I remember watching Highway Patrol, Perry Mason, and Columbo; I often heard there is no such thing as a coincidence.

It might be him.

Using a dogsled team to escape could also explain why the Musher Man murders occur in the winter and why no one ever sees him. The murders always occur on a snowy night.

Damn. He could be the guy.

Before I could process any more information, the man came back in and closed the door.

"All fed." He smiled. "Now it's time to fix something for us. Good news: I rescued most of the deer meat from the plane. Venison will go great with these pork and beans."

He turned to the stove and sideboard and began preparing our meal. Taking the opportunity of his obvious good mood and distraction while making dinner, I began to gather some information.

"You called me Keith earlier; how did you know my name?"

He turned his head. "I managed to remove your shirt but had to cut the rest of your clothes off to check the damage to your leg and arm and search for any other injuries. I chucked the clothing scraps." He motioned to the door. "They are all in a trash bag outside. Don't worry. I emptied your pockets. Your wallet and other items are over there." He pointed to a small basket on a shelf near the stove. He said my identification gave him my name, and on his second trip to the plane, he found my initials on a duffle bag and brought it back. He gave me a smile. "I haven't checked yet. With luck, you have another pair of pants in your bag."

I nodded. "Okay, I understand about my pants, but why am I naked?"

"Oh, that." He bobbed his head back and forth; redness tracked up his cheek. "Um, you soiled your pants during the accident or sometime later when unconscious. I had to cut your pants off for disposal. Getting them over your injured leg would have been difficult," he rubbed his forehead with the back of his hand, "and messy." He went on to tell me he did not want to embarrass me but could not leave me in the soiled clothes.

As he sliced up some of the venison, he recounted to me about the accident site and how the plane had been skewered by a snag and hung midair, teetering against a large boulder. Due to the precarious perch of the plane, he could not retrieve the two bodies and left them for an official recovery team, though he did recover their wallets to hand over to authorities when he reported the accident. He hesitated as he relayed the story, leaving me with the feeling he left specific things out about what he found at the crash site.

"You know my name. What's yours? I'd rather not have to say, "hey you," every time I need to talk or ask a question."

I realized my words and tone sounded snitty and apologized. Although part of me worried I sat in the presence of a serial killer who killed my girlfriend, I also realized the man saved my life and deserved better.

I can do better for now.

"Denali Darkcloud. But everyone calls me Denny." He plopped the slices of venison on the stove top and stirred the beans.

As Denny continued to prepare the meal, he cut up the venison, mixed chunks of the cooked meat into the pot and let the flavors stew together for a while longer. He brought me a bowl of steamy goodness. Everyone struggles to find actual chunks of pork in most cans of pork and beans. I smiled, grateful this did look like venison and beans. The aroma accentuated my hunger, my last meal being a rushed breakfast before the attempted escape from the meadow. My tongue made love to the venison stew.

"Is there enough for seconds?"

I thanked Denny for the meal as he gathered the bowls and spoons.

"Is this your cabin?"

He chuckled. "No, this is an old cabin my cousin's family stumbled upon years ago." He gestured to the room. "It's available for any passing hunter or hiker. When they found the cabin, it showed little signs of occupancy or recent use, and my uncle found it useful whenever they came down to Montana for hunting or a rest stop when training dogsled teams, long distance."

He walked over to the canvas flap. "Over the years, they made a few improvements and modifications. This canvas dog door in the bunk room is the most convenient thing my uncle added to the cabin." He walked back and pointed to a broom. "I arrived yesterday and planned to sweep the floors today, but your chaotic arrival rearranged my priorities."

I recalled the cloud raised by Loki and Odin when they guarded me. "I can understand how it provides easy access for the dogs to go outside to conduct their business or drink water, but doesn't it also make it possible for unwanted animals to enter the cabin, too?"

"That's one of the reasons why I left Loki and Odin. Whenever they leave the cabin with no one here, my uncle has wooden slats to block access to the canvas door. It prevents destructive animals from entering." He explained he left it open for the two guards.

I am amazed by the training of these dogs. And now I know his family trains dog teams, so his cousin or uncle could be the Musher Man.

"Down to Montana? So, you're from Canada?"

"No. My cousin lives in Canada. I have a house down near Stryker."

I remember the news reports after they found Vicky's body. They identified the Musher Man's first victim as a woman near Stryker.

Shit. He is the guy.

Not wanting to appear to be interrogating a psychotic killer, I shifted to talking about my injuries and his treatment. He said he has had substantial training in first aid and other medical emergencies. His mother, an exceptional nurse, taught him many things as a child.

Did she teach you how to kill someone?

"My cousin will be arriving in a few days," he said. "We planned on spending a week hunting and sprucing up the cabin. Every time they visit, they bring a few items to make the cabin more functional and comfortable." He nodded and smiled. "Thus far, none of their work has gone to waste. If any other hunters or hikers have happened upon the cabin, nothing has gone missing."

"This is my first trip here. So far, my only contribution consists of fixing the spring gutter, giving us an easy source of water at the porch."

"Spring gutter?"

"It's an uncomplicated design, using several hand-carved gutters, allowing fresh water from a spring to flow to the cabin."

I nodded. "Nice. Not to be rude, but when can I get out of here?"

"Here's the deal. I need to go to Eureka for help and since you are movement impaired, I cannot leave you alone." He shook his head. "The distance is too far to take you on a bumpy sled ride with your leg in its current condition. Continued bouncing up and down, unsupported in the basket of my sled, could cause permanent damage." He pointed to the door. "I used a wing from your plane as a makeshift sled to get you here, but I don't think we can manage the distance to Eureka by dragging you the whole way."

He sighed and looked through the window. "So, we wait for my Cousin Paul."

In Eureka, Denny said he would ask authorities to send an aid vehicle or helicopter, and until they arrived, I would be fine in Paul's care. He told me he would deliver the two wallets to the authorities and let them know what happened when it happened and where the crash site could be found. He said he had no way of knowing when they might try to recover the bodies, whether after the storm or wait until sometime next spring.

I shivered, considering my situation on the upside. It occurred to me that the Quad's will never know I slipped off a log and filled my snow boots with icy water.

CHAPTER 39

DENNY

It has been three days since the crash, and Keith is doing better. Well, a little better. His leg remains swollen. I'm worried about that, but he says he can tolerate the pain until we try to move him.

Going to the toilet has been our biggest problem. I could fashion a crutch for him to use, but the cabin's exterior facilities, distantly reminiscent of an outhouse in only its rudimentary purpose, would be far too difficult for him to manage, even if his leg had little pain. And assuming he could walk with a crutch, his arm splint would limit his movement. For now, we are using an old bucket, and I carry the waste outside for disposal.

Glad it doesn't leak.

Keith has been acting strange the last couple of days, and I hope his mood comes from his embarrassment of having to poop and pee in a bucket. I am not so sure. No doubt, he still grieves for his dad and worries about what his mother must be going through. She could only know they both missed their planned return by several days and must be going crazy. Since the first morning after his arrival, other than eating, peeing, and pooping, every time I try to talk to him, Keith's eyes close as if he is falling asleep.

***

Some time ago, my Uncle John told me he had no idea who built the cabin or when. "I think loggers working in the area built the original cabin," he said. "This would explain the larger stove. It's versatile for cooking purposes and functions as a winter heating source. If we brought the appropriate ingredients, we could even bake bread in the oven."

With him in mind, I decided to roast some of the venison.

The cabin has a small bunk room off the main area, with two sets of three bunks opposite each other, three stacked from bottom to top. The bottom bunks sit inches off the floor, and the uppers about two and a half feet from the sloped roof.

"Here you go, boys and girls."

I chuckled as my dogs claimed the lower and middle bunks when we arrived. I knew Paul and Uncle John used the upper bunks for storing things or to keep them off the floor, away from the dogs.

The back wall of the main cabin has a bed, too. "With just the two of us, we had no need for the large original cabin table," Paul said. "We removed the legs and lowered the tabletop onto its opposing benches. The table legs remain underneath, and it could be reassembled if needed. We moved the two upper bunk mattresses there." He told me with a chuckle. "It's a bit cozy for the two of us but functional for a few nights." He went on to explain, "For one or two people, the small three-legged table is sufficient. We brought it in from the porch."

After his first night on the floor, and with a bit of ingenuity, I maneuvered Keith to the main bed so he could get better sleep. I'm using one of the skinny upper bunks in the bunk/dog room, cushioned by the sleeping bags. Pixie sleeps on the bunk below me and nudges my hand whenever my arm hangs over the side.

Keith has one good leg and one healthy elbow. When needed and with my help, we slide him off the bed as he supports himself on his good elbow. This allows him to use the bucket. It's not the best of circumstances, but better than trying to fashion a bedpan. The only usable items in the cabin for a bedpan are plates and bowls or the cooking skillet, and using any of them is out of the question.

***

Late afternoon on Tuesday, another alert from Copper got my attention. He and several others took advantage of a few moments of sunshine and laid down to sun themselves off the porch. Any dog not already outside shuttled through the bunk room flap. I stepped through the cabin door and met a cavalcade of yips, excited whimpers, prancing paws, and wagging tails. Minutes later, two lead dogs rounded a drooping copse trailed by rows of others in ganged harnesses until Paul's toboggan sled came into view, followed by a smiling, waving Paul.

I turned to Pixie, sitting next to me at attention, and pointed.

"Greet."

She took off, followed by the other eight, and they surrounded the harnessed team, and a sniff-sniff yip-yip reunion erupted. Laughing, Paul pulled up next to the cabin, dropped his snow hook and stepped down from the sled. The two of us began to disconnect his team leads so his dogs would be free to move around in the enthusiastic meet and greet. Their harnesses could remain on for a while longer. They all shuffled around, sniffing and reporting to each other on their journey, or the status of the cabin, or the strange-smelling boy inside, or whatever it is they passed back and forth to each other in their chaotic dance of salutation.

Several of his dogs ran over to the trough and drank their fill.

Paul gave me a hug and laughed. "Well, if any bears happen to be in the area, I am sure all this excitement has warned them off." He rubbed several necks and greeted Pixie. "Deer and other game animals, too."

"It's good to see you, Pala." He smiled when I used his real name. I asked him about arriving early, and he explained my Uncle John kept watch on weather reports and convinced him to take advantage of a short and reasonable weather window to come down early. "The forecast indicates the next few days are going to be nasty. Papa figured we could work on the cabin during the worst part of the storm." He laughed. "Or we can chat and play cribbage while we wait on our hunting until after the worst of the storm cleared." He sighed, rubbing bobbling heads with hanging tongues. "In addition, the extra time gives my team a chance to rest."

One of Paul's lead dogs, I forget his name, came over and nudged his hand, gave a snappy bark, and tried to pull on his sleeve. "What's up, Buster?" he said, rubbing the thick fur in his pooch's neck. I do not remember a dog named Buster; he must be a new lead dog.

Answering the question, I motioned to the door. "We have a guest. Our hunting trip may need to take a hiatus for a while. Come on inside." I led Paul through the cabin door, and a wet, pungent aroma assailed my senses. "Whew. We have plenty of moist heat sources now. I think we should leave the door open for a while."

I grabbed the water pot and took it back out to the spring gutter, filled it, and set it on the stove.

"I'll heat some water for coffee."

Paul began removing harnesses from his team and hung them on a series of pegs and nails opposite the tiny window from where my team's harnesses hung. The window overlooked the porch and gave a clear view of the pond, its white edges getting wider. The encroaching snow accumulation and freeze made the pond appear to shrink. Paul stepped back out to the porch and shook his coat as he pulled it from his shoulders, lowering it with one final shake before hanging it inside, as well.

Although taking glimpses of Keith as he cared for his team, he remained silent until he took a seat at the table. I brought in the other stool and gestured to and from my patient. "Paul, Keith. Keith, Paul."

Scanning the boy lying on the bed, arm in a sling and leg in a splint, Paul crinkled his forehead. "I would say it's nice to meet you, but I think your current situation is not so nice. Still, I am glad to meet you." Paul leaned over and shook the hand of Keith's good left arm.

In a scratchy, hushed voice, Keith nodded.

"Yes. Me too."

Paul looked from me to Keith and back. "So, who's gonna tell me what happened?"

Keith let out a sigh and looked at me. I took his acquiescence as a sign for me to talk, and although I did convey most of the tale, Keith added detail when he felt I missed an important piece of information. We recounted aspects about the storm, geese, plane crash, the death of the pilot and Keith's dad, and his rescue. Paul sat there in silence, listening. Pixie and his two lead dogs lay on the floor near us. Most of Paul's other dogs snoozed in the bunk room. Some of them whimpering, legs twitching, chasing rabbits in dreams. I heard occasional laps of water from the trough outside and knew Copper, Loki, and Odin attended porch duty, keeping us safe.

"Okay," Paul said with a ripple of breath, his eyes moving between Keith and me. "No hunting, but not a wasted trip. Had we not planned this trip when we did, there would be three victims of the crash." He settled on me with a squinch on his cheek. "What's plan B?"

I explained my thoughts of taking my team to Eureka for help once he arrived and admitted his report of two nasty days of weather could impede my idea. We might need a plan C.

I sighed. "A cautionary part of me wants to wait out the storm, but the swelling in Keith's leg has not gone down as much as I would like. I am afraid to wait any longer. I'll head out tomorrow morning, regardless of the weather." I looked at Keith. "Paul can care for you until help arrives."

Wheels turned, gears ground, dominos fell, and Paul shook his head. "Don't be an idiot." He turned and held his arm toward Keith. "If anyone should stay with Keith, it should be you. What do I know about first aid? Short of a bandage and aspirin, of course."

"Wait a second." I gestured to his two leads, sleeping near his feet.

"You just arrived, and you said the storm would give you the opportunity to rest your team."

I began to shiver. The room had aired out enough, so I got up and closed the cabin door.

"Yes. I did say that. However, you forget who these dogs are." He reached down and petted Pixie. "Nothing against Pixie, and I can say this out loud now because my two leads are sleeping. She must be the smartest lead dog we have ever trained. Smart, but slow." He sat back and opened his arms. "And no disrespect to your team, but they are more pets than race dogs," he saw a flush move up my cheeks and added, "when compared to my team, which we are training for sale to international dog race teams."

He rolled his head, and I heard his neck snap. He went on to remind me the Iditarod can last longer than a week. His team has been on the road for a couple of days. For them to go to Eureka, tomorrow will be nothing more than one more leg of a race and damn the weather. It would be good training. He could get to Eureka and be back to the cabin in the same amount of time it would take me to drive my team one way. Paul made sense.

"Okay. You go."

From the corner of my eye, Keith's movement drew my attention. He grimaced, his face contorted, and I heard a moan.

"What's wrong? Are you in pain?"

"No, no." His forehead distorted. "It's, it's nothing. I'm fine. Just gas."

We talked for a bit more, and I asked Paul if he wanted to unload his sled. “No, it can wait.” He turned to the stove. “I’ve been meaning to ask what smells so good.”

“I’m experimenting.”

Realizing the deer meat had escaped my storytelling, I went on to tell him about recovering the wrapped meat at the crash site and hoped he liked my attempt at a venison roast. Since we had a fresh supply, we might as well indulge.

“Well, it smells fantastic.”

CHAPTER 40

PAUL

At Papa's suggestion, I drove my team out of Canada between storms and followed our regular path through the valley and foothills to the winter cabin. Experimenting over several trips, we discovered an easy route across several snow-covered fields in the valley and then a series of forest and old logging roads, some maintained, some not. Once the foothills began to exert their presence in a more dramatic way, the logging roads showed increasing signs of disuse, most becoming overgrown. In the late afternoon, we passed, where Denny stopped for the night with his team. By nightfall, we stopped at an easy location for water and shelter, a couple of miles southeast of Glen Lake.

During the second day, the entire route consisted of one forest or logging road after another. Switchbacks became common as the roads tended to follow the least path of resistance as they worked their way into and around the mountains. Although we used a trail map of the area, my dad and I came up with a quick way of recognizing the best direction to turn when roads forked. In some instances, the trip could be completed either way, but we determined the best path and marked our preferred route. On a noticeable tree, snag, or infrequent post, we hung sections of yellow-colored rope with large, looped knots. One knot means take a left turn or the left fork. Two knots indicated to go right.

I found the route unusual for this trip because of the absence of trees to remove from the path and realized Denny must have taken care of any obstructions when he passed through. During most of my previous trips, I found an occasional tree or large branch on the road, needing to be removed to allow my team passage. Smaller branches could be dragged off the road, but I have my trusty bow saw strapped across the back of my toboggan for easy access, just in case. The jagged blade has a strip of garden hose sliced down its length, lashed over the sharp-edged teeth, to keep my knees from getting cut when we go over bumps.

Although there has been significant snowfall since Denny passed by, ruts left in the snow remained noticeable. He did well on his first trip out here. The subtle path gave my lead dogs a clear view of our heading. It provided good training, too; it simulates following another sled team in a race and the lead dog's sense of urgency to keep going cascades through the entire team. We crossed Williams Creek a second time now and have only a few more forks in our route. All of them, to the right. We will be at the cabin before dark. The trip took under two days. It's not bad for the new lead dogs.

Long before I could catch the smell, my leads sensed the smoke from the cabin, and their excitement became evident. Sensing their destination within easy reach, they picked up their pace. When the cabin came into view, I saw Denny and his team lined up on the porch.

Trained to maintain order in the greeting chaos, my team continued until we arrived at the cabin. Although not arduous, the day seemed long, and I wanted to release my hounds from their constraints. Inside, we had supper, and Denny told me about Keith.

"It's getting late. We should go out and unpack the toboggan and get our supplies out of the weather." I stood up to grab my coat. "Then we can clean up from supper."

Denny followed me out, and we started to unpack and carry items into the cabin. Since Keith slept in the main room and we could not use two of the upper bunks for storage, we packed some of the supplies under the main room bed and in the void between benches. I went out for the last load, and Denny stood there, staring at my sled in a trance.

"What's up?"

"Your sled."

"Yes." I tilted my head. "It's a fine sled. So what?"

"How long would it take you to get to Eureka if you leave tomorrow morning?"

"Well, we have a clear path to Glen Lake. We both passed through there this week. Assuming the storm doesn't bring down any trees before tomorrow, I can reach the lake by noon or so. After a short rest, I can head over to the highway and follow it north to Eureka. The highway shoulder is wide enough and will give me an easy and unobstructed route to town. Under normal conditions, I would never use the shoulder of a highway. But this is not a normal situation."

Picking up the last item in the toboggan, I turned to Denny.

"It'd be a long day, but most of the trip is downhill. I could be in Eureka sometime tomorrow evening. Why? What are you thinking?"

"We can transport Keith in your toboggan." Denny walked over to his sled, standing on edge at the far end of the porch. "Due to the basket seat of my sled, I couldn't transport him because I had no way to support his leg. It would stick straight into the backside of my wheel dogs." He walked back to me and reached down to squeeze the side of my sled. "Keith could sit propped up or can incline in your toboggan, and his entire leg would be supported either way."

"So, rather than wondering when or if a medical team could come out here, we could get him to the hospital by tomorrow night."

"Yes."

We both turned our heads when we heard Keith.

"Hey, guys. Sorry, but I gotta go."

Denny looked at me and chuckled. "You might want to stay out here for a bit." With a big sigh, Denny grabbed a musty bucket and went back into the cabin. After the sounds of the bucket scraping on the wooden floor, a few moans, and groans, Denny stepped out and waved me off with a hold. He went back in when Keith called again. After more groans, he came out with the bucket. "I got lots of practice doing this back home."

I'm not sure if he laughed or whimpered as he turned, holding the bucket away from his body, and tiptoed over to the dilapidated outhouse.

EUREKA

CHAPTER 41

KEITH

Winter Cabin, January 1972

My trials of pooping and peeing in a bucket would soon end. Denny told me they were going to use Paul's sled to transport me to Eureka.

"After tomorrow night," Denny chuckled, "an attractive nurse will help you poop using a real bedpan." Just my luck. "Oh, and she will give you a sponge bath too."

Wonderful. Well, I did need a bath, but not an embarrassing end to this disastrous hunting trip.

Paul joined the teasing. "Of course, instead of a pretty nurse, it could be an ugly male orderly."

Great. Just what I need.

Besides seeing my mom again, I had only one other thing to look forward to when we reached Eureka. As soon as possible after getting to the hospital, I would tell the police about Denny. They would hear my story.

After dinner, Paul and Denny explained how they planned to load me into the toboggan. Between the two of them, they assured me they could do it without difficulty. Denny suggested using the wing as a stretcher for the two of them to carry me out of the cabin. Once there, they could tip the wing to the side, allowing me to slip off and into position on the sled. By sliding me from the right side first, my good arm can help control my descent by holding onto the wing, and my good leg can slide in first and support my splinted left leg as it slips off the wing.

If only we could leave now. Still, tomorrow was just one more uncomfortable sleep away.

***

Morning came early with the scurry of dogs, yawny whimpers, barks and yips, heavy panting, and licks to my ear. What is it about dogs and licking ears? After everyone had breakfast and did their morning business, and I mean everyone, Denny carried in the wing and set it on the floor. Rather than using a second sleeping bag as a cushion on the wing this time, he spread it across the bed of the sled.

We managed to slip a clean pair of underwear over my splints to minimize my impending emergency room embarrassment, followed by my pants. They sliced one pant leg to get it over my splint. In the hospital, he reminded me, they would cut everything off anyway and put me in a gown, leaving nothing to the imagination.

I could not wait.

Oh yes I could.

Taking a great deal of care, the two helped me down onto the wing. I must admit, the serial killer had a kind way about him. They squatted down and picked up the wing ends, and Paul backed out the door. They lined me up to the left side of the sled and began a careful tip to my right. I anticipated a bunch of pain in my leg, but the slip into the sled cavity went easier than expected.

"Do you want to sit up or recline?" Denny asked.

"It's a long journey, and I'd go crazy laying on my back for the whole trip. At least sitting up, I could see things as we approached and brace myself when needed."

Denny picked up my duffle bag and propped it against the end of the toboggan for me to lean against.

"I've slipped all the wallets and other things from your pockets into the bag."

As Paul hooked up his harnessed dogs, I heard the two cousins talking.

"I'll clean up our breakfast mess, secure the cabin, and head out after an hour or two," Denny said. "I know my journey to Eureka will be an overnighter."

Paul shook his head.

"Wait for the storm to pass. With the expected heavy snowfall, it could take you two days to get to Eureka or more. You and your team are not prepared for the onerous conditions."

Denny crossed his arms and opened his mouth. Paul held out his hand before Denny uttered another word.

"Look, you have all the supplies we brought down for a week of hunting with two teams. You could stay for a couple weeks if you had to." He took a deep breath. "I don't want to find you frozen to Pixie under some damn tree." Paul put his hands on his hips and gave Denny a parental look. "Yes. I know you would release your team, and the other dogs could survive, but Pixie would never leave you." Denny nodded in agreement, shoulders slumped.

"Okay. I'll wait for the weather to clear."

Relieved the musher man would be staying behind and be separated from me for at least a couple of days, I relaxed for the first time since waking up at the cabin.

He cannot escape. Justice is coming.

Oh, fudge! My Navy enlistment starts next month.

CHAPTER 42

DENNY

Watching Paul leave, I let out a deep breath. Soon, Keith will get the care he needs and be on the path to recovery. He sure had shown me two different sides of his personality over the last few days. In one moment, he shows appreciation for the aid given to him, be it meals, medical, or poop patrol. Then, moments later, he acted as if I was a leper, turned his head and feigned sleep. I know the loss of his dad must bother him, but goodness, what did I do to make him dislike me so much? In any case, he needs to get to the hospital. Tonight, he will be safe.

I might as well sort through the items Paul brought down from Grasmere and see what I can do while stuck here.

Back in the cabin, I squatted next to the bed in the main room and pulled out the bundles we shoved in there last night. The bulky ones contained a hefty mix of canned goods, additional nested pots and pans in assorted sizes, and sealed tubs of dog food.

The innermost pot had a rope with hooks coiled inside it. Once unwound, it took me several minutes to ascertain its purpose.

"Ahh, I know what this is for."

I fastened the looped end over a large nail pounded through an overhead roof joist near the stove. The hooks cascaded down from the ceiling, and I hung the few pots, pans, cups, and ladles we had from the spaced-out hooks, with the larger items lower on the rope.

Hanging bulky pots and pans on the rope provided more space on the shelves against the back wall for all the canned and dried goods. Plates leaned against the wall.

"Nice."

"Woof?"

Pixie rolled her head and sat next to me, her ears forward.

She heard me talking to myself again and appeared worried she had missed a command.

"Oh, Pixie. It's nothing. I'm just pleased with myself for arranging the shelves."

I gave her rubs on her neck and ears. She snapped her jaws shut and turned. A few seconds later, I watched her tail going through the bunk room flap. She has more important business to deal with, getting reports from the guard dogs, no doubt.

The remaining supplies consisted of a few blankets, nails and screws for repairs, a few extra tools for maintenance, and more dog food. I shifted all the food to the upper bunks. I can sleep in the main room now.

Returning to the main cabin, I looked at the bed and imagined Keith sitting there, slouched, wrapped in blankets, brooding. "I better take these blankets outside, shake them, and let them air out for a bit." I hung them on a nail under the porch overhang to keep them from getting wet.

Back inside, I lifted one end of each mattress and used a foxtail and dustpan to remove accumulated dirt and debris. Shifting to the other side, I flipped the mattresses end over end. A sheet of paper flipped out onto the floor. It came from the corner of the bed where I placed Keith's duffle bag when I brought it back from the plane. It must have fallen out when he searched for his clean underwear. I picked it up.

"What the…?"

CHAPTER 43

PAUL

Although I did remove one snow-laden branch from the road before we could pass, we had no problems on the first leg of our journey. The trip still took longer than I hoped to reach the junction beyond Lick Lake, where I would take my alternate route. During any other trip, I would turn north, following our normal path back to Canada. This time, I needed to head west and work my way over to the state highway.

After a brief stop for rest, a bit of food, and taking care of biological needs, I hooked my team back in their places and put one foot on the back of the sled.

"Oops. Almost forgot."

Keith looked up. "Forgot what?"

"We're heading over to the highway. It will be dark before we reach Eureka. I have a reflective sign to hang on my back when traveling on highways." He stepped around to the front of the sled. "Sorry, but it's under your feet, somewhere. I will try to keep from hurting you." Stretching my fingers under his legs and feeling around, I found the sign and pulled it free. As I hung it over my shoulders and tied the strap around my waist, I turned to Keith. "As fast as my team is, we are no match for automobiles or trucks. I want them to see us and steer clear."

Back on the sled, I raised the snow hook and stepped off the brake. "Marche."

CHAPTER 44

KEITH

Paul told the truth.

What little daylight could filter through the snowy skies started to fade before we reached the highway. With the heavy snowfall, I could not follow the sun and had no clear shadows to provide clues to the time of day. Then I realized the heightened level of my hunger and thirst allowed me to assume my normal dinner time had passed.

Normal dinner time.

The idea of normal changed when my dad died. How can anything ever be normal again? Even with Bruce and Peter, my dad had always been my best friend. His death provides one more reason to report Denny to the police. If he had not killed Vicky, I doubt my parents would have arranged the hunting trip, and my dad would still be alive.

Focus, Keith. Focus. Calm down. Just get to Eureka.

Every so often, a car or truck passed us on the highway. Sloshy snow at best and dirty, gritty snow at worst splattered over everything and everybody. Some of the drivers issued a quick honk, in a friendly greeting to the uncommon conveyance or as an apology for the obtrusive spray.

Every honk caused me to jump. The dogs never wavered and never gave any indication of being distracted by passing vehicles or spraying debris and stayed resolute in their task. Impressive. If nothing else, Paul's family did an excellent job in training these sled dogs. For the first time in my life, I regret never having a dog. I can see the allure.

They are amazing.

Even the murdering Musher Man had dogs who cherished him. And their behavior gave no evidence they belonged to a serial killer. Then again, how does a killer's dog act? To be honest, I guess they would act like vicious junkyard dogs. Pixie, Copper, and the others are well-trained working dogs and show no vicious signs.

Stop it, Keith. Just stop it. Focus.

Denny did it, and if he did not kill Vicky and the others, the police would figure it out. He will be their problem, not mine. If I can help solve the case, it will be all the better. The world will thank me.

My stomach continued to demonstrate its level of discomfort, and the increased growling provided further evidence of the late hour. The evening snowfall began slowing to a whimper, allowing occasional glimpses of distant lights to peek through until glowing murmurs of a town started to emerge and broaden.

Eureka.

I felt Paul tap on my shoulder.

"We're getting close to town. I've been here before, many times, so I'll head straight to the emergency room."

Paul stayed on the highway and took me through the center of town. Experiencing minimal traffic, he saw no reason to take a side road and avoid the highway.

Our arrival drew no attention from inside the medical facility. The dog team had no flashing lights or sirens, and no one expected us. Paul dropped the hook he used several times when we stopped along the way, although the cleared driveway under the clinic awning offered it a little perch. With the level surface, I am sure he did not need to use it, but God loved him. He wasted no time and scurried through the door.

Minutes later, a yawning orderly pushing a gurney followed a doctor still pulling on a white coat out the door. Paul hurried over to his team to keep them calm and to check on their condition after the long day's journey. The doctor assessed my condition, what little he could observe through the sleeping bags, and asked me some questions. Being tired, half asleep, and cold as hell, I have no clue what he asked or what I said in answer. I seem to remember Paul telling him I had a broken arm, a screwed-up leg, and something about a plane crash.

Motioning for the orderly to lower the gurney, they moved it next to me, and the next thing I knew, warmth enveloped my face, and bright lights accosted my eyes. The sleeping bags disappeared, followed by my clothing, and they draped a blue gown over me, slipping my one good arm through.

Just as Denny predicted.

They moved me down a corridor, removed all the splint materials on my leg, and took X-rays of both my leg and my arm. The orderly moved me into a small room and left me sitting there alone.

Hope he isn't the one to give me a sponge bath.

Although the room temperature remained low, compared to the last several hours, I felt comfortable and dozed off. When the doctor gave me a gentle shake, it took me a moment to realize I woke up in a safe place, under medical care. His brow peaked.

"Whoever treated you before you arrived saved your leg. However, you have an infection and need more treatment and surgery. This is beyond our small facilities' capability, and I'm arranging to transport you to the hospital in Kalispell."

He turned to leave.

I tried to shout and managed to crack out a scratchy whisper. "Police."

Stopping, he turned back to me. "I'm sorry, what?"

"Call the police." I struggled, and the doctor handed me a cup of water with a straw. After taking a sip, he set the cup aside and leaned in closer. "I need to talk to them. Before you send me to Kalispell."

"The man who brought you in has already talked to the police. They know about the plane crash." The doctor turned his head and looked out the window. "I heard them talking and understood the sheriff knew the location of the old cabin. Your friend says the crash site is close by. When the storm clears, they plan to launch an aerial search for the crash site."

"He is not my friend. I just met him." I began coughing, and the short fit caused me to jerk my body. My leg throbbed. The doctor observed my groaning. "I need to talk to the police about something else. It's important."

"Okay." The doctor stood to leave. "But first, I'll give you something for the pain."

CHAPTER 45

SHERIFF HASTINGS

"So, you're telling me Denali Darkcloud, also called Denny, is the killer known as the Musher Man, and he murdered your girlfriend last winter."

"Yes," the boy said. After trying to clear his throat, he scratched out a struggling whisper. "He lives, or lived, in Stryker, where he killed his first victim."

"And this Denny character drives a dogsled, like the young man who brought you in last night."

"Yes." He drew the word out in a low hiss.

"And this guy is still out at the old cabin with his team of dogs?"

Keith nodded. "His team is younger than Paul's team. Or less experienced." The boy blinked and shook his head. "I'm not sure. I heard them say Denny could not keep up with Paul, so he stayed behind. They wanted to transport me for treatment, and Paul could get here in one day, plus his sled could support my leg. Denny would follow after the storm cleared."

"I see. Well, thank you for the information."

The boy waved his one good arm. "Be sure to send someone out to arrest him. He has avoided capture for years."

I tipped my head and squinted at the boy. "I understand and will take care of everything. Thank you. Now, try to rest. I understand your mother will be here soon."

After the interview, I went back to the station. As I pulled in, I confirmed the other dog team remained safely sequestered in one of our open garages. We removed the vehicle to give them an open space to relax and rest out of the direct weather. The dogs wandered about, stretching and drinking water or sleeping prone by themselves, legs twitching or in clumps together. The young man, Paul Whitehorse, stayed with them and relaxed, reading a book in his toboggan sled.

In the office, I asked my receptionist, accountant, dispatcher, bottle washer, and all-around office manager, Martha, to call my son to the station and connect me with Sheriff Jacobson in Whitefish.

Her voice echoed through my office door.

"Sheriff Jacobson on line one."

Picking up the receiver, I spoke to my old friend.

"Chris. I have some things going on you need to know."

I went on to explain how a boy, Keith Brown, from his town, had survived a plane crash. Paul Whitehorse gave me the two wallets of the men who had been killed in the crash, and I gave Chris their names and our plan to locate and recover them when the storm allowed.

"There's something else." I took a long breath and exhaled. "The survivor claims his rescuer is your notorious serial killer the papers refer to as the Musher Man." I could hear him stammering through the phone. "I know. The stories might be true." After telling him about the man named Denny, who saved Keith from the crash, he gave an audible gasp. "Now, the plane crash is in my jurisdiction, but I know the winter killer belongs to your office. As soon as I have him in custody, I'll turn him over to you."

Before hanging up from the call, I asked one more question.

"Are you still in contact with the FBI agent from the field office in Salt Lake? It's up to you, but you might want to give him a heads-up."

Moving to the breakroom coffee pot, I poured myself a cup of overheated black sludge. The short amount of dark amber fluid in the clear vertical tube indicated this as the last cup from this morning. Tasting the burned bitterness provided instant clarity, and I shivered.

"Is this coffee or motor oil?"

Martha chuckled. "Don't worry, boss. I'll make a fresh pot."

Nodding, I went back into my office. A short while later, Martha opened the door and brought my coffee cup over to my desk.

"Your son has arrived."

"Thanks, Martha. Send him in."

"You must be heavy into thought, Pops. I'm right here." Michael said.

I realized I missed hearing my son's identifying scrape and thump as he walked the hall to my office, following Martha. His artificial leg and cane made a regular clip, clap-scrape as he walked.

"Sorry, son."

I sipped some coffee, burning the roof of my mouth and tongue. Wincing, I motioned for him to come in and sit.

"You're lucky it's my day off."

Sitting forward at my desk, I leaned on my elbows, forearms crossed, and focused on my son. "Tell me again, everything you can remember about the medic who saved your life in Vietnam." For the next twenty minutes, Michael relayed his story of Denali Darkcloud or Doc Denny and what he had learned through letters since returning to the States. I knew most of what he told me, but I found the latest information significant. "So, he remained in Vietnam and didn't return to the States until 1971?"

"Yes. June. After his discharge, he came through Eureka back in September and continued up to Canada to stay with his cousin's family until this winter. He needed snow to bring his dogsled team back down. He plans to return to his home near Stryker." My son smiled. "He has a surprise waiting for him."

"Yes, yes. Quite a surprise." Reaching over to my phone, I picked up the receiver and rang Martha. "Martha, could you bring me the Whitefish winter serial killer file?"

"What are you thinking, Dad?"

"Just hang on. Trust me."

After Martha handed me the file, I opened it and scanned the names and dates of the unsolved murdered women attributed to the Whitefish winter murderer or Musher Man. I printed their specific information on a notepad:

- Panacaea Clarke, November 1967
- Amber Batchelder, December 1969
- Vicky Tisdale, December 1970
- Sandy Morris, December 1971

Based on the general reports, they attribute all four killings to the same person. I turned the note to Michael. "From what you tell me, unless Denny Darkcloud somehow found a magical way to get to and from Vietnam and Montana without anyone detecting his absence, he could not be the killer. This could be why they listed him as a material witness in the first murder and not a subject or formal person of interest in the crime." Closing the file, I looked at my son. "They wanted to talk to him, not arrest him."

Standing up, I walked my son out of the office. As he slipped into the driver's seat of his car, I leaned in before closing the door.

"Denny is out at that old logging cabin east of town. He has his dogs with him. If he doesn't come to town in the next few days, we should be able to go out and get him. We just need this storm to break." I reached in to squeeze Michael's shoulder. "Don't worry. I have no intention of arresting him either, but I do intend to ask him some questions."

Before going back into the office, I walked over to the makeshift dog kennel and found Paul Whitehorse feeding his dogs. The dogs made noises as I approached, but none of them seemed concerned about my presence or acted threatening. Two of them wandered over to sniff me and get momentary rubs before going back to eat.

Paul looked up and smiled. "Thank you for the use of the garage, sheriff. I'll try to get out of your hair soon." He walked out and held out his hand, catching several snowflakes. "I would go back to the cabin, but I know Denny will head out this way when the storm breaks. He says he has some things he wants to talk to you about."

"I'm sure he does." I tipped my head. "You live in Grasmere, right?"

"Yep."

"Less than an hour away."

"Not by dogsled, but yep."

Looking at his sled, I blinked. "Yes. Of course." I turned back to him. "Have you used the cabin before?"

He nodded. "My dad and I come down most winters when training our dogs. We visit so often; we're doing some repairs to the cabin."

"I see." I began turning and stopped. "When you get your team fed, could you leash them up and come into the office for a moment? I have a few questions about the cabin and the plane crash for you."

"Sure. There's little more I can tell you. Denny did all the work, but give me a few, and I'll be right in."

"No hurry." When I got back to the office, I asked Martha to call in my deputy.

"He's outgassing up his cruiser and should be back any minute."

"Perfect."

I poured another cup of coffee and waited. Deputy Langston walked in as I burned my tongue again and lurched, spilling drips of coffee on my desk calendar, placing a big brown blob on January 15. My written notes for the day smeared as I wiped up the mess.

"Sheriff, Mr. Whitehorse is here," Martha said, her voice calling from down the hallway.

I told Langston to stand by and asked Martha to send him into my office. When Paul stepped in, he glanced over at Deputy Langston, and a momentary fold appeared on his forehead. He turned to me and asked what I wanted to know.

"Mr. Whitehorse, I need to know if your family has a truck to come down and pick up your dogs and sled." The crinkle returned, and his jaw dropped open and closed. "And if so, I suggest you make them your first call. You are going to be with us for a while. As he jumped up, I gestured to my deputy, who blocked the door. I asked my deputy to read Paul Whitehorse his rights. "Paul, you're under arrest for the murder of four women." I read their names.

After his phone call, my deputy put Mr. Whitehorse in the holding cell, and I asked Martha to connect me with Sheriff Jacobson. Although out of the office, she told me Deputy Daniels answered the phone and asked me if I wanted to talk to him. "Line one."

"Good afternoon, deputy." He confirmed his awareness of my earlier conversation with Sheriff Jacobson and asked me if we got our man. "Yes. But I believe he's your man, not mine." I gave him a little chuckle. "I doubt you all plan to interrogate his dogs. They will be returned home later today." He laughed back. "When can you come get him?"

Deputy Daniels told me he would be on his way to pick up the suspect as soon as possible.

CHAPTER 46

BILLY

Stepping out of the shower, I had my pants on, and my uniform shirt laid out when my father-in-law, Steve Daniels, called. "I know your shift doesn't start for a while, but could you come in early? I need to make a run to Eureka to pick up a suspect and hope you can come into the office." I heard him sigh. "Your dad took a sudden drive to Kalispell, and you know he doesn't like us to leave town without an officer's presence in the office."

"Sure." I flexed my arms, admiring my profile in the mirror. "Who are you picking up?"

"You'll never guess." His tone ended with a gleeful chortle. "You might not be as crazy as people say. Your Musher Man story is panning out. They have the suspect up in Eureka, dogs included. Sheriff Hastings just called."

Knowing my stepdad loved nothing more than sitting behind his desk and eating a donut or three, I offered to go pick up the suspect for him. Although my dad asked him to head up there if the Eureka police called, without hesitation, he agreed and said he warmed up his cruiser. He planned to drive up there as soon as I arrived.

I finished buttoning my shirt and headed out to my car. Jumping in my trusty black beauty, I headed into town. Parking my baby at the station, I walked in. Although Deputy Daniels warmed up his cruiser, I told him I preferred to take mine, put on my weapons belt, and snatched my keys from the hook.

As I turned to leave, he offered me his thermos, filled with fresh coffee for the cold trip. He likes to sip hot coffee when driving in winter weather. Thanking him, I headed out and started up my cruiser. With the thermos rolling back and forth on the seldom-used passenger seat of the police car, I headed north to Eureka and pondered about how to take care of business.

When I arrived at the Eureka station, Sheriff Hastings mentioned he expected Deputy Daniels to be picking up the suspect. I chuckled and told him the deputy was still working on his morning donuts. The sheriff's forehead creased, then nodded. He asked his deputy to bring out the suspect.

I had not seen the retard in four years and never did get a clear look at him. The first time, my head had been rung like a bell, and I felt woozy from both the hit on my head and from the crappy powdered substance Pansy made. He stood across the room from where I sat, nursing my head and arm, his blurry silhouette eclipsed by the outside light. I suppose my distorted vision could have caused the fuzzy halo.

I remember long black hair, tanned skin, and slumped shoulders. I only caught a momentary glimpse of him the second time as the bright kitchen light blinded me, and then a distant look outside in the shadows across the yard. Again, I remember darker skin and long hair.

The man Deputy Langston escorted out of the holding cell fits the bill. His dogs out in the garage confirmed everything I needed to know.

Looking over, I noticed a blank look on his face. Just as I remember. The retard.

"Other than when he made his phone call, the suspect hasn't said anything since we arrested him," Deputy Langston said.

I reached out to put my handcuffs on the young man. "Doesn't surprise me." Cinching the cuffs tight, I turned to Langston. "It's a long drive. I'll take these off when he's in the car."

Langston accompanied me to the station door and watched me walk the suspect out to the cruiser. I walked around to the driver's side and paused for a moment, pretending to remove the cuffs, and followed proper procedure by covering the suspect's head with my hand as he settled into the back seat.

"See you around."

I gave the deputy half a wave.

As Eureka disappeared from my rear-view mirror, I glanced at the retard's reflection. His face still showed no signs of interest, recognition, or concern. I turned my head.

"It's nice to see you again."

He looked out the side window, harrumphed and tipped his head until his neck popped. After a few moments, he adjusted his position due to leaning back against his handcuffed wrists.

About fifteen minutes out of Eureka, close to Stryker, Montana, where my troubles all started, the highway followed a section of Summit

Creek. Intermittent turnouts became available for people to park their cars and hike down to the creek for fishing. I glanced up at the retard and noticed him shifting again. Perfect. I pulled over at a small turnout, big enough for two vehicles and stopped centered in the graveled space. My strategic location and the fact that it is a police car would discourage anyone from trying to pull into the same turnout. I turned to face the Musher Man.

"You have helped me out a lot over the last few years, Denny, and I want you to know I appreciate the assistance."

He gave me a slight glance and a momentary raised eyebrow, then a stone face returned. He "Harrumphed" as more of a groan than an utterance.

"Sorry, I forgot to remove those handcuffs before we left. I can do so now, and you can be more comfortable if you promise to be a good boy." He looked at me and let out a deep breath. "Good enough." Not carrying if his excessive exhale meant he understood, I got out and walked around to the creek side of the car and opened his door. "Get out." He sat there, staring forward. "Get out, and I'll remove those cuffs. Then we can get back on the road."

He exhaled again, shifted his legs and scooted out. I pushed him behind the car, facing toward the creek. Holding on to the cuffs with one hand, I pressed against his back with the other until he bent over.

"I'm going to remove the cuffs now. Behave." I removed the clasp on my holster and, with the key, unlocked his cuffs and backed up one step. "Now turn around."

As he turned around, I unholstered my sidearm, stepped up close, put the gun in his stomach and fired. His eyes went wide, and his body wobbled. Before he could fall, I pulled him into a half-bear hug and fired again.

Wincing, his forehead wrinkled into a tight knot.

"Why?"

I smiled, kept a tight hold of him, and followed him down to our knees as his legs buckled. When we hit the ground, I leaned back and pulled him over on top of me. I wriggled my body, getting my backside dirty and my front bloody.

"Because I can."

Satisfied, I pushed him off, and he rolled over the turnout embankment into a bush. I got up, climbed into my cruiser, and poured myself a cup of Steve's coffee.

After thinking for a moment, I spilled a splash of coffee on my lap and on the floor of the driver's side and poured the rest of the cup alongside my open door. Grabbing the thermos, I walked several yards down the embankment, avoiding snow by stepping on rocks or fallen branches, to the creek and poured about half of its contents into the passing stream. I returned to the cruiser and got in, sat there for a moment, and picked up the microphone to my car radio.

"Officer needs assistance, Highway 93, north of Stryker. Send M.E."

I heard a scratch on the speaker, followed by Deputy Daniels acknowledging my call and saying help would be on the way. Some thirty or so minutes later, Sheriff Hastings pulled up behind my car, and several minutes later, back from Kalispell, Sheriff Jacobson and Daniels pulled up in separate vehicles. Much later, the contract medical examiner arrived.

"Steve, we've got the creek-side lane of the highway blocked by official vehicles with lights flashing. Put out some flares and manage passing civilian vehicles," my dad said.

After each sheriff took photos of the scene, they walked over to me and took more pictures of me. My dad frowned.

"What happened."

I explained how the drive had been pleasant, and I had poured a cup of coffee to sip on. The suspect said he had to pee, and I told him to hold it. We would be at the station in Whitefish soon enough.

He startled me by getting up on his knees and said he would pee in my car if I refused to stop. When he unzipped his fly, I hit the brakes, spilled my coffee, and pulled over at the first available turnout. I gestured at the coffee stains on my pants and car floor and told them I dumped the rest of the cup on the ground when I opened my car door.

"When I let the retard out, he walked over to the slope there," I pointed to the area short of where he laid by the bush, "and made like he intended to pee," I told them how I heard his zipper again, assuming he would take care of business. "That's when he turned around and rushed me. He had me on the ground before I could react."

I turned and pointed to my back with my thumb and told them I somehow managed to pull my service weapon and shoot him twice. I brushed at my blood-soaked shirt. Looking between my dad and Sheriff Hastings, I wiped my forehead and continued my story.

"I pushed him off me and took several breaths, grateful to be alive. I think I lay there, shaking for a couple of minutes. When I got up, I came over and called it in. You know the rest."

The medical examiner confirmed the suspect received two gunshots to the abdomen and said he would perform the postmortem examination when he got back to the clinic. I helped him load the body. He got into his vehicle, made a quick turn, and headed south.

CHAPTER 47

SHERIFF JACOBSON

Assessing the scene and adding to my notes, my mind began to wander back to the Stryker woman's grisly death. How convenient; the presumed Musher Man gets caught and killed before anyone familiar with the case had the chance to question him. My son had a part in the first winter murder, and now he silenced the original, unlikely person of interest. I never believed the boy killed the Stryker woman.

***

I met her once, long before her murder. Rumors and innuendo circulated through town, and Sheriff Boyer tasked me to interview the Stryker medicine woman. No one knew where she came from, but rumors indicated she provided more than medicinal help. Teenage boys had been bragging about late evening sexual encounters, and those claims of indecency reached the ears of town officials and then the police.

Sometime in the summer of 1966, I drove out to the farmhouse to interview her and see if I could uncover any evidence the stories had a basis in truth. The woman offered me a cup of tea and, after a cursory conversation, allowed me to examine her herbal lab.

"What are these dry materials."

"Poultices," Ms. Clarke said and showed me several jars of ointments, most opaque with tints of white, green, or brown, and some clear. "These are tinctures," she explained the kinds of treatments she could create and pointed out her nurse certificate, framed and hanging on the wall of her lab above a worktable. A small, folded cot leaned in one corner. "For the occasional overnighter."

She showed me two bedrooms upstairs, one for guests.

"If a woman has a baby, she can stay here until she's ready to leave. The bed is more comfortable than the cot below."

"I've been blessed with considerable family funds and no longer need to work as a nurse in an established clinic or hospital."

She intended to provide medical services to Native American clientele in the area and any other area women who had difficulty finding or could not afford medical help elsewhere.

"If any money changes hands," she held up her hand, "I accept only enough to reimburse the cost of the materials used."

The woman did not look like any local Kootenai I'd met, and guessed she had little, if any, Native American blood.

"What's your connection to the area?"

She explained her only association came from the young Kootenai man who lived with her on the property. I nodded and told her I had heard of the young fellow and asked to meet him. She opened her mouth and closed it again. Although I picked up on clear hesitation, she smiled and nodded.

"Sure, but he won't be back until early fall," she explained how he spends the summers with his cousin's family in Canada. I would have to come back in late August or September. "Of course, you could always drive up there."

Finding the woman charming, attractive, and innocent of all rumored indiscretions, I thanked her for the tea and the tour and left for the station. I drafted a full report for Sheriff Boyer. Other things took priority over the next summer, and I never made my way back to meet the boy.

***

The highway scene brought back more memories of the medicine woman's murder. Images of the farmhouse scene flashed through my mind, the bloody hands and footprints surrounding a gruesome body covered by a shawl, a plucked goose in the sink, blood on a drawer handle, and a closed kitchen door. The last image did not flash by as my mind settled on the burned remnants of sneakers blown clear from the back of an old truck. Something does not add up, and my math is leading me down an unwelcome path.

A thought occurred to me, and I opened the passenger door of my son's cruiser and picked up the thermos. Taking a deep breath, I turned the green Stanley Thermos around in my hands until the worn initials "SD" appeared along its side. The thermos bottle felt light, and I twisted the top open and peeked in. Almost empty. I ran my finger around the wet inner neck of the thermos, raised it to my mouth, and licked it. Sweet coffee. Screwing the lid back on, I placed it back in the car and shut the door as my son headed back after helping the doctor load the body.

Shaking my head, I addressed my son.

"Get in your cruiser and go back to the station. I want to see your incident report on my desk when I get back. Deputy Daniels will follow in a few minutes." He arched his eyebrows and gestured to the bloody stains on his shirt. "You can get cleaned up after you complete the report." He stood there with a frown. "Go. Now."

Sheriff Hastings crossed his arms as I closed my notepad and slipped it into my pocket.

"A little tough on the lad, don't you think?"

I called Deputy Daniels over, and as he walked toward us, I pulled off my hat and wiped my brow. Even in this cold, my forehead glistened with sweat. I shook my head at my friend.

When the three of us stood together, I shifted my gaze between them before lowering my eyes, noticing road sludge on my shoes.

"Gentlemen, we have a problem."

I exhaled and kicked a rock down the embankment. Bits of ice splattered my pant leg. Rubbing my chin with my hand, I looked back up at the two men.

"We need to talk."

CHAPTER 48

ABE

My day started like any other day in Eureka. Normal. After eating a healthy breakfast made by my wife, who insists on helping me lose weight, I headed to the office. On my way, I stopped at the little bakery a block over. Trying to keep from completely undoing my wife's low-calorie breakfast, I settled on a bagel with cream cheese rather than my usual indulgence. I smiled, acknowledging my unusual self-discipline. She would be proud of me if she knew. Then I stopped.

If she knew, I would be dead.

I finished the bagel in my car before going into the office. My receptionist and my wife are best friends. Sally smiled as I walked in.

"Good morning, Sally."

"Good morning." Her eyebrow bounced. "You missed some."

"I'm sorry. What?"

"Crumbs on your coat and trousers. You missed some."

She gave me an evil-knowing grin.

Curses.

I will be in the doghouse tonight, and since we do not have a dog, it will be on the couch. I frowned, brushed the remaining evidence from my clothing, and sighed.

"Don't worry, boss. I won't squeal. She just asked me to hold off on bringing any sweets into the office while you are on your diet. She never asked me to report on any indiscretions." Sally chuckled and poured a cup of coffee. She handed the cup to me with another grin. "You did good. Here, wash it down. Bagels go well with coffee."

"Bagel? How did you know?"

"The dry white crumbs rolled right off when you brushed them. Your usual bear claw crumbs are darker and tend to stick and smear."

"Guess I better pay more attention to my diet, else there will be hell to pay. Thank you for being such a loyal employee." I winked at her. "And friend."

Sally beamed her normal bright smile and nodded as I stepped into my office. "Oh, Mrs. Whitehorse called earlier. She needs to talk to you; says it's important."

Sally turned and went back to her desk.

With a bit of care, ensuring my hot coffee stayed where it should be, I set my cup on a coaster beside my new desk calendar mat. A couple of weeks into January, and so far, I tapped my wooden desktop. No spills on the calendar. I reached over to my Rolodex to pull up Dyani Whitehorse's number. Sally heard me twirl the wheel and called out.

"I put her number on your calendar. Today's date."

I glanced down, saw the number, and pulled back my arm. As I did, my sleeve hit my cup, and the dang thing started to tip. Good news, good news, and bad. The good news, I somehow managed to steady the cup before it toppled. The other good news, nothing landed in my lap. And, of course, the last week of January 1972 now has a sugary, light brown smear. I grabbed a tissue to sop up the bulk of the spill and could see the coffee soaked into the bottom of each successive month in the calendar. I will have eleven more months to remind me about my clumsiness. Each calendar month in the year will have a coffee streak across the bottom. Sigh.

"Thank you."

I shook my head and dialed the Grasmere number.

Dyani Whitehorse picked up on the second ring and wasted no time giving details on current events. Although I knew from Denali's letter about his planned hunting trip, I let her tell me again. Her son Paul followed a few days after, and the two planned to hunt in the mountains east of Eureka.

After several minutes of me nodding and speculating about the point of her initial call, she told me Paul had been arrested in Eureka. She began a dreadful wailing, and the conversation became difficult to understand. Her tirade might have included some Kootenai words. At last, I managed to calm her down and get her to focus on what happened.

"They arrested Paul for the murder of four people. Can you represent him and find out why the police think he's involved?" She let me know her husband John had left earlier for Eureka to pick up Paul's dog team and sled. The police held them at the station. "Talk to him before he leaves if you can."

I took a quick swig of the coffee and grimaced at the heat. "Ouch."

Standing up, I rushed out and turned to Sally. "Hold all my calls. We have an emergency. The police arrested Denali Darkcloud's cousin for murder, and I need to sort this out."

"You don't have any calls."

"Well. Just the same. Hold them."

I waddled to the car as fast as my short legs could manage, got in and drove to the station. As I pulled around the corner, I could see a large open truck with a canvas cover near the police station's motor pool garage. The whole station has a small footprint, and all the buildings are close together. I parked and hurried over to find a man walking the last dog up a ramp to the truck bed. I could see a long sled in the middle and on either side, several wagging tails and lolling tongues marveling at their change of transportation.

"Mr. Whitehorse, I presume."

"Yes. You must be Abe." When I nodded, he reached out to shake my hand. "I'm glad to meet you, but under the circumstances, sure wish it could have waited until sometime next summer at a picnic."

I let out a breath. "Me too. Have you talked to the sheriff yet?"

He shook his head. "The lady in the office directed me out here to collect the dogs.

"Will they be okay in the truck for a bit?"

"Hours."

"Okay. Let's go find out what's going on."

We walked into the police station and found Deputy Langston and Martha huddling at her desk, him leaning on the desk, his back to us, and her sitting with one elbow on the desk, chin in hand, looking up at him. When they heard us, they stopped talking. She sat back while the deputy stood, pressing his hand against the wall to prevent falling.

"Deputy. I'd like to talk to my client, Paul Whitehorse." He gave me a blank stare. "Now. Please. Thank you."

"I'm sorry, Abe. Um, counselor. Mr. Williams." For a quick moment, he glanced at Martha and put his arms to his sides, palms out. "He isn't here. The Whitefish Police picked him up earlier."

"Okay then." I turned to Martha. "Let Sheriff Hastings know I'm here and would like to talk to him." I tipped my head from side to side and leaned in, placing my hands on her desk, and whispered. "Martha, it's more of a must than a like."

Until I leaned in, I did not notice Martha's pale face. Her normal pink glow had evaporated. I do not know if she started to go pale when we entered or if the blood began draining from her face before we arrived. Standing there, leaning in close, I could see a distinct new line of red moving up her cheeks.

"Abe." She glanced at the deputy and turned back to me. "He isn't here. He's out on an emergency call."

I leaned back and turned toward Deputy Langston. "An emergency call, and you're sitting here leaning against Martha's desk." I looked back at Martha. "I'm not buying it." I spread my legs, crossed my arms, and gave the two of them my standard courtroom glare. "Tell me what's going on."

Martha stood up and tried to give me her intimidating look. She crossed her arms, mimicking my stance. Seconds later, she rubbed both of her arms as if she caught a chill, straightened her dress, and sat down again.

"I … I'm sorry. He left on official business, and we are not authorized to say anything more." Her chin went up, she tilted her head and raised her eyebrows. "You'll just have to wait." I relaxed my arms, knowing they had made up their minds to remain vigilant on passing more information. "I will let him know you stopped by."

When John and I stepped outside, I walked with him to his truck.

"I got this. I am not happy with the bull they handed down back there. First, it's an emergency call, and then it's official business. I will find out what they are trying to hide from us and let you know."

"Okay." He massaged his neck with one hand. "Financially, we are doing well and are able to cover all of your costs defending Paul. Just let us know how to proceed."

Shaking my head, I held up my hand.

"Panacaea Clarke put me on retainer years ago. Paul is family."

I wished him well on his return to British Columbia and promised to be in contact as soon as I had more information.

CHAPTER 49

DENNY

With her phenomenal extra sense of knowing my thoughts and worries, Pixie woke me with licks and pulled on the sleeve of my woolen sweater. She had something important to show me and would not take lounging around in the cabin as an excuse to ignore her. She held on until I got to my stocking feet. Herding me to the door, she sat, waiting for me to open and go outside.

"What's up, Pixie? Has Paul and his team returned?"

She snapped her jaws with a bop-bop and moaned a whimpering "Rawr-rawr," with the second 'rawr' concluded by another bop.

"Okay, I'll go outside."

Rubbing her ears with one hand, I pulled open the door and stepped onto the short porch, my stockinged feet prickled by the damp threshold.

Backed up to Krinklehorn Peak, the cabin faced east. My eyes squinted at a myriad of sparkles across the pond. Pixie came to my side and nudged my leg with her nose and sat, tipping her head. One ear up. Her eyebrows, too.

"I see it, Pixie. Clear skies. We can leave." She bopped her jaws again and bounced up on her front legs. "Can I have some coffee and breakfast first, girl?"

"Rawr."

She bounded around and ran through the flap. Rallying the troops, I decided.

Having kept my gear ready to travel whenever the weather allowed, getting the sled packed took little time. I checked the cabin, ensuring nothing remained inside to spoil and draw the undesired attention of wandering critters by its decaying odors. I am sure my team has left ample markings to discourage most animals for quite a while. Their not-so-subtle messages to passing predators are, "We've claimed this area. Get lost."

I double-checked the stove. Only smoldering now, the banked fire from last night would be out in a few hours. With my pooches fed, I turned to Pixie.

"Let's go to work."

I blocked off the flap access, lifted their leads and harnesses from the cabin pegs, and assembled my team.

We spent the next night close to where the road forked. If Paul had stopped here on his trek to Eureka, any impressions of sled tracks or dog prints could no longer be seen. Although clear, the evening sky became dark, a waning crescent moon rising; a good omen, I hope.

The following afternoon, Pixie led us into Eureka. As the outskirts of civilization came into view, I slowed my team to a crawl, and my thoughts turned to where to go first. I no longer needed to rush to the hospital. Paul took care of Keith. Besides, Pan provided all my earlier medicinal care, and I preferred not to wander all over town looking for the medical building. My second thought, checking in with the police, hit a similar chord. I'd never been to the police station, either. Although I was sure they wanted to ask me questions about the plane crash, after waiting more than a week, a few more hours would hurt no one.

While I did have business at the bank, it could wait until after I was home and could assess its condition. I was sure the explosion destroyed One Buck, so I would need to buy something new. At least something new to me. Aunt Dyani still had all my paperwork. I would need it before going to the bank anyway.

The hardware store, grocery, and bakery were the only other places I knew. Of course, we often stopped at the service station. No need to stop now. I had other priorities.

I headed for the office of Abe Williams. It's at the south end of town, near the bakery. Absent the last time I dropped by, I hoped he would be there now. If not, I would have had to start searching for the hospital to check on Keith or the police station. Whichever one I found first wins.

Abe's office had been a small, two-bedroom home at one time. As the town grew, the location, near the old railroad tracks, fell out of residential favor. When we met him years ago, he told Pan he picked it up for a little ditty. She laughed. Although I joined in the mirth, I never understood what he meant until much later.

Before I could get my team moving again, I heard a car honk behind me. Thinking it warned of an approaching vehicle, I glanced over my shoulder to check. I could see no threatening traffic, so I waved in the general direction of the sound, thanking them. As usual, Pixie and the team ignored the noise. Several minutes later, we crossed over the highway, and Pixie led us, scurrying down the road to Abe's law office. We continued to the corner of 1st Avenue and 1st Street. I chuckled, always wanting to say the corner of first and first. We stopped in front of Abe's office.

The unplowed street, devoid of cars, showed tire tracks and icy, slushy ruts yielding their path from one direction to another. One unblemished set of tracks skirted over to the gate in front of Abe's office, and a clear set of odd prints led from there to his front door.

He painted the house. It's gray now.

It had fresh white trim and dark gray shutters. An open sign could be seen in the front porch window. His 'Attorney at Law' sign dangled from chains hung between two porch posts. Two cars, speckled with splotches of snow, sat in the drive beside the office. As memory served, they would belong to Abe and his assistant.

I set my snow hook, walked to the front of my team, and rubbed Pixie's neck and ears.

"It could be a while girl. Wait here."

I heard a sound and turned to see Abe and a woman standing on the front steps of his office. Someone stood behind them. Between the shadows under the porch roof and the glare from the snow, I could not see well enough to recognize the other person.

Walking toward me, Abe called out. "Denali. It is so nice to see you. Thank God." He opened the gate of his white picket fence and stepped under the curved arbor. "Please, release your dogs in the yard. The fence surrounds the house. They can wander around and stretch. I have a big back porch, too. Sally is bringing out some water for them. They can lay down out of the snow." He walked out and gave me a hug. "Please, hurry. We need to talk."

While leaving the harnesses on my team, I released their leads and motioned for them all to follow Pixie and Abe through the gate. Thick strands of dormant vine laced through the arbor and provided purchase for accumulated snow. Glancing up, Abe and Pixie looked like a picture framed in white as they stepped through.

Okay, the rear view of the picture.

The team bounded through, some prancing one way, others twisting another, and yet others stopping to stretch and move on their own, even if for a short while. Splotches of yellow snow scattered across the yard. Abe and I watched them frolicking as we walked to the back of the old house, where he opened a screen door on the enclosed back porch. We stepped up and both stomped our shoes on a doormat, slush splattered.

Sally came through the back door and set a pot of water on the floor.

"I'll have another one in a minute. It's filling now. They'll have plenty to drink."

She propped the porch door open so they could go in and out.

Abe gestured for me to follow Sally through the back door, and I entered a roomy kitchen with a standard red and white checkered pattern on a worn linoleum floor. The room had been modified to serve as a storage and filing cabinet space, as well. Most of the kitchen cabinets showed labels indicating note pads, paper, file folders, etc. Too many for me to read in passing.

"Hang your coat here," Abe said.

Turning, I removed it and noticed someone sitting at an aluminum table at the other end of the room. With a big smile, he raised a cup of coffee.

"How're you doing, Doc?"

He set his cup down and stood.

Although the cane, hanging on the back of his chair, and his false leg were new, I would recognize his voice if nothing else.

"Lieutenant!"

He blinked.

"It's just Michael now."

"Okay, then it's just Denny."

He laughed, closed his eyes, and shook his head.

"I'm sorry. You will always be Doc to me."

Smiling, I gave him a return chuckle. "Well then, I'm sorry too, Michael. You just might hear me call you Lieutenant from time to time."

He laughed again and opened his arms. I stepped forward to greet him with a big hug.

CHAPTER 50

ABE

After everyone got coffee or refills, I ushered them into my office, including Sally. I asked her to take notes of our conversation.

"So, here's what I know." I looked at Denali and sighed. "Through a series of unfortunate miscommunications and misinterpretations by me and me alone, I failed to see or read the letter you left me four years ago. It wound up in the back of your family file, unnoticed and unopened." He shook his head. "Although I had occasion to review the will and power of attorney for specific reasons. Until recently, I did not realize the letter existed in the correspondence section of your family folder." He closed his eyes and let out a deep exhale. "I owe you a profound apology and am truly sorry."

"No problem," Denali said, squeezing one eye shut and arching the opposite eyebrow. "Now I know why no one ever came to talk to me while in boot camp." He continued to explain why he expected a visit by the authorities. "By the time I finished initial medical training and transferred to Camp Lejeune, I assumed authorities caught the killer without my help or the evidence."

I nodded for a moment and stopped, blinking and thinking about what he had just said.

When he finished, I turned and looked between Michael Hastings and Sally before returning to Denali again.

"About that." I took a deep breath. "Panacaea's killer is still at large. For years, the papers have reported on a brutal killer who has attacked and killed a woman each of the last three winters. There are four victims, with the last three killed and mutilated in the same way as your mother."

"They have a nickname for this killer." Rubbing my cheek, I looked at Sally again for courage. "An anonymous source claimed the first victim had a witness who saw the murderer escape on a dog sled. They refer to the killer as the Musher Man."

Denali jumped up. "That anonymous scum killed my Pan." He waived his hands. "My mother. He saw me leave because I ran away. He wanted to kill me, too."

He began rubbing his forehead and walking in circles, one hand moved to stroke his scalp, fingers combing through hair much shorter than I remember before it settled on the back of his neck.

I asked him to sit and calm himself. It took Sally and Michael, both grasping arms from either side, to escort him back to his chair. Denali pulled a piece of note paper from his shirt pocket and handed the crinkled thing to me.

"I guess this explains Keith's drawing. He left it under the bed covers at the cabin."

I straightened the sketch and saw bold and scattered scratches around a series of hand-drawn dog paw prints. Multiple lines of ink traced over the words 'MUSHER MAN' so many times the pen threatened to tear through the paper. I knew Keith was the rescued boy.

"So, Denali." I needed him to focus on what he knew, not how irritated he felt. "You can identify the killer?"

"Yes."

"Do you know his name?" He shook his head.

"But I know what he looks like and can identify him." He looked at my black coffee cup sitting on my desk. "And his car."

I bopped my forehead with the back of my hand. "Earlier, you mentioned having evidence. Your letter didn't say anything about evidence."

"I guess I forgot to write it down." He gestured with one hand. "I have his high school letterman jacket. He left it at the house the second time he came over. When I went back to get some things after he killed Pan, I took it."

"Where is it? Can you get it?"

Denali smiled. "Of course. It's in Pan's old chest up at my aunt's house in Grasmere. I can call and ask her or my Uncle John to bring it down. Or my Cousin Paul. He should be around here somewhere. He could have it here in a few hours," Denali laughed and added … "depending on whether he uses a vehicle or his dog team."

"Oh, Denali." I took another deep breath. "The police thought he might be the Musher Man and wanted to hold him for questioning. Your Aunt Dyani called me to represent him after his arrest." Shaking my head, I continued. "Before I got involved, a Whitefish deputy picked up Paul to transport him to their station. "Something happened, and Paul is dead."

Denali's shoulders slumped, and his head lowered, chin swaying on his chest. After a moment, he stood up, walked to the window, and placed his forehead against the pane. A frosty glaze of moisture began spreading from the contact. Wiping his eyes, he came back and sat down again, taking deep breaths.

"The sheriff tells me the Whitefish deputy has been suspended pending an investigation, and both police stations are working together to determine what happened."

Denali leaned forward, his hands rubbing both thighs.

"I understand an FBI agent will be participating, but not as a direct result of Paul's death. The FBI gets involved in serial killer cases, and the agent has been making intermittent visits to the area since the second murder. The arrest of a suspect drew his interest."

Denali looked up at me. "What happens now?"

"Well, a couple things." I held up a finger. "First, I'll take you over to the police station. Sheriff Hastings asked me to bring you in to see him if you showed up. I believe he wants you to make a statement." I scratched my chin and leaned in toward Denali. "He didn't want me to call the Whitefish Police. He will contact them."

"Why?"

"He has given me the impression something is amiss, and your safety is of concern." I gestured to Michael and asked him to come too. "I'll drop you off at the store, and you can follow. You will need your car."

"Hold on." Denali turned to Michael. "Lieutenant … I mean Michael, how did you get here then, and how did you know I would be here this morning?"

"We've been expecting you any day since the storm died down. I asked my friends to watch for you. When they noticed a dogsled team coming into town, they honked at you and rushed over to get me. I only arrived minutes before you."

"How did you know I would come here first?"

"I didn't."

"We hoped," I said.

Denali turned to me. "What's the second?"

"Pardon?"

"You said I had a couple of things to do. What's second?"

"Oh, sorry. Yes. When you're done with the sheriff, you should take your team back to your home outside of Stryker." I looked over to Michael. "This is why Michael should come with us to get his car. He needs to go with you to the farm."

"I'll let him explain."

Michael waved me off. "The full explanation can wait." He smiled at Denali. "I'll drive ahead and open the house and get the stove fired up."

"Which one, the stove in the kitchen or out in my workshop?"

"You'll see." Michael squinted, and one cheek peaked into half a grin.

I motioned to Sally, who got up and gathered the coffee cups. "We should go. The day is not going to get any longer. Can we leave your pooches here?" Denali nodded, and as we passed through the back porch, he kneeled in front of one of the dogs and gave its neck and ears rubs.

"Stay here for a bit, Pixie." He turned to two of the other dogs. "Copper, Loki, protect." Raising my eyebrows, I opened my mouth, and Denali answered my unasked question. "They will stay here until I get back and won't let anything happen to Sally or your office." He smiled and stepped off the back steps while sticking an arm through his jacket. "You're not expecting any other clients, are you?" He added with a grin and a wink.

CHAPTER 51

DENNY

Abe dropped Michael off at his workplace, the local hardware store, and we headed to the police station. En route, Lieutenant Mike told me after all his physical therapy ended, and when he returned to Eureka, he managed to get rehired at the hardware store where he worked before the war. In lieu of his old job of running the cash register, helping customers, and sweeping floors, the owner rehired him as assistant manager. The store manager never had an actual assistant before. He established the position to train Michael to manage the store. The owner planned to retire and leave Michael to run his store. In addition, Michael plans on making an offer to buy the store.

"Excellent," I told him. "So, you worked at the hardware store before Vietnam?"

"Yes."

"I think we met a long time ago. My mother and I brought in a rifle and shotgun for service. You helped us and taught me how to take care of the weapons."

He smiled, eyes rolling up. "I remember. That was you?"

***

At the police station, Sheriff Hastings ushered us into his office. He put his left hand on my shoulder and offered to shake hands with his other.

"Before we talk about anything else, I wanted to thank you for what you did for my son in Vietnam. He gives you a lot of praise and credits you with saving many lives over there, not just his."

"Thank you, sheriff." I sighed and lowered my gaze. "Just doing my job. It's what my mother trained me for."

"You did more than your job, son." He turned and shifted to the chair behind his desk. "Please, sit." He gestured to the two chairs in front. "Now it's time for me to do mine." He looked at me. "It starts with keeping you safe."

My head wobbled as my wide eyes blinked. "Why?"

"There have been three additional murders since Panacaea Clarke. Until this week, we had no clue she was your mother. Four years ago, a material witness or person of interest in her murder went missing. People described him as a simple-minded boy named Denny. Many thought it possible the murderer killed him too and disposed of the body."

"I remember Sheriff Boyer calling me about a challenged boy named Denny just after the murder. I had no clue who he asked about," Abe Williams said. "Until today, I didn't know Denali had a nickname." He looked at me. "Simple-minded, I'm confused."

"I can explain." I spread my arms, elbows tucked and told them how Pan home-schooled me to keep me from attending public schools. "She feared how other children would react to my mixed heritage and hid my talents and capabilities from her clients by promoting the idea I had a mental handicap."

I nodded to Abe. "Abe, you knew me as Denali Darkcloud, an intelligent young man enlisting in the military. Everyone else, including the killer, knew me as Denny, a challenged farmhand with dogs."

"The real killer needed to create a false trail to divert the blame to someone else. He chose the simple-minded farmhand and left false clues to lead authorities to think Denny killed Panacaea," Sheriff Hastings said. "The killer must be behind the anonymous newspaper stories about the Musher Man, as well."

The sheriff went on to explain how Sheriff Jacobson, a deputy back then, examined the original crime scene. "We had a lengthy conversation the other day, and the sheriff admitted he never believed the boy with the dog sled killed Ms. Clarke. Although some evidence at the site tilted toward the boy, he said too many inconsistencies led him to believe the boy either witnessed or arrived after the murder. In any case, as a person of interest, he wanted to interview the boy."

I leaned forward. "So why did you arrest Paul for the murders?"

"Only Sheriff Boyer, then Deputy Jacobson, and the FBI agent knew the full details of those early suspicions." He showed me a notepad with names and dates. "Based on the dates of when the four murders occurred, I knew Denali Darkcloud couldn't be the killer. Two of the murders happened during your time in Vietnam. You have the perfect alibi."

"We now know Denali Darkcloud and the missing person of interest, named Denny, are the same person, and now we know with certainty Denny also has the perfect alibi."

The sheriff lowered his eyes. "Still, we knew, or thought, the killer operated during winter on a dog sled. Paul showed up with a dogsled team, transporting an injured plane crash victim, and he lives a short distance over the border." The sheriff shook his head. "Paul admitted to me he comes down during the winters to exercise dog teams. It would be easy for him to transport a disabled woman in his sled. Please realize the last victim died last month. The case became fresh and urgent."

"Since the killer evaded capture for over four years, it seemed prudent to detain Paul Whitehorse for questioning." He took a deep breath and exhaled. "I had no way to know events could, or would, turn out the way they did."

Abe watched us during our chat, shaking his head on occasion and nodding at other times. "Sheriff." He cut in. "Earlier, I think you said Sheriff Jacobson has a new subject." The sheriff nodded. "Can you tell us more, the suspect's name, anything?"

"No, I'm sorry." He twiddled his pencil through his fingers. "They have a suspect, but they are short on evidence. Thus far, they do not have enough cause or evidence to get search warrant approval."

"Denali, I mean, Denny does. He witnessed the murder and can identify the killer. He can also identify his car. The killer drove a shiny black Oldsmobile." Abe raised his hand, pointing his index finger to the ceiling. "And Denny has the killer's high school letterman jacket."

"And I know how he burned his shoulder," I said.

CHAPTER 52

SHERIFF JACOBSON

February 1972

Like he did every day, Deputy Daniels sorted through the mail. I heard him dropping envelopes on his desk, most of them labeled to the sheriff's office. I watched him through my office window. He looked at one official envelope addressed to him by name. The return address indicated it came from the crime lab in Missoula, Montana. He leaned against his desk, grabbed the letter opener, sliced open the envelope, and pulled out a formal report. He stared at the report for several moments. His eyes closed, and his face paled as his chin sank to his chest. Turning, he walked down the hall and knocked on my door. "Sheriff." He pulled out a handkerchief and blew his nose. "We need to talk."

***

Looking at myself in the men's room mirror of the Whitefish police station, I stopped counting creases around my eyes; I needed more fingers on my hand to continue further. Where did they come from? Can the stresses of being sheriff be showing on my face already? Turning my head, the distinct lines of my aging skin smoothed out as they slid under the now graying hair at my temples.

Or were they just hiding under there? Either way. Damn.

I stood back from the mirror above the sink and took in my full body reflection in the mirror on the door. Better. With my legs spread, fists at my side, and chin up, I still had a better physique than the old TV Superman. At this distance, no one could see my creases.

Chuckling, I believed it best to just keep folk from getting too close. Other than my darling bride, keeping people at arm's length should be easy. Now for the interview.

***

"Tell me, Deputy. What do you remember about 22 November 1967, the night you found the body of Panacaea Clarke in Stryker?" FBI Agent Carl Winfield said as he put two cups of coffee down on the table and slid one toward my son.

Billy huffed. "Why are you here, asking questions? Where's the sheriff?"

"We decided it best for me to do this interview and avoid any conflict-of-interest issues. Now answer the question."

From the observation room, I watched my son scratch his chin with one hand while the index finger of his other hand rubbed against the cuticle of his thumb. He developed the telling nervous habit as a child. His mother describes it as playing a tiny violin. We knew it as a sign and what it meant.

"I drove up to the old witch's farmhouse." Billy gestured with his arm. "I saw something burning in the back of a pickup and a young man leaving in the distance on a dogsled."

"In the dark?" The agent tipped his head. "How could you see anything through the distance under the bright outside light?"

"My headlights!"

"And you saw the sled straight ahead of you, beyond the burning truck, in the distance?"

"Yes."

"How did you know the person on the sled was a young man?"

"Well. I … I'm not sure. He must have turned toward me and looked young. Anyway, I heard about the young retard with dogs who lived out there, and guess I made the connection."

"I see." The agent wrote in his notepad. Billy's finger played a faster tune on his thumb. "Then what?"

"I pulled up closer and saw a dead woman on the kitchen floor. A plucked goose blocked the door open so I could see in."

The agent worked his pen on the pad and looked up.

"A goose? You sure? Most people fix a turkey at Thanksgiving."

"It looked narrow, like a goose."

"And you didn't go in?"

"No. I never left my car."

"You didn't touch anything?"

Billy's knuckles began turning white. "No."

"How did you know the body was a woman?"

Billy sputtered, and his hands went limp before rubbing his thighs.

"I dunno. Who else could it be? I thought the witch lived alone."

"Alone?" The agent squinted his eyes. "Didn't you just say the young man lived there?"

"Well … yes. But he lived in the workshop." Billy blinked and shook his head. "Or so I heard from someone." Both of Billy's index fingers began playing a duet.

One of his hands gave a subtle shake as he reached out to the cup of coffee and took a sip. His face grimaced, and he turned his head and spat out the liquid, splattering the floor under the mirror.

"Sweet coffee. I can't drink that crap."

"Oh, sorry." The agent said and glanced toward me behind the mirror, raising an eyebrow. "I must have mixed up the two cups when I brought them in."

He pulled Billy's cup back and pushed the other one forward.

The agent eyed the deputy. "How did you know the medicine woman was dead?" He tipped his head. "She might have been injured, unconscious, and needed help. She might have had a heart attack. For that matter, how did you know the body wasn't the boy? It could have been a woman on the sled rather than a young man."

"What's all this about, Carl?" Billy's ears shifted up and back. "Or should I say, Agent Winfield?"

The agent leaned back in his chair, crossed his arms, and stretched out one leg. His eyes studied my son. "Two things, Deputy William Jacobson." He tapped an extended finger on his temple. "One, when then Deputy Christopher Jacobson arrived at the farmhouse that night, he found the kitchen door shut. Yes, he did find a raw, plucked goose," the agent squinted, "in the sink."

Carl leaned in.

"And two, he found the woman covered with a large shawl. If open, from a car window outside, under a bright mercury lamp, you couldn't tell the gender of the body or even differentiate it from a simple pile of laundry."

He placed pictures of the shawl-covered body on the table.

Billy's eyes moved left and right before he responded in a mocking tone. "I don't know what to tell you." He crossed his arms. "Maybe the retard came back and covered her."

"Why do you suppose a simple-minded fool, already in the process of escaping the scene, would come back to cover her with a shawl after he knew someone saw him leaving?"

Billy nodded and grinned. "Like you said. He's a simple-minded fool."

"Third, the killer flayed open all the other victims and left them uncovered, naked." The agent studied my son. "Why do you suppose the fool would cover the first victim and not any of the others?"

"Hell! I … don't … know. Maybe he only had one shawl, and I thought you said two things."

He turned his head to look toward the mirror and stuck his two violins in opposite armpits.

"Fourth!" The agent held up four fingers, knuckles toward Billy. "Why do you suppose the killer would bother to burn his coveralls and sneakers to destroy them, yet leave his bloody shirt in the workshop to be found? It makes no sense."

"Simple-minded. Remember."

"Fifth!" The agent pursed his lips. "The bloody sneakers left clear impressions in the snow, going to and from the workshop. By measurement, they indicated a size 12. In a lucky circumstance, the gas can in the back of the truck exploded and forced the sneakers out into the snow. One shoe tongue survived the fire. Its label confirmed a size 12 shoe."

He paused and shifted forward, leaning on his elbows.

"Additional footprints went to and from a snow sled at the front door. Photos show a parallel track from a sled, with dozens of paw prints in the snow, as well." The agent squinted at Billy. "Since you witnessed a man on a dogsled leaving the area from behind the house, this appears to confirm he came back to the farmhouse."

Billy's grin went wide, and one eye winked. "See! I told you. The bastard came back." Billy dropped his hands on the table. "This proves my story."

"Maybe." Winfield glanced at his notes. "It could explain all of it; it might explain only part. You see, then Deputy Jacobson measured those snow bootprints, too." He raised his eyebrow. "A size 12 snow boot leaves a larger impression than a size 12 sneaker. We have determined the boot to be closer to a size 9. As it turns out, he found old size 9 shoes in the workshop." He tipped his head and tugged on his ear. "You see, we know the sled returned to the farmhouse. However, from the size of the boots, we ruled out the sled operator as the killer years ago."

Billy plopped his hands on his thighs. "Well, there you go! It's obvious." He began rubbing and squeezing his legs. "He had an accomplice. I should have guessed."

"Perhaps." The agent leaned back into his chair, hands in his lap, fingers interlaced. "Seventh! You know we kept the evidence. After it became clear we had a serial killer, the importance of any evidence increased." He continued studying his quarry, who gazed at something in his lap.

"We always hoped to find some new clue to help us determine the identity of the killer. He succeeded in destroying the overalls. Besides remnants of the burned sneakers, the original evidence included the shawl found covering the body and a bloody flannel shirt discovered in the workshop. And lots of blood, of course."

The agent's head tilted. "At the time, we verified blood on the shirt as the same type as the victim. Since then, nothing has been found to connect the killer to any of the other three victims."

He tipped his head again until I heard a muffled crack from his neck.

"So, like I said, we have the shawl, a bloody flannel shirt, and the half-burned sneakers from the original crime scene." He paused for a moment and blinked twice. "Oh yes. We also have fragments of the woman's blouse. Its buttons had spread across the room. Deputy Jacobson found most of them on the kitchen floor, all but one." He looked up at my son. "And then there's the saliva."

Billy's head swung up from his lap; his squinted eyes focused on the agent. He shifted in his chair, his feet wiggling. I wondered if his toes played the violin, too.

"What saliva?"

The words cracked, and his voice changed into a high excited squeak.

"The medical examiner found tiny specs of saliva on the first victim's face." The agent placed one hand on the table, fingers splayed. "He found some on the flannel shirt sleeve, too, and mucous. Back then, the town doctor, acting as a part-time medical examiner, determined the fluids did not come from the victim. This leaves only the simple-minded farm hand." Again, he studied my son. "Or the killer."

Agent Winfield pulled in his legs and sat forward, sitting his elbows on the interview table.

"We didn't know about DNA back then. Recently, Deputy Daniels had reason to pull the evidence and send all the blood samples, mucous, and saliva to the DNA lab in Missoula." He raised his eyebrows. "He got the results back two days ago."

"Come on. It takes forever to get DNA results."

"I put a priority on it."

"Great!" Billy's lips thinned. "Did you match it to the dead dog-boy?"

"No. It did not match the young man." The edges of the agent's mouth curled into a tight frown. "And the dead boy is not the young man who lived on the Stryker farm with the late Panacaea Clarke."

Billy's eyes blinked wide for a brief second. He smiled and leaned back. The fingers of his hands relaxed. He wiped his forehead and flicked his wrist as if tossing off sweat.

"The accomplice. No wonder he tried to escape." He let out a breath.

"The dead young man's name is Paul Whitehorse, and he lived in Grasmere, British Columbia. He is a cousin to the young man who lived on the farm." He held up his hand, palm toward my son. "Before you ask, the two cousins are not a DNA match."

"Wait!" Billy arched his forehead, and his ears moved up. He pinched the bridge of his nose, and I noticed a sweat stain expanding on his back. He dropped his hand, and his index finger went to work again.

"How can you be sure? Anyway, where did you get Denny's DNA?"

The agent's frown relaxed as his right cheek eased up. "He gave us a sample."

Billy jumped up. "Excuse me?"

"Sit!" The agent said, pointing to the empty chair. "He's in Stryker, on house arrest. He turned himself in."

He sighed and leaned back in his chair again.

"You got him! Great!" Billy pumped his right arm. "When do we pick him up?"

"Pick him up … like the last suspect?"

"No, no. That was different. He tried to escape. I'll let this guy piss in my backseat if I have to." Billy sat back and breathed. He closed his eyes and spoke in a hushed tone. "So, we're done? You got him."

The agent shook his head. No emotion is showing on his face. "We are not done." He took a deep breath and exhaled. "In your earlier statement, you said you went out to the farmhouse to get medication for your burns, right?"

"Yes. As I've said, over and over, I heard the medicine woman could make healing ointments or salves and hoped she had one to reduce scarring from burns."

"If you can remember back then, tell me about how you burned your arm and what happened to your letterman jacket."

"My jacket?" Billy fidgeted and wiped his nose with the back of his hand. "I've explained all this before. And what the hell's my jacket got to do with dog-boy butchering the damn witch?"

The agent deflected the question with a lie. "I don't know. Tell me, anyway."

Billy retold the story of how he stopped to drink some beer in the park and started a bonfire. He got lighter fluid on his jacket, and it burned through to his arm before he could take it off.

"Are there any witnesses to the fire or the injury?"

"No." Billy's fingers continued fidgeting a silent tune. "I just got back from losing the Brawl and was in no mood to be with anyone."

Agent Winfield sucked his upper lip inside his lower, then pinched it between his thumb and finger. "What did you do with the jacket? People tell me you loved the thing and never wore anything else around town for years."

Billy sighed, tipped his head, and shifted from the violin to tugging on his ear. "It got ruined. Both its arm and shoulder got burned through. I tossed it." He began rubbing his temples. "I don't remember where. I might have tossed it in the bonfire. Besides, my football life ended, and the damn thing reminded me. I didn't want it anymore."

"All right. A couple of things have bothered us since the original Thanksgiving murder."

Billy crossed his arms, hunched back in his chair and snickered.

"Yeah. What?"

The agent squinted again. "Back in your initial interview, you identified a man leaving on a dog sled and referred to him as the Musher Man. You never said anything about the young, simple-minded handyman who worked at the farm. Now, you are certain he is the Musher Man." He lowered his head and peered at the deputy. "Did you know this handyman?

Had you seen him before? Did you meet him"?

"No, no, and no."

"Why are you so certain then? What makes you connect the Musher Man to this dog-boy? And just minutes ago, you referred to him as Denny. Why?"

"No! Wait." Billy shook his head. "I never met him. I don't know him. It must be from the kids who told me about the medicine woman. They mentioned the retarded boy who lives there with a bunch of dogs." He squeezed his drippy nose between his thumb and finger and wiped them on his trousers. "They must have told me his name."

"So, what you're saying now is … you don't have any evidential reason to claim the boy is the actual killer?"

"Well, then, why did he leave? Seems like a guilty move to me." Billy tried to smile, his cheek twitching. "Why didn't he come back? Where's he been hiding?"

The agent deflected again. "We'll get to those answers soon." He crossed his arms. "The other thing bothering us since the first murder, a woman has been killed every winter, including this year, all attributed to this mysterious Musher Man, except for the winter of late 1968." He continued studying the deputy's reactions. "Why do you suppose that is?"

"For cripes sake, Carl! How do I know?" Moving his eyes around, he leaned forward, rubbing his hands on his legs. Billy took a deep breath and let it out through pursed lips, and raised his hands to the side. "Maybe the retard got lost and took a year to find his way back."

"Perhaps." The agent tipped his head side to side. "Maybe." He stood. "One thing's for sure. He's back now." The agent looked at my son, the corner of his mouth curled. "Do you remember where you spent the winter of '68?"

"No. Why should I?"

"Does the Montana Law Enforcement Academy in Helena ring a bell?" He squinted at my son. "Although a body has never been found, a young woman disappeared in Helena during a snowstorm in late 1968."

***

At my request, Deputy Daniels arrested William (Billy) Jacobson for the four Musher Man murders and the homicide of Paul Whitehorse on Tuesday, the 14th of March 1972. I could not face him, and it bothered me how I let my love and trust for my son dissuade my gut feelings on this case for years. At least three more innocent women and a young man died because I trusted my son. How could I have been so blind?

There is only one thing left for me to do.

Agent Winfield brought up some of the issues bothering me from the Stryker crime scene, but not all. Evidence showed the killer interrupted the victim while preparing a meal. Dried sliced vegetables sat arranged on the cutting board. I did not notice back then, but after reviewing photos of the crime scene later, I realized we never recovered the knife.

I took a swab of blood from a drawer handle in the Clarke kitchen. At the time, we knew it did not belong to the victim. Wrong blood type. DNA had now matched the blood on the handle to the saliva on the shirt sleeve and on the face of the victim. They all matched my son.

With the DNA evidence in hand, and while Agent Winfield interviewed Billy, Deputy Daniels, the Eureka police, and a second agent from the FBI field office executed search warrants of William Jacobson's Oldsmobile, his cabin home, and Deputy Jacobson's police cruiser.

In the garage of Billy's home, on the workbench, in the bottom compartment of a fishing box, wrapped in a fragment of a bloody blouse, they found the kitchen knife of Panacaea Clarke. We matched the fabric remnant to her blouse. They found size 12 shoes in his closet.

Also in the garage, in a shoebox, on the bottom shelf of the workbench, in the back, behind cans of engine oil, they found four women's gloves, one fuzzy light blue, one black leather, and one woolen mitten. One from each of our local victims. We suspect the fourth, a narrow brown leather glove, belonged to the Helena victim.

In a painstaking search of Billy's black Oldsmobile, in the trunk, in a fabric seam, under where the left rear taillight sits, they found a blood-stained button. The buttons matched those from Panacaea Clarke's blouse. A later DNA test matched the blood to Ms. Clarke. We believe it stuck to Billy's clothing and fell inside the trunk when he changed clothes.

In the trunk of the deputy's cruiser, they found part of a balled-up tissue. DNA later matched it to Vicky Tisdale.

John and Diane Whitehorse delivered an unburned letterman jacket to Attorney Abe Williams in Eureka. According to Denali Darkcloud, the killer left the jacket on the vestibule floor of their home during his second visit when he first assaulted Panacaea. Denny hung it on a peg after the man left. At some point, Panacaea covered it with a spare apron. She disliked looking at it. Initials on the inside label of the jacket read WJ.

As I left the station, I handed an envelope to Deputy Daniels.

"Steve, at your earliest convenience, would you please deliver this to the mayor?"

He looked at me and rumpled his forehead. "Tell me this isn't what I think it is?"

I shook my head and stepped out of the office, leaving my badge and weapon on my desk.

CHAPTER 53

DENNY

Two Weeks Earlier

When Pixie and the team stopped in front of the porch for a moment, I thought we had arrived at the wrong farm. Is this my house?

Michael leaned against the vestibule door, arms crossed, grinning, with the screen door open and hooked into its winter position. The vestibule had a new exterior door. Then I noticed the house had been repainted. Even in the fading light, the white gleamed. Michael walked out and gestured to the barn and workshop. Bright red paint stood out against the white snow and gray sky.

"Michael. You've been busy." Stepping down from my sled, my body shivered as if hit by a cold breeze. "What's all this?"

"The beginning." He led me around the house. Behind where the temporary water tank used to sit stood a water tower with a standard farmhouse tank. "You'll have plenty of water now and at proper pressure, too. We refurbished and repaired the windmill. It no longer screeches."

Michael chuckled and did a hop on his good leg. He pointed toward the back.

"We turned the small area off the side yard into a septic field. You have an indoor toilet now."

"Lieutenant, this is too much. What did all this cost?"

"Hardly anything, Doc." His smile filled his face. "The windmill required minimal repair and lots of grease. I found someone who planned to demolish their old tank and tower system. They needed a larger capacity system for their expanding farm, and I convinced them to donate their old one. They let me take it for free. They seemed happy not having to bear the cost of removal."

"It still must have cost a lot. What about all this work?"

"About that."

Michael smiled and whistled. I heard both the vestibule and barn doors opening. In the next several minutes, several people walked into view. Hidden behind civilian clothes and clean smiling faces, I could not recognize anyone in the lights and shadows; immediate recognition failed to register. Many limped, and some had missing limbs.

The last time I saw them, they had dirty, blood-streaked faces and wore the disheveled uniforms of wounded and exhausted Marines. They walked with some of their friends and families. Hoots and hollers accompanied them as honking vehicles pulled out from behind the house. The last vehicle, a truck, came out of the barn. The bed of Pan's old truck had been repaired, and One Buck had a new green coat of paint.

"I've had plenty of volunteer help. Gunny here did most of the hard labor."

"Hi yah, Doc." Gunny's voice added to the cacophony, shaking Denny's hand with one arm and embracing him with the other. "Hope you like your new roof."

As the guys and their families meandered around and I passed out handshakes and more hugs, I heard the ringing of a phone. Michael tapped my shoulder. "That would be Abe. He arranged for the installation of a phone line and wanted to be the first person to call you when you arrived." I turned toward the porch and noticed a striking young, dark-haired woman standing there. "Is there a Denny Darkcloud out here somewhere?" She motioned at the crowd, snickering. "He has a call."

Michael put his hand on my shoulder. "Let me introduce you to Tayen. She's a Native American nurse who needed a place to work." He shook his head. "No. Not Kootenai." Abe recognized the importance of the services Panacaea provided, and since the house had everything Tayen needed, he arranged for her to relocate here and set up shop.

"She's been living and working here for over a year. He checked with your Aunt Diane, and they both felt sure you wouldn't mind."

When I looked up, Tayen's eyes met mine across the yard. They sparkled, and when she smiled, my breath stopped. Behind her, above the house, clouds cleared, revealing the new moon.

END

Made in the USA
Monee, IL
22 December 2023